Dear Mystery Lover,

I am very pleased to introduce Donna Huston Murray and Ginger Barnes. *The Main Line Is Murder* is the very first DEAD LETTER paperback original and the first in a charming amateur sleuth series set in the tony suburbs of Philadelphia.

When I first read *Main Line*, I was struck by the authenticity of Ginger's voice. It seemed to me that I was sitting in a friend's kitchen listening to her adventures over a cup of coffee and a nice piece of pastry. When I spoke with Donna about the book, my warm feelings proved to be on the money. Like Ginger, Donna is the wife of a headmaster at a private school and has innumerable stories to tell of her years in the 'burbs.

Donna's depiction of the Main Line is very much like other suburbs around the world—full of homespun charm with a touch of malice. Wherever you may live, folks like those who populate Ginger's community may be right down your own block.

Look for the next Ginger Barnes mystery, *Final Arrangements*, in March of 1996.

Keep your eye out for DEAD LETTER—and build yourself a library of paperback mysteries to die for.

Yours in crime,

Shawn Coyne
Senior Editor
St. Martin's DEAD LETTER Paperback Mysteries

**At Bryn Derwyn Academy
there are plenty of
crusty curmudgeons on staff.**

**And when contemptuous attorney
Richard Wharton is murdered,
there are plenty of suspects . . .**

Businessman Kevin Seitz, who claimed Wharton's legal maneuverings led to his father's bankruptcy and suicide.

George Kelly, who blamed Wharton when Mrs. Kelly walked out on him.

Algebra teacher Jeremy Philbin, who described his marital woes down to the last excruciating detail for avid listener Wharton, only to be told the attorney didn't handle divorces.

Randy Webb, who vied with Wharton for the affections of Tina Longmeier.

And Tina's husband, Eddie Longmeier, who was very displeased to learn that Tina preferred Wharton.

Dead Letter mysteries by
Donna Huston Murray

THE MAIN LINE IS MURDER

FINAL ARRANGEMENTS
(COMING IN MARCH 1996)

The Main Line is Murder

Donna Huston Murray

St. Martin's Paperbacks

This book is a work of fiction. Names, characters, places, and incidents are products of the author's imagination. Any resemblance to actual events or locales or persons, living or dead, is entirely coincidental.

THE MAIN LINE IS MURDER

Copyright © 1995 by Donna Huston Murray.

ISBN: 0-312-95637-1

Printed in the United States of America

St. Martin's Paperbacks edition/November 1995

10 9 8 7 6 5 4 3 2 1

To Ruth M. Huston Ballard

I know you know, but this makes it official.

Acknowledgments

My most sincere thanks to those who generously shared their expertise whether it was convenient or not: Helen and Ian Ballard, Calvin Bonenberger, Ralph Brown at Wolfington, Mariandl Cabell, Don Nypower, Dorinda Shank, and Dr. Ken Zamkoff.

Also, I'm especially grateful to my trusted "first" readers Terri Anderson (who isn't a relative), Robynne Murray, and Hench Murray (who are).

—Donna Huston Murray

※ *Chapter 1* ※

Despite what happened during the next hour, three PM, Friday, December 3, started off pretty normally—I was annoyed with myself.

Barney, our aging Irish setter, caught the expression on my face and stopped wagging his tail. After I finished rummaging around under the kitchen sink, I reached out to fondle his chin.

"Ginger Struve Barnes, the oldest living Girl Scout," I told him, shaking my head with disgust. "Maybe some day I'll learn not to rush in."

I slam-dunked a bottle of all-purpose cleaner into my canvas carryall with the rest. Barney eased back several inches and lifted his eye wrinkles.

"Even for a good cause," I added, aware that my vow to reform sounded unconvincing, even to me.

The Post-it note I stuck to the TV screen read, "Mop Squad duty—again. Love, Mom."

At ages nine and twelve Garry and Chelsea were more than capable of finding the cookies by themselves. Also, the school their father now headed loomed over our house like a dump truck over a tricycle. If necessary, a ninety-second jog would put the kids inside Rip's office. Finding me would be only slightly more difficult.

A glance at the December dreariness outside reminded me to flick on the porch light before I headed out. As I hurried through the chilly air, the loaded carryall bounced painfully against my leg.

"This place stinks," our son had announced the first time Rip ushered Garry and me into the lobby of Bryn Derwyn Academy, one of the smaller private schools on Philadelphia's Main Line. The inaugural family tour took place one Sunday last March, right after Rip accepted the job as headmaster. To protest the family's relocation "across the river," our daughter had opted for a movie with friends.

"Shhhh," I warned our son.

"Well, it does," he complained, and rightfully so. The place smelled of dank carpet and dusty drapes. I'd also seen better matched furniture at a yard sale.

"Has possibilities, don't you think?" Rip remarked, unable to repress a grin.

"Yes," I agreed with a reflexive nod. Mentally, I had already rented a steam-cleaner and made new drapes to remedy the school's first impression, "rushing in" to support my husband's career. Such is the seduction of the chronically understaffed, under-endowed private school. It needs you. Like the National Debt needs taxes, it needs you.

Today a seasonal six-foot pine temporarily displaced the blue sofa and walnut coffee table I had found for the middle of the lobby. An antique mirror and some graceful walnut chairs decorated the inside auditorium wall, and behind me cream-and-blue Waverly print drapes dressed the tall front windows. Much to the dismay of Rip's inherited secretary, I made the drapes from remnants and pirated everything else from other parts of the school back in August, when anyone who might want to form a committee had been on vacation.

Friday afternoon classes had ended forty-five minutes

before, so teenagers in school uniforms showing the wear and tear of the day, if not the week, milled around waiting for transportation. Parents leading lower-school children by the hand headed for their waiting Jeeps and Mercedes. Rip's secretary rocked back and forth on tired feet behind the receptionist's desk, her usual post after the receptionist went home.

"T.G.I.F., Hank," I greeted her, using the nickname that had helped Joanne Henry and me to become friends.

"Aren't you about done?" she asked, eying the carry-all. "The place looks great."

"Two more weeks, kiddo—then never again." Rip had invited the parents to tour the "new improved" school the evening of December 16, prior to the holiday concert; so I considered that to be the "Mop Squad's" deadline.

Joanne's attention had strayed. When I looked to see why, I noticed tears magnified by her fashionable glasses.

"What's wrong?" I asked. Joanne's eyes were usually hard as flint.

"Oh, Gin," she lamented. "You won't believe what I did this morning." Her fine, beige hair remained perfect, her dark rose knit dress contoured her compact, middle-aged body without one unflattering dent or bulge; but here she was, Rip's fencepost of secretarial stability, undeniably flustered about something that had occurred hours ago.

"I spilled coffee on my computer keyboard," she confessed. For emphasis, her eyes widened until they were distraught, gray puddles.

I shrugged my confusion. Give me a chandelier to hang or a garbage disposal to replace and I'm in business, but technology any further evolved than the elementary household appliance I leave strictly to the professionals.

"Did you get a shock?" I asked uncertainly.

"No."

"Was the computer trashed?"

"No." She clicked her tongue with exasperation. "The screen froze and I lost the document I was working on."

"Oh." That was it?

"We have to get a new keyboard."

Okay, I thought. No big deal. The school wasn't rich, but it could probably afford one measly keyboard. "I'm sure you didn't mean to . . ."

"Gin," she interrupted. "I wasn't there when it happened."

"You weren't?"

"I mean, I must have been, but I don't think I was."

"Where do you think you were?"

"In morning assembly." The daily, school-wide gathering where announcements were read, birthdays fussed over, academic achievements and sports victories cheered; Rip had instituted the morning ritual to help the two hundred thirty-nine students and twenty-seven faculty members get to know each other—and him.

"So somebody else walked by and knocked over the cup . . ."

Joanne pressed her lips tight and slowly shook her head. The tears behind her glasses sparkled. "We were all in assembly for Peggy's birthday." Peggy was a particularly shy secretary who handled the work of three busy bosses almost without speaking. I would have gone in, too, if only to watch her squirm.

"Maybe you did it without realizing—maybe on your way out."

Joanne's perspicacity was beyond challenge. If she knocked an elbow into a mug and wrecked a computer keyboard, she would have been aware of it. Unless, as older people fear, she was losing it—clearly her reading of the situation.

"I guess I must have," she reluctantly agreed.

I, too, would sooner have believed the school had poltergeists, but nothing was to be gained by dwelling on one relatively small incident. A diversion seemed to be in order.

"What's with the mittens?" I asked, jerking a thumb toward the fragrant Christmas tree. Obviously that month's service project, it was covered with twenty packages of jockey shorts and girls' panties clipped on with red, yellow, and blue clothespins.

Joanne blinked away her self-doubt, scanned the tree, and finally spotted the two pairs of mittens dangling among the Hanes and Fruit of the Loom.

"Oh, them," she snorted. "A couple of mothers must not have believed the memo." Idiots, her scowl conveyed. Who wouldn't believe that orphans needed underwear more than they needed mittens?

"Hi, Mrs. Barnes," chirped a fifth grade girl, who I swear used her pink glasses to look straight through me. Her mother had chosen Bryn Derwyn for its sheltered, family-like environment, and rightfully so. Already the worldly wisdom in the girl's eyes suggested the ability to blackmail at will.

"Hello, Elaine," I replied as if I weren't the least bit afraid of her. She smiled smugly, pivoted at the tree and swaggered down the left-hand hall. Below the dark-green Bryn Derwyn uniform sweater, her white shirttail blocked out a sizeable patch of plaid kilt. Mata Hari in a Norman Rockwell disguise. Elaine Wrigley made me shudder.

Joanne had answered the switchboard, so I wiggled my fingers good-bye and proceeded down the right-hand hallway where Rip had established offices for Development and for Kevin Seitz, the new business manager he hired over the summer. Both doors stood open, but Kevin, whose family knew my family, had his back to the hall while he spoke into his phone.

Randy Webb, the Director of Development, nodded a curt hello as I passed. I felt my back straighten and my face freeze. "Randy," I said as cordially as possible.

Not yet thirty, his looks were usually considered pleasing—wavy blond hair, blue eyes feathered with curly lashes, nice bones. His rolling stride made women aware of his broad shoulders and narrow hips. To me, his suavity came off as detached, possibly even arrogant.

Of course, I chose to be especially hard on him. Last month I caught him pulling out of a clinch with the aunt of one of the students. Both Randy and the woman, Tina Longmeier, were married—to other people, it went without saying. Both were horrified that I chose that particular moment to see if the copy room required the services of the Mop Squad. And although I did not mention the incident to Rip—after all, what had I actually seen but two adults blushing furiously—Randy and I were destined to remain polite strangers.

Beyond those two doors across from an empty fifth grade classroom stood a sort of all-purpose meeting space containing a rectangular table large enough to accommodate a dozen chairs. The Board met here as well as the Bryn Derwyn "Community," the body of volunteers who initiated everything from fund-raisers to picnics for the kids.

In a corner someone, probably Randy Webb, had deposited a box of pamphlets and a brand-new groundbreaking shovel adorned with a large green bow—the optimistic symbol of the current fund-raising campaign. Since Kevin and Randy both used the room to meet with contractors or alumni or whomever, there was also a coffee corner showing signs of careless daily use.

As my mother will testify, I'm not really a neatness

freak, but even I understood that for a school trying to foster self-esteem, sloppiness transmitted the wrong message. Bryn Derwyn desperately needed to recover from the retired head's myopia and the neglect of his equally elderly, and also departed, maintenance man. When Rip had lamented the unbudgeted expense, naturally I volunteered without thinking. Now after months of scrubbing, both with and without help, my halo tilted precariously over my ear.

Yet this afternoon the cobwebs and ingrained dirt were not my primary interest. On a rainy day back in August, Jacob Green, the new maintenance man, had run around trying out a bunch of unidentified keys he found. One had opened the wall full of four-foot-wide cabinets that constituted the Community Room "closet." Inside was quite a lot of old merchandise nobody had touched in years. I wanted to see whether any of it could be salvaged to sell at the school store the night of the holiday concert. Cleaning, it went without saying, as I went along.

I dumped my coat and purse on a chair, kicked the carryall under the table, unlocked the far left cabinet, pushed up my sweater sleeves, and began unloading a shelf.

One box of XL T-shirts, white with green school logo. They were huge, explaining why they were unsold. Maybe the faculty could wear them when they played the students in soccer or softball. Or maybe not. I set the box behind me on the corner of the large meeting table.

A spool of telephone cord? Give it to Jacob. Partial boxes of pencils, notebooks, and erasers. Never out of date, although I couldn't remember the last time I used a block eraser. I found a dozen green eyeglass cases with the school's logo in gold, a gross of frosted shot glasses etched with the logo, and a brown bag contain-

ing about fifty brass scarf rings from when the younger
kids' uniform included a Girl Scout-type scarf. I'd seen
yearbook pictures; the kids all wore suitably self-conscious expressions, every last one.

There were also a hundred wool baseball caps, which
would surely sell since they were a nice quality and also
right in style.

Nothing remained on the first shelf but dust balls and
mummified bugs. I grabbed my purse and went in search
of Patrice, Jacob's helper, who would know where to
find one of the five hand-held vacuum cleaners purchased to help perpetuate the Mop Squad's efforts.

She recommended borrowing the one from the
Faculty Room, remarking cynically, "Lazy bums'll never
miss it." After so many months of helping her do her
job, I agreed with the sentiment.

When I returned with the faculty's Dustbuster, (Black
and Decker's latest model), the Community Room door
was closed and quiet voices were coming from inside. I
couldn't tell whether it was coffee talk or a meeting
because of the curtain on the door. So I rapped with a
knuckle, and Kevin Seitz peeked out through an eigh-
teen-inch opening. Behind him I could see the school's
attorney, Richard Wharton, showing papers to a couple
I knew to be three years behind on their tuition, another
detail the retired headmaster's trifocals missed.

"Hi, Gin. What is it?" the business manager asked.

I waved the Dustbuster in the direction of the junk on
the table.

"Oh, sorry, Gin. Didn't realize you were working
here. Would it be possible for you to come back in an
hour?"

I agreed, and Kevin quickly shut the door. Obviously
a sensitive discussion. Since both Kevin and Richard
were involved, I assumed that payment arrangements
were being negotiated.

The Dustbuster was too bulky to carry around for an hour, so I set it on the floor next to the door. If the little-used exit at the far end of the hall had been unlocked, I might have sprinted the short distance from there to our house. However, it had already been chained closed for the weekend, and my coat remained inside the Community Room.

So I wandered back to the lobby. From the adjacent auditorium I heard the distinctively off-key, off-beat voices of a bunch of kids singing "Silent Night" and decided to kill time listening to them rehearse.

Rip sat about five rows back, slouched in his seat with his straight dark hair fallen down to his green eyes, fingers tented in front of his lips. Rather than disturb his concentration, I moved in behind him by a couple rows.

The performance appeared to be a run-through staged for his benefit because with only a sweep of her graceful hand, the part-time music teacher signaled for three gangly sixth grade boys to launch into "We Three Kings." Never mind that they were awful, the parents would swoon.

Rip shifted in his seat to relieve some tension.

Tension? A closer look told me he was angry as hell.

About a cherubic bunch of kids trying to sing?

During "Joy to the World" I monitored faces, especially the precocious Elaine Wrigley, who sang with the sobriety of the entire Salvation Army. Somehow Rip managed to ignore her.

Halfway through "O Little Town of Bethlehem," I got it. Then for the next twelve minutes I stewed and squirmed and desperately wanted to leave.

However, leaving would have insulted those who sang. It was the ones who mouthed only a few words who would have understood, and it was on their behalf that Rip was furious.

After the final "Jingle Bells" with full and enthusiastic participation, Rip congratulated the kids, dismissed them, and circled the music director with a fatherly arm. She was two-thirds his size and twice his age, but forgave him for both, smiling graciously with a face that obviously expected praise.

I sat still, several yards away from their pocket of privacy, made more private by the racket of children dispersing.

Rip's head wove back and forth sadly as he delivered the bad news. The woman stepped away, shock freezing her features.

"But we've always . . ." she began her defense.

More murmured discussion, then an audible, "We're a nonsectarian school, Nora. Not all our students are Christian."

Nora's eyes widened. By now only the three of us remained in the huge room. "Well, I'm sure no one minds singing a beautiful carol. Why would they mind?"

I thought of the Jewish boy whose behavior had proven my guess was right. He simply stood there until a song came along he wanted to sing.

Rip stepped back, summoning patience. "I'm sorry, Nora," he said. "You'll have to change the program, and if there isn't time to do that, you'll have to cancel."

Nora inhaled. I could hear her huffing from the middle of the auditorium. "No, Mr. Barnes. No. I'd rather quit," she said. Then she scooped her purse off a chair and marched up the aisle. The door compressor wheezed with relief as it swept her through.

"Hi," I said, alerting Rip to my presence.

"Oh," my husband said. "You heard."

"Did you have suspicions?" I asked. "Was that why you came to watch?"

He nodded. "I saw the program. Joanne was running it off on the copier."

"What will you do now?"

Rip stuffed his hands in his pockets. I noticed his tie was crooked.

"I really hate to ask this," he said. His eyes were also puffy with fatigue. "Really hate to ask. But do you think Didi could fill in? Just until the concert?"

My first thought was, why not? Didi, my dearest friend, *could* sing, and every moment of her life was conducted as if she was on stage.

However, Rip appreciates Didi the way Mozart might have enjoyed rock and roll—in very small doses, if at all. So my second thought was that Rip was desperate.

"You sure?" I pressed.

"Sure. Even Didi's got to be more politically correct than Nora."

My nutmeg-colored bangs obscured the doubt etching grooves into my forehead. Heck, everybody's new at their job for a while, even Rip. And this probably wouldn't be *that* big of a mistake.

So I ran home without my coat after all because Didi's latest phone number was somewhere under the lunch menus, lace snowflakes, and cartoons stuck all over the front of the refrigerator.

The police didn't consider my next twenty minutes to be especially significant; but as I mentioned, everybody has the right to be wrong—Joanne, Randy Webb, Rip, Nora, me.

Why should they be any different?

❊ *Chapter 2* ❊

Shivering after my underdressed run from the school, I shut the front door behind me. Barney rushed to sniff me over while conveying a hopeful, "Is it dinner yet?" with his eyes. I ruffled his neck with two hands and told the dog, "Hello to you, too."

With one last shiver I called Chelsea and Garry to reassure myself that they were home. Thanks to the first Bryn Derwyn student who greeted Garry with a snide, "So you're the headmaster's son," we had decided not to transfer them from the private school where Rip previously worked. Their bus was reliable, but delivery times varied with traffic.

Garry emerged from the kitchen, a cold pizza crust in his raised hand.

"What's the matter?" I asked, instantly alerted by his expression. The dog began to hop around under the crust.

Rip's four-foot-tall near-replica shuffled into the living room and flopped into a TV chair. When Barney delicately removed the pizza crust from his fingers, Garry didn't even notice. Deep, nine-year-old depression.

"Dave lost my World Series hat."

His beloved, expensive, commemorative hat from when the Phillies won the Pennant, inchcs from reaching the top of the top. The hat had been integral to Garry's persona for almost a year now, adjusting as he grew, resting on his bedroom shelf at night, dusted, caressed, folded in the professional batter's manner during school, popping back into shape upon its owner's head at every opportunity. Garry looked adorable in that hat . . .

"How did that happen?" I asked.

"Dave's Mom got him one of those haircuts, you know, sort of long on the top?"

I knew. Long on top, shaved close from about the eyebrow level down. The current dust-mop style required a certain *je ne sais quoi* personality to bring it off. Since Dave was a relatively shy fifth grader, it was safe to assume the haircut made him excruciatingly self-conscious. "He asked to borrow your hat," to ease the adjustment, no doubt.

"Yeah, just for outside after lunch. That big guy Christopher from sixth grade was giving him a hard time . . ."

"So you said yes."

"Yeah, but just for one hour, one time. And he lost it, Mom. Put it down somewhere and *lost* it. How could he *do* that?"

"I'm sure Dave didn't mean to be careless."

"It was my favorite, Mom. How could he be so . . . so stupid?"

I was sitting across from Garry, the dog now at my feet, irresistible conditions for a mother.

"So which do you think is more important," I opened. "Your best friend or your best hat?"

"But, Mom . . ."

"I know. You're really angry."

"Yeah. He knew I liked that hat, and he *lost* it." *Al-*

lowed it to be stolen, was probably more accurate, but I decided not to mention that.

"Not on purpose, he didn't."

Garry fidgeted. "Yeah, but . . ."

"So which is more important—your best friend or your hat?"

No answer.

"Okay. Then which is more important, Barney or the rug?"

Grudgingly, "Barney."

"My purple sweater or my elbow?"

"Your elbow," said with a grimace.

"Dad's golf clubs or your sister?"

"Tough call," delivered with a smile.

I slapped him on the knee. "Go feed the dog before he faints."

"We decorating the tree tonight?" Garry asked on his way into the kitchen.

"You bet," I replied. "Why don't you dig out the decorations from the attic room upstairs while I finish up at school."

The slightly asymmetrical white pine we'd bought at a Boy Scout stand waited in front of the already faded burlap drapes I'd made for the living room.

If the school had needed redecorating, the headmaster's house had needed—everything. Since the retiring head had lived elsewhere, we found the house provided on campus filled with dusty cartons of textbooks and assorted junk. In fact the place was so devoid of domesticity I worried whether it was even habitable.

Now, in spite of the booby-trapped fixtures, the clunking heater, and all the nest feathering yet to do, I counted on trimming our Christmas tree to finally make this former storage bin feel like home.

"Hi, Mom." Chelsea hopped down the stairs from her bedroom where she had changed into jeans and a sweatshirt. I watched closely, looking for signs of more trouble on the school bus. The eminently popular Beth-something, the only girl her age who lived nearby—actually her back yard met our side yard directly next to the house—had excluded Chelsea to the extent that it had become difficult for her to converse with anyone. Now that it was a few months into the school year, I wondered whether the situation had improved; but I couldn't ask. Asking about it would only emphasize Chelsea's rejection. Since her mood seemed neutral, I assumed she was adapting one way or another.

She proceeded to sit down at the dining room table with a bottle of pink nail polish and a box of tissues. Winter afternoon sun set off her golden red hair with a candlelight glow. Against the new wallpaper—thick strips of flowered branches and stylized birds—our blossoming pre-teen appeared painfully young.

I leaned against the doorway. "Listen, ducky," I said, "I have to call Aunt Didi and then go back and work at school for a while. Can you please make sure Garry doesn't eat our dinner before I cook it?"

Chelsea grudgingly agreed to try.

Didi's current work number was stuck on the refrigerator under a coupon for Froot Loops.

"Amigo," Didi greeted me. Presently, she was hostessing for a Mexican restaurant down the pike from the beer distributorship she owned, a convenient arrangement from a transportation standpoint and one of her more logical reasons for taking a job.

I told her why I was calling.

"This was your idea, right?" she asked skeptically. Already her voice had time-warped me to pigtails and back.

"Rip's," I admitted.

"Really? He must be desperate." A statement. A true statement, so I acknowledged it as such.

"Okay, I'll do it. Hang on a sec." She moved the phone away from her mouth. "Mario," she shouted loud enough for me to hear. "Mario, dear, I'm terribly sorry but I have to quit." Mumble, mumble. "Family emergency." Mumble, mumble.

The lie felt like a shadow passing across my back.

"What's it pay?" Didi asked when she came back on the line.

"Haven't a clue." Or maybe I had; this was Bryn Derwyn Academy we were talking about. "Very little," I amended.

She asked me a few questions, such as how long the program was supposed to be, how many kids were involved, their ages, and so on. They were sensible questions, so I allowed myself to be reassured.

After we rung off, I called something endearing to the kids, put on an old jacket, and did one abominable little ballet jump Didi taught me on the way back to school.

Both the lobby and outer office were deserted. Through Rip's opened office door I saw him and a few teachers gathered for a meeting. Joanne seemed to be taking notes. Probably just everyday business. I waited outside the door until I caught Rip's eye, then I gave him the thumb's-up signal to indicate that Didi was on board. Rip grinned and nodded, his eyes conveying that special warmth he reserves for me and the kids.

So I was feeling a bit warm and glowy myself when I headed back to the Community Room. I also felt a bit rushed because it was pushing four o'clock and I would have to hurry to get much done before it was time to go home and cook dinner.

Once again the Community Room was closed, but this time I heard no voices. When I knocked, no one answered. Kevin's and Randy's offices had been empty when I passed by, so I assumed they both had left for the weekend. The couple the school's attorney had been negotiating with was also gone, but not Richard Wharton.

When I opened the door, he was sprawled face down across the conference table, the back of his head a shattered mess.

❧ *Chapter 3* ❧

*M*y hand flew off the doorknob. The soft click of the door latch spooked me further into the room. I was alone with Richard's corpse.

Suppressing the need to run, I hugged in a deep breath then whistled it out through pursed lips.

Calm your breathing, that's right. Then try to think.

Okay. Finish looking. Finish looking and then you can go.

The position of Richard's body appeared benign, as if his death were a passing whim of fate. One second he had been sitting at a table collecting a pile of papers; the next he was sprawled forward, his skull shattered, the papers again in disarray.

Moved by sympathy, I reached toward Richard's arm, my hand anticipating the rough tweed of his brown sport jacket even as I brought myself up short. Television police forever warned about disturbing a murder scene.

Murder. My mind grappled with the incomprehensible. How could anyone do this—ever?

Soon I would force my frozen body to leave, to report Richard's death and set the process of the law into motion. Meanwhile, my heightened sensitivities continued to record the room. Although I probably spent only half a minute assimilating Richard's appearance, those thirty seconds had made an indelible impression.

Now I noticed that the most visible paper on the table bore the name of the couple who was delinquent with their tuition payments. The box of extra large T-shirts remained on the table at the same angle as before I left. The pencils and erasers and bag of scarf rings—everything appeared untouched. The overhead lights remained on. The five chairs at Richard's end of the table had been jostled, probably used by Kevin and the couple to whom Richard had been speaking.

Only the groundbreaking shovel was out of place. Looking incongruous and unnaturally clean, trimmed with a large, loopy bow in the school's trademark dark green, it had originally rested in the corner near the box of brochures. Standing, it might have been waist high to me, and it had a Y-shaped metal thing fixed to the top end with a wooden handhold like most short gardening shovels.

Now it lay on the floor near where I'd been working. A small smear of blood suggested it skidded or bounced a few feet after the killer flung it behind him. Or her. I was not an especially large woman, but with a nicely balanced little shovel, I could cause plenty of damage if . . . if what?

It was time to get the hell out of there and call the police. Let them ask if, and what, and why.

I pulled my jacket cuff down over my hand before I opened the door. Then I sprinted down the hall into the lobby, nearly colliding with Jacob, the maintenance supervisor.

I put both hands on his chest to steady myself, to reassure myself he was real.

"What's wrong?" he asked.

"Something terrible, Jacob. A man's been murdered.

I'm going to call the police. Please stand at the front door and keep everybody here."

Jacob's complexion had turned ashen all the way back to his remaining band of dark hair. Sweat beaded his upper lip.

"Who?" he asked. "Where?"

Already jogging toward the main office, I answered over my shoulder in a hushed voice. "Wharton. Richard Wharton. He's in the Community Room. But don't say anything. Just guard the door and tell everyone Rip will be right out."

Jacob wiped his lip with his hand and nodded solemnly. When I glanced back again, he had stationed himself between the two main doors. He wasn't much bigger than me, but if I had come face to face with him just then, I would have stayed put—if only to find out what was going on.

Joanne and the teachers who had been with Rip had scattered around the outer office, one reading mail, two chatting quietly. Joanne spoke into the phone.

"Stay here," I told them all. "Don't move an inch."

I entered Rip's office and shut the door tight behind me.

My husband rose slowly from his chair. "What's wrong?" he asked. Instinctively, he gravitated toward me.

What I said stopped him like a slap. His eyes widened and stared. His body swayed slightly, and he spread his fingers on the desktop to steady himself.

He said nothing, just reached for the phone with the same stunned expression, punched 911 and handed me the receiver. Then he tightened his tie and straightened his back and opened the door to the outer office.

Just as our emergency call was answered, I could hear the gasps of shock from the people Rip informed. One of the women began to cry.

The crying braced me, toughened me. It's been that way ever since Chelsea was born. Somehow I learned to cope first and crumble later—preferably in private. I calmly and succinctly told the dispatcher there had been a murder at Bryn Derwyn Academy, adding that the people on the premises were being asked to stay until the police arrived.

After that, I made a second call to our house. The kids would see and hear the police roar into the school driveway, and they needed to be warned. To my relief, Chelsea answered; being the younger of the two, Garry might have panicked just from the stress in my voice.

"There's going to be a bit of commotion over at the school," I said as calmly as possible.

"What?" Chelsea interrupted.

I took a deep, time-consuming breath. "Something happened to Mr. Wharton, and the police have to check it out."

"Is he dead?" I could visualize my daughter's face wide with awe, flushed with the thrill of life's drama. She did not sound scared. Tell her the truth?

"Yes, Chelsea. I'm afraid so."

"Ohmigod."

"Dad and I are fine. Everybody else is fine. Please just wait at the house for us. We'll tell you whatever we can when we get home. Go ahead and get something to eat if you want."

"Like, how did he die, Mom? Was it a heart attack or something?"

"Probably not."

"Then what, Mom? Mr. Wharton was old, but not *that* old." Fear was infusing itself into her voice. I could almost hear her thoughts: If somebody Mr. Wharton's age could die suddenly, so could anybody.

"It was more like an accident." The expedient white lie.

"Look," I added before Chelsea could quiz me further. "I've got to go now. Just hang in, and I'll be there as soon as I can."

When I got home, I would obliterate the white lie with the whole truth, and probably spoil some additional innocence as well. It wouldn't be easy, and I felt certain both kids would require generous portions of reassurance for weeks to come.

My eyes rested on the familiar cover of Bryn Derwyn's present-year directory, tucked under Rip's phone for handy reference. It reminded me that, for my husband, there would be 239 students, their parents, the faculty, the board, and the whole alumni body to reassure.

"Phew," I remarked to myself. "Lucky thing Richard was a bachelor."

Was a bachelor. I began to tremble, but one more glimpse at the directory shamed me out of that.

When I emerged from the office, the three waiting teachers ambushed me for more details. Joanne saw my face and held them back like a no-nonsense crossing guard.

I proceeded into the lobby, a robot now with only so much juice left to operate my limbs.

When he caught sight of me, Rip stopped speaking with Jacob and just watched.

There was an oak bench along the far wall. I went to it and began to pull. Rip recognized what I was doing and helped me close off the hallway leading to the Community Room.

Then wordlessly, we sank onto the bench side by side. Rip covered my hand with his. I allowed myself to meet his greenish-brown eyes just a second, just a second for sustenance, and that did it. Next thing I knew I was sobbing into his shoulder.

After I had finished venting, finished wiping and

blowing, while all of us who had gathered in the lobby seemed stuck in that suspended-time state of waiting, it occurred to me that I had always considered Richard Wharton educated scum.

I disliked him the day we met, and nothing he had done in the six months since had improved my opinion.

※ *Chapter 4* ※

That Tuesday morning back in August we had been living on the Main Line less than two months, so I didn't entirely understand why I was putting on my best summer skirt outfit, stockings, and heels at eleven AM.

"Do I really have to go?" I asked Rip, who was around the corner fixing his tie at the bathroom sink. "I'd like to be here when the plumber looks into that leak."

For ten days the laundry room floor had been wet. I knew the problem wasn't with the washer or the utility sink, because I had experimented by putting dry sheets of newspaper under them.

"Jacob can talk to the plumber. And you should come to lunch because Michael D'Avanzo specifically invited you." Rip had returned to our bedroom looking especially sexy with his hair combed wet and his cheeks glowing with fresh aftershave. Unfortunately, I would have to hold that thought till later.

I proceeded to put in some tastefully dressy "midday" earrings, little gold shells that just showed under my acorn mop of hair. "Who is this guy anyway?"

"Grandfather of a student. Wealthy."

"So we're schmoozing?"

Rip shrugged into his maize summer blazer. I knew the color because I had just cut the cardboard label off the sleeve. "We're schmoozing," he agreed. "Get used to it."

"Bet I was invited so you won't be able to talk business for the whole meal."

"Maybe. Maybe the guy wants to show off his restaurant. Maybe he likes women. Maybe he just wants you to get out of the kitchen. I know I do."

Rip referred both to my dubious cooking skills and the fact that he'd been entertaining groups of three and four guests at our house for lunch three times a week beginning five days after we moved in. Most were for the admissions people of other nearby private schools and, if possible, their heads as well.

Rip needed to familiarize his peers with Bryn Derwyn's program and who it was designed to help. That way, if his school appeared to be a better match for an applicant, the other admissions people could make an informed recommendation.

Although the lunches were a little like applying for the same job over and over, Rip seemed energized by them. Me, I was feeling a little worn—and I didn't even have to sit in. Being pampered by an older gentleman actually sounded wonderful.

Since I still needed a local map to get to the nearest grocery store and home again, I had no idea where La Firenze was located. It looked like a plantation on an immaculate rolling lawn. The foyer floor consisted of an intricate inlaid marble pattern depicting a lion and a guy with a sword and a gold shield. Chamber music whispered in our ears and so did the maitre d'. Dining was going on in all of the several rooms on the ground floor, and judging by the waiter laboring up the broad staircase with a loaded tray, more diners were accommodated upstairs.

We were shown to an intimate little cubicle about twelve by fifteen containing one rectangular table, our host and Richard Wharton.

Before entering, Rip breathed deeply, preparing to conduct himself well in front of a man he knew primarily by his formidable reputation and another whose behavior he had begun to question.

Both men rose as Rip and I approached the table. Wharton shook Rip's hand and leered hello at me with the smug amusement of a cat who has discovered the mouse cannot escape.

While Michael D'Avanzo kissed my hand, I squinted at Wharton distrustfully, causing him to chuckle.

"Welcome," D'Avanzo told us. Then he swept behind me to help with my chair. He was a beautifully fit man of about sixty, immaculate white hair above a perfectly tanned square face with broad black eyebrows. He wore a flattering navy blue suit, a smooth white shirt and a plain red tie. In his breast pocket a matching silk handkerchief folded into two peaks completed the look.

When he bent down to ease my chair in behind me, I inhaled an interesting masculine fragrance dominated by lime. It smelled so good I involuntarily turned toward it, only to meet Michael D'Avanzo's smile. In contrast to the cockiness exhibited by the school's attorney, D'Avanzo's expression was warm and appreciative. After spending most of my time elbow-deep in moving boxes, soapy water, or paint, I responded with every feminine fiber I owned. Every platonic fiber, of course. I could easily believe I was invited for every reason Rip had guessed, including the one about getting me out of the kitchen.

"Thank you for inviting me, Mr. D'Avanzo," I told him. Let the schmoozing begin.

He beamed behind his clasped hands. In place of the usual wedding band was a roughly tooled gold ring enclosing a diamond three times—make that, six times—the size of my engagement ring.

"My pleasure," he schmoozed right back. "And, please. Call me Michael. I'm not really such an old man."

I raised an eyebrow, thinking, "I believe it." Michael's grin broadened as if he had read my mind.

Meanwhile, Richard Wharton, on whom I had been briefed but had not previously met, waved to the waiter who stood by the doorway. "May I treat us to a bottle of wine?"

"Oh, no no no," D'Avanzo complained. "You are in my restaurant. You are my guests. But, please. Order whatever you want."

Wharton began a murmured conversation with the wine steward. Briefly, our host observed his original guest with a penetrating expression of cold calculation, which he replaced almost instantly with a smile.

He turned his attention to Rip. "So I finally get to meet the well-respected Robert Ripley Barnes," he said, as if it had taken years to arrange rather than days. "I've heard quite a lot about you."

"Thank you," Rip replied. From a minuscule stiffness in his shoulders, I knew he was thinking he should have met D'Avanzo back in May when the philanthropist was first approached about helping to fund a new gym. Another waiter set a water glass in front of my husband, and he reached out to touch it.

"Ah, I see that you are concerned, possibly annoyed about my little gesture toward your school."

Rip's alarm was restrained, but clear.

D'Avanzo patted the table twice and looked over Rip's shoulder. "You are quite right, of course. You should have been consulted." He leaned forward on his elbows and met Rip's gaze. "But I assure you my little gesture will grow on you, as they say. Your Bryn Derwyn will be better off. And yes"—here he leaned toward me and stated—"you'll pardon my bold honesty, please. Humor an old man . . . and yes, my grandson will have an arena to exhibit his athletic ability . . ." Again, to me: "Nicky is the apple of my eye, as they say, the world to me, as surely a mother can understand . . ." Back to Rip: "And yes, even my son-in-law will benefit. God knows with a wife like my Tina, he needs all the help he can get." He wagged his head, perhaps over a difficult daughter who was still very well loved.

If any of my discomfort over being present while the men conducted business remained, this exchange erased it. Michael D'Avanzo was quite skilled at holding two or more private conversations simultaneously. Rip's at business level, mine at the confidential personal level, and others I was certain at will, although he seemed to merely tolerate Richard Wharton. If he addressed the man again, I looked forward to gauging D'Avanzo's attitude.

To the waiter, D'Avanzo nodded and said, "We begin." Menus were passed around. Mine was without prices, as I supposed the others were.

I settled on something involving artichoke hearts and parmesan cheese then set the menu aside, glancing toward our waiting host to indicate that we could pick up the conversation.

"My daughter," he continued smoothly, "is rather headstrong. Spoiled." He spread his hands. "My fault, I'm sure. Her mother, rest her soul, did her best to control our Tina, but I could never bring myself to punish such a treasure. Now? Now is too late and we must do the best we can.

"Her husband, Edwin, does excellent work, but there must be work before a man can do it. You see?"

I nodded and sipped at the crisp white wine that had just been poured. Rip had waved his away, as had the restauranteur. More for Richard Wharton—and me, if I wanted it.

We paused to order, Richard choosing a full heavy meal, Rip a pasta dish with scallops and cream. Our host limited himself to an oyster hors d'oeuvre and a salad. Catching my surprise, he filled his chest with air and winked as he ran his hand down his tie. I returned a rather giddy smile. It had been some time since anybody flattered me with such genteel flirtation. I made a mental note to leave the wine to Richard. I didn't need it.

D'Avanzo now addressed Wharton, who sat close beside me. "Is the wine to your satisfaction?" he asked his guest. Perhaps it was my imagination, but I felt that D'Avanzo was asking as a matter of form, including the attorney in the conversation as any host would include every guest, whether or not they were in favor.

Wharton seized the opportunity to rave about the vintage, explain why he preferred it to another, and generally show off. I plastered on my polite smile and stopped listening, observing instead every visible detail about Richard Wharton plus a few invisible ones. I already knew my husband both disliked and distrusted him.

His age: about forty. He was deeply tanned, nothing unusual for August, but this tan suggested that the owner might not spend quite as much time in the office as my husband, for a handy example. Odd, because I always thought people who charged by the minute tended to consider a billable minute the only one well spent. So Richard Wharton either had unusual priorities for a lawyer, or he owned a sunlamp.

He had a nice jaw with a hint of beard; I'd have bet he kept an electric razor in his top right-hand desk drawer. His nose was perfectly straight, his eyebrows sunbleached and full, but flat and unobtrusive, positioned just right above his dark-lashed eyes.

The man's eyes were beautiful. The irises were a golden brown edged in deep brown, the whites whiter than his shirt, his teeth whiter than his eyes. And naturally his hair was a wavy dark taupe with coppery highlights from boating or whatever. Probably boating because his tie was covered with those colorful signal flags flapping on a navy background. He wore a plain old navy blazer and tan Salty Dog pants you usually expect to see without socks.

There was no trace of deference toward D'Avanzo, which meant Wharton either considered himself financially equal to the restauranteur, or sufficiently prominent in his field that he didn't have to kiss anybody's . . . ring. I was just beginning to wonder why he bothered with Bryn Derwyn, which must have been comparable to charity work to him, when he noticed my stare and raised one of those eyebrows a fraction.

"Ah," D'Avanzo, said when the waiter delivered my plate. "Let us eat."

Between bites Rip began to discuss locker rooms. "I studied the blueprints, and I think we could use more space for the girls, maybe eliminate that extra set of rest rooms in the vestibule."

"Perhaps you are right, Mr. Barnes," D'Avanzo addressed Rip formally, another form of sexist flattery but respectful in its intention. "Why don't you meet with my son-in-law personally and describe any concerns you may have. The drawings are preliminary, of course."

Rip nodded, and then engaged D'Avanzo in a discussion of the timetable for the project.

That's when Richard Wharton put his hand on my knee. It was his left hand, so the extracurricular activity didn't affect his ability to feed himself. Neither did it appear to diminish his intense interest in what the other men were saying.

What to do? While I chewed and pretended nothing

awkward was going on, I realized that the folds of the tablecloths—there were two, a long and a short—prevented Rip and D'Avanzo from noticing anything. For all they could see, Richard Wharton's hand rested on his own knee.

"Could I please have some more wine?" I asked, thinking the stretch would force the creep to let go long enough to let me shift my chair. Or else the intoxicant would give me some of the nerve it had obviously given Richard Wharton. Blushing, sipping, I thought wryly, At least now I know one of his priorities.

Any other time I would have slapped the offending paw a stinging blow and verbally cut the guy off at the knees, but this was the chairman of the fund-raising committee. He was responsible for soliciting from the heavy hitters, most of whom he probably knew personally. I couldn't afford to offend him.

That's why I lifted his hand by his shirt cuff up to eye level and said, "Pardon me, but I think you dropped this."

Captured red-handed, so to speak, Richard Wharton chose to burst into laughter. Some of the fancy white wine he had just sipped went up his nose, too, because he did a double-take and snorted and went for his handkerchief. Rip smiled with painful good-sportsmanship. Our host chuckled his polite appreciation of my reprimand while aiming cold oyster eyes at Richard.

Thereafter, I was always "Mrs. Barnes" to the attorney with ironic emphasis on the "Mrs."

Unfortunately, Rip's quarrel with Richard Wharton predated mine and contained far more substance.

And that was the thought the police interrupted when they wailed into the school driveway.

Chapter 5

*A*s it happened, the police and attendant support staff swarmed the front entrance of the school just as Bryn Derwyn's victorious boys' basketball team began to jump and jostle out of their bus. The juxtaposition of realities made me sorry I was an adult.

The kids wore short wool coats or ski jackets over their baggy sweat pants, sloppy socks, and white high tops. One or two wore baseball caps. The sight of the four official vehicles silenced their carefree camaraderie, although one six-footer exclaimed, "Whoa, check this out."

"This doesn't concern you, son," a uniformed policeman told him, herding the tall boy backward toward the front door. The rest of the team sidled inside with wary over-the-shoulder glances.

Meanwhile the JVs trickled out of the bus. Win or lose, the younger players always came home elated. Now their chameleon faces were wide with the TV-show display of drama. "Wow," was the most common response.

An officer accompanied both teams to the locker room, possibly to control the gossip, probably to insure that nobody broke loose and contaminated the crime scene. "Disturbance," was the only explanation I heard anyone give the kids, and the youngsters didn't believe it any more than they were meant to.

One uniformed cop canvassed the lobby taking names and addresses while another few searched the building for stragglers. The most authoritative person, a Lt. John Newkirk, nodded to Rip and me before leading his small army down the hall to view the remains. After determining that my call was indeed legitimate, he relayed a request for the coroner, set the forensics people and the photographer to work, then returned to the lobby.

He shook Rip's hand. "You're head of the school?"

"Yes," Rip admitted. If his clothes, a white shirt and patterned tie over charcoal wide-whale corduroy slacks didn't identify him, the glances of the other surrounding adults did. "Better you than me," their expressions said, and, "Thank goodness I just work here."

"Any more kids around?"

Rip eyed his watch. "Girls' basketball won big yesterday, so the coach gave them today off. Might be a few students working individually with teachers, but four-thirty is late for a Friday. Probably this is it." He pointed his chin at the cluster of teachers and staff. The roundup had gathered two more teachers and three more students; Kevin Seitz, the business manager; the lower school secretary and a computer repairman; Patrice and two boys who had been serving out detentions by helping her clean.

The lieutenant turned to me. "You placed the call, Mrs. Barnes?" He was imposing in a bulky way, about six-two with thinning dark hair and a broad reddish mustache, black eyes, pasty cheeks that made you think of a poor diet or the British complexion; but then he wore a fairly new London Fog overcoat with the lining in, and maybe that suggested the comparison. He projected a bored, low-key competence that made you want to pound something to rivet his attention or maybe continue speaking until you finally said something that woke him up.

"Yes, I . . ." I hesitated to mention that I found the body; it sounded so canned.

Fortunately, Newkirk filled in the blank, nodded to cut me off and said, "Can we speak in private?"

"Of course," I answered.

"My office," Rip offered with a wave of his hand. Then he squeezed mine, lowered himself to the bench, and rested his chin on his fist. I know because just before I would have lost sight of him I glanced back. He looked miserable, and it occurred to me to wonder what I looked like myself.

Newkirk quietly closed the door behind us and directed me into Rip's chair, a big swivel thing covered in a durable tweed. Rip had chosen it to fit his leggy height, and in it I felt more like a little girl in the principal's office than I would have in one of the visitor's chairs. It was hard to say whether that was a calculation on Newkirk's part or whether he just thought I'd feel less threatened with him in the subordinate position.

"Where do you want to start?" he asked.

My attention skipped over the paraphernalia of Rip's office as if I'd never seen it before, as if I hadn't decorated it myself. Understated blue-and-burgundy plaid wallpaper with a tan linen background, a framed lithograph of a country school on election day. Tan linen-like drapes. On the corner credenza a collection of family photographs huddled in their brass frames. The incidental table between the two visitors' chairs supported a bowl of dried flowers I had supplemented with graceful grass stalks and fern pods collected from the unkempt garden in front of our house. Shelves of books filled a tall case—T.S. Eliot, John Irving, Sonia Sanchez, Theodore Dreiser, Alice Walker, F. Scott Fitzgerald, Pat Conroy, Dorothy Parker, and more—poets and authors Rip had once taught his English students and might teach again, books that spanned the range of human sensibilities, writers to hold your hand under any condition. I wondered which one would be appropriate for the death of an attorney.

Newkirk tapped his pen.

"I guess I should start with when I first saw Richard Wharton in the room," I answered.

"Okay."

I explained about the Mop Squad and how I planned to clean the Community Room closet looking for things to sell the night of the holiday program. I told him I went out for a minute and when I got back, Kevin Seitz and Richard were speaking to a couple I knew were late with their tuition.

"Their names?"

I told him, even spelling the last name; but then I added, "You won't embarrass them, will you? I'm not certain that's what they were talking about."

"But that was your assumption."

"Well, yes."

"No guarantees, Mrs. Barnes, but we'll be as tactful as possible. Go on."

I swiveled, unable to stop fidgeting. "I thought about going home for an hour—we live just beside the school —but my coat was still in the Community Room, and the door closest to our house was already chained shut, so I decided to watch the music rehearsal." I continued to explain how I went home without a coat anyway because Rip asked me to phone Didi. "Then I spent a few minutes talking to our son, Garry, and finally came back here. When I got to the Community Room, Richard Wharton was dead."

"Did you touch anything in the room?"

"No, not even the inside doorknob." I explained how I covered my hand with my sleeve before I left.

"Anything look odd to you, aside from the victim and the murder weapon?"

"No." I thought about that again. "No."

"Why did you leave the room the first time?"

"To get something to clean the shelves."

"Did you pass anyone in the hall?"

"No."

"Who else was in the building that you remember?"

I told him about the rehearsal and the music director quitting.

"When you left, your husband was alone in the auditorium?"

My pulse picked up. Was he? "No. No, we walked toward the office together. By the time I came back he was meeting with three teachers. Joanne was also there taking notes or getting instructions or something. It looked as if they'd been there a while."

Newkirk nodded noncommittally. "Know any reasons why someone might want the victim dead?"

"First hand reasons? Provable reasons?" I asked.

"Any reasons."

I considered that. What I knew or thought I knew was all of a damagingly personal nature. Furthermore, the so-called information had been obtained through gossip. If the police couldn't do better than that, we were all in trouble.

"He wasn't well liked," I remarked vaguely, wondering whether I should add, "except by some women."

"Why not?" Newkirk asked with a raised eyebrow.

"I guess because he didn't care who liked him and who didn't."

"Arrogant?"

"Self-assured."

"Antagonistic?"

I shrugged. "He was a lawyer. That was his job."

Newkirk flipped his notebook closed. "Getting cold in here," he remarked.

Outside the day's light had faded into our early winter dusk. Down on the road car headlights streaked by—the last rush hour of the week. I could sense relief in their efficient speed, or perhaps I was simply happy that Newkirk seemed to be finished with me.

"Let's see who's still out there," he suggested.

It was Rip, Joanne, Kevin Seitz, and only three teachers. Newkirk's assistants had weeded out the groups who vouched for each other, Patrice and the detention boys, another teacher and her two student appointments, leaving a sad collection of potential information sources hugging themselves warm and waiting to be interviewed. All the adjoining halls except the one to the Community Room were dimly illuminated by safety lights. Even the lobby was shadowed and unwelcoming.

"Cold in here," Newkirk repeated to Rip. It seemed to be a question.

"The thermostat automatically goes down for the weekend."

Newkirk nodded as if it was an answer he expected, but not one he liked. "Can you turn it up?"

Rip made a little grimace. "Wouldn't it be easier to talk to these people over at our house?"

"Maybe. Yeah, probably." He called over a nearby officer and said, "Harv, help these people find their coats then take them over to the Barnes' house. Back over there?" Newkirk asked, indicating the proper direction with a jerk of his head.

"I'll show them," I remarked cooperatively.

"Coffee?" he asked with a pathetic expression that passed for "please." "This might take awhile."

To the nearest officer he added, "Meet you there."

Then he guided Rip toward his office with a wide-spread paw. "A word with you first," he informed my husband, which threw my thoughts back to the uncomfortable place where they left off.

❧ *Chapter 6* ❧

With Rip and Lt. Newkirk closeted in Rip's office and the witnesses and their official chaperones off collecting briefcases and coats, I sank onto a lobby chair and allowed my mind to skim over the details of July 9, an awful Friday that began with Wilson Flagg complaining about having to fix our bedroom ceiling and ended with Rip learning about his problem with Richard Wharton.

Yes, I decided. That was right. Technically, our daughter's birthday camping-out party didn't get ruined until early the morning of July 10, when some jealous kid or irritated neighbor squirted Chelsea and her girlfriends with a garden hose from behind a bunch of trees. Back inside, their wet-hen stomping and screeching loosened Wilson's brand new ceiling patch, which crashed onto our bed about 2 AM. On Monday morning when Wilson learned that our house required another repair, he quit right on the spot.

But at ten Friday morning when Rip phoned, the elderly maintenance man had just begun to bitch. "Don't see how I can keep up with all that extra stuff your husband wants done over the school if I'm here every day. Only so much one man can do, if you catch my meaning. Nope. Won't be ready for September if this keeps up."

I gauged Wilson to be about sixty-five, give or take a decade. His head was summer-tanned and freckled, with a sparse amount of wispy brown hair. Broad ears supported wire-rimmed glasses. Wide nose, thick lips, and oversized dentures. He was just over my height by a couple inches, maybe five-foot-eight, but he stooped into his concave chest as if avoiding a punch. I could have taken him easy.

In fact, I was just preparing to point out rather emphatically that I was not responsible for the woeful condition of our house or, for that matter, the thunderstorm that had worsened the leak in the roof that caused the hunk of ceiling to fall down in the first place. He was lucky I had to answer the phone.

"Did I tell you about tonight's dinner with the Bodourians?" my husband asked cautiously, the Bodourians being Rip's esteemed predecessor and his wife.

"Impossible," I adamantly maintained while pacing through chunks of plasterboard in my socks. "You'll have to cancel; Chelsea's party is tonight." The birthday sleepover was my effort to mollify our sensitive preteen, who had moped and groused about our relocation to a hair-graying degree through much of the spring. Glory be to old girlfriends, the party appeared to be turning the emotional tide.

"That's tonight?"

"How could you forget? She's talked about little else for two weeks!"

Rip sighed heavily. "Bill Bodourian invited us three weeks ago, Gin. I'm sorry I forgot to tell you, but it's just too late to cancel." Because Bill Bodourian would think Robert Ripley Barnes was an idiot, not at all the type of person to entrust with thirty-two years of one's life's work.

I clutched my hair, suddenly aware that Wilson Flagg was listening from the top of his ladder, aware also that Rip had forgotten pretty much anything a family member had told him since he started his new job on June 15. The man was maxxed out. My turn to sigh.

"I think Didi is between men," I told my beleaguered husband. "Maybe she can supervise the party."

She could, and she did.

That night, as the valet eased our car away among the oaks and azaleas of the Bodourian's club, I remember glancing at Rip. No admiration for the immaculate landscape, not even the slightest anticipation of a fine meal. His eyes were narrowed and his lips pressed tight.

"What?" I asked.

"I was just wondering," he said as he guided me through a broad doorway into an illusory passage to the country club's dining room. Looking closely, I realized that artful clumps of early black-eyed Susans repeated themselves in the mirrors that lined the right hand wall.

"Wondering what?" I asked as we were drawn toward a collection of heavily draped tables overlooking a golf course.

"Wondering what information could be so sensitive that Bill Bodourian needs to tell it to me here."

"Nothing good?" I guessed.

"Nothing good," Rip concurred.

The witnesses and their police escorts were now gathered in the lobby looking at me expectantly. I stood.

A young officer with a weak chin and glasses nodded and held open the school's front door for me. All of us paraded out into the dark cold like a band of silent, somber refugees.

While I led the way down the middle of the parking

lot across the right side of the school, my mind was free to recall the Bodourians' dinner conversation.

We had been ushered to a table against the window overlooking the putting green. Since Rip and Bodourian had met during the interviewing process, the imposing, white-haired gentleman rose and extended his hand to greet me specially. His clothes suited him and his chosen environment—a moderately wild madras sport coat and an Aren't-I-the-daring-one? yellow tie.

His tiny wife, Claire, remained seated. Her tastefully embroidered mint-green dress was garnished with a pearl choker. Every last perky silver curl had been sprayed into obedience by someone other than her.

Drinks were ordered, and Rip and I were given a moment with our menus.

Claire laid a pink paw on my wrist. "Try the Tuna Dijon," she mothered me.

I pretended to think about it.

"Lamb chops, medium," I told the waitress, whose lips briefly twitched, then recovered.

The seating arrangement put Claire across from me next to the window, Rip facing her husband toward the inside of the room. The chatter of the other diners made listening to the men's conversation slightly difficult, especially since Claire's snapping blue eyes and personal questions commanded that I pay attention.

"Now do you have children, dear?" she asked.

"Yes, two. And you?"

"Oh, my yes. Three boys and a girl. Lawrence is a law professor at Princeton, and Maggie is married to a pediatrician . . ."

I zoned out what the others did while I tried to catch the drift of Bodourian's exchange with Rip. Something mild and ingratiating about finding the office in order.

"Quite well organized," Rip replied, making me realize the question had called for a compliment. Bodourian preened and dried the bottom of his water glass on the creamy linen. Long fingers. Buffed nails, perhaps?

Claire proceeded onto grandchildren, and my gaze strayed to the elderly man trying to make a twenty-foot putt on the green down below.

"You look to be in good health," Claire told me.

I sipped my house wine and considered the question, an odd one to pose to someone not yet thirty-five. "Yes, so far so good." When I looked back, the man was putting from the opposite direction.

"So important. So important. When your health begins to go . . ."

Bodourian accepted his salad from the waitress with a nod. "Finished your hiring, have you?"

"Well, no," Rip admitted, and I could tell he wanted to add that he'd been on the job less than three weeks. "I'd rather not make any snap decisions."

"Fourth grade will be easy. Could have taken care of that myself but thought you'd like one of your own in there." He flicked a finger, giving the impression that he really hadn't felt like bothering with that one. "However, the middle school math opening—too bad the fellow I found went elsewhere. Fine young man. Middlebury graduate. You'll have trouble doing as well."

"I'm hoping to get someone who can coach."

Bodourian's left eyebrow arched behind his thick, black-rimmed trifocals. "Good idea," he grudgingly admitted. "Always good to double up like that." His lack of enthusiasm telegraphed his distaste for athletics.

"I was curious," Rip began, "why you limited the extracurricular activities. Financial considerations?"

Bodourian puffed up but wouldn't meet Rip's eye.

"Don't believe in distractions, old boy. Eye on the ball, to use one of your sports metaphors. Give them the basics and send them off to college prepared to study."

His voice imbued the word "study" with a dramatic intonation, not unlike the emphasis a TV preacher I once heard put on the word "God."

My eyes met Rip's briefly. We both believed childhood was too short to rush.

I thought Rip might launch into his Ph.D. candidate discourse on why well-rounded students are better prepared to face higher education and the world, but our dinners arrived about then, and he probably thought his energy would be better spent addressing his salmon encrusted with horseradish.

While three of us occupied ourselves chewing, Claire filled the open air time with the medical saga of her bursitis. Nibbles of stir-fried chicken (she had also skipped the Tuna Dijon) were interspersed with "and then he told me to's" and "so I told him's." Perhaps it was the house wine, my underlying desire to be at Chelsea's party, or the oppressive attitudes of our host and hostess, but I was dying to liven up the meal. At home we had had more amusing dinners right after Garry got a tooth pulled or Chelsea broke her arm.

"Seen any good movies lately?" I asked Bill when Claire paused for a nibble.

"I'm afraid Claire and I don't go to the cinema nearly as often as we once did. Isn't that right, Mother?"

Mother blinked. Her mind had been working out what happened at the next office visit.

"Too much nudity and sex for us old timers," the retired headmaster admitted.

"Awful," Claire concurred. "Just awful what they call entertainment these days. Children know all about sex way too young, if you ask me."

"But they have to . . ." I began, but Rip caught my eye. Not worth it.

"That reminds me," I said instead, "about the day

Chelsea's health class had sex education and, you know, basically got the whole story."

I glanced around the table. Rip, who knew where I was going, folded his arms to watch me perform. Claire had leaned forward the better to hear, and Bill squinted at me impatiently. I opted for the short version.

"Chelsea jumped off the school bus mad as all get out." I raised my voice appropriately. " 'I found out what you and Daddy did,' she yelled at me. 'I think it's dis*gust*ing. And you didn't just do it once—*you did it twice!'* "

Rip and I leaned back and smiled, amused once again by the old family standby. Claire seemed bewildered. Her husband offered a good-sport chuckle.

"I don't know why they have to teach *children* . . ." Claire lamented.

"Now, Mother. We've been through this . . ." Abruptly, he asked me, "Do you care for dessert?"

I thought the answer was supposed to be no, so that was what I said.

"Fine. How about coffee? There's one item I need to mention to your husband before we let you get home to your . . . delightful . . . children."

I nodded and told the waitress iced decaf.

"Interesting, your mentioning your fondness for athletics," Rip's predecessor began, not at all inconvenienced by what Rip had actually said. The old head was 100 percent authority figure now, the patriarch beyond questioning, and I braced myself to finally hear what was worth the price of our meal.

"Did your little ones ever get chicken pox?" Claire asked hopefully.

"Excuse me," I told her confidentially, "but I'd like to hear what Bill's saying."

"You've heard talk about building the school a new gymnasium?" Bodourian questioned Rip.

"A few people mentioned it during the interviews."

"I take it you were for the project?"

"Sooner or later," Rip admitted. "The present gym seems adequate for now."

"Do you . . . ?" Claire tried again.

"No, I never have," I told her apologetically. Her face pinched together as she tried to read sense into my premature answer.

Bill Bodourian pressed his lips into a pout. "Many of the parents, especially the ones on the Board, don't have your patience," he told Rip. "I received quite a bit of pressure to raise funding as soon as possible."

"But with such a modest-sized student body . . ."

"Yes, I quite agree. In fact I felt a theater would have come first, but many people insist that athletics make or break a school. They certainly offer an outlet for all those teenage hormones." Bodourian glanced toward me as he emphasized the last word. I suppose the accompanying smile was meant to show he, too, had a sense of humor.

Rip waited quietly for the retired head to continue, something Bodourian seemed reluctant to do.

"How was it left?" Rip prompted.

The older man took a breath then dove straight in. "Quite on their own, mind you, some of the parents— led by a Board member, of course—approached Michael D'Avanzo. Do you know who he is?"

"I've heard the name."

I watched the two men over the top of my iced coffee, afraid to miss a word of their delicate conversation.

"Lots of contacts I was told. Very 'connected,' I believe was the phrase. Anyway, his grandson, Nicholas, lives with him. D'Avanzo formally adopted him after his parents—D'Avanzo's daughter and her husband—were killed in a car crash. Nicky's the apple of the old man's eye. He's been at Bryn Derwyn for a year now and is coming up on seventh grade. Quite an athlete."

When Claire opened her mouth for one last try, I gave her the palm-up stop signal I use on the kids.

"The parents who approached D'Avanzo were very smart. They argued that a new gym would benefit no one so much as it would young Nick. The upshot of it all was that D'Avanzo agreed to foot half the bill if the school could raise the other half. He would give a certain amount up front to pay for architectural plans, the rest would be matched in installments as Bryn Derwyn proceeded with its fund-raising campaign."

Rip had become still as low tide. "How much?" he asked.

"Million and a half total according to the first drawings."

Rip reacted with mild surprise. "So you've proceeded that far?"

"D'Avanzo's was a very generous offer. No one felt we should turn it down."

"Why wasn't I told right away?" After he had been hired back in February, he had been kept informed about almost everything else.

Bodourian leaned forward. "This more or less is right away. Negotiations continued up until my last day. I thought you'd be pleased to be out of it; and frankly, a newcomer wouldn't have been able to bring it off. All in all I think you'll find you've been handed quite a good deal."

Rip appeared unconvinced. Perhaps being forced to raise $750,000 for a project he didn't endorse accounted for his reticence.

"There's one condition," Bodourian continued somewhat sheepishly.

"Yes?" Rip's dissatisfaction was undisguisable now.

"D'Avanzo wants us to use his son-in-law as the contractor."

Rip tilted his head. "Is that legal?"

Bodourian's chin rose. "Richard Wharton will see to it that our by-laws are not violated." He eyed Rip without much regard, like a man who knew he held all the trump. "Richard Wharton was really the key man. In fact I appointed him chairman of the committee in charge of raising the balance."

"Who's Richard Wharton?" I couldn't resist asking.

"Lawyer. On the Board," Rip answered.

"And if we don't use the son-in-law? What's his name?"

"Longmeier. Longmeier Construction. Reputable firm. On hard times like most of them. Their bid was competitive. Nothing to worry about there."

Like hell, Rip's face said. "Thank you for telling me this, Bill," Rip said aloud. He glanced at his watch. "Getting late. I'm afraid Gin is throwing a birthday party for our daughter, and we should get back to light the candles. Lovely of you to invite us . . ." He stood and shook Bodourian's hand, nodded at our hostess. "Claire."

"Goodnight," Claire cooed. "So nice to have met you."

"Good night," I echoed.

When I looked back, Dr. William F. Bodourian was signaling for the waitress, probably not for coffee.

"What was all that about?" I asked as I trotted to catch up with Rip's lengthy stride.

He did not respond. Outside the heavy, arched doorway he grabbed his car keys off the valet's rack, tipped the gawking college kid and strode off.

"But sir," the valet called, starting after him.

I extended my arm to hold the parker back. "Let him go," I said. "My husband needs the exercise." I smiled and shrugged, knowing the young man had seen the fire in Rip's eye.

"Yes, ma'm." Then I waited, my clutch purse gripped tightly between my sweating hands, hoping my husband wouldn't forget to pick me up.

He remembered, but it was several miles before I dared to ask why he was so furious. Despite what "connected" usually meant around Philadelphia, I felt certain Bodourian merely meant that Michael D'Avanzo was into networking. The older man just wasn't good with slang, that was all.

Except that wasn't it.

"I should have been informed right away," Rip complained. "You don't saddle a new head with a million-and-a-half project without warning."

"You're worried about raising the money?" I asked, still confused by Rip's anger.

"It isn't just that. We do need the gym. I'd have waited to build it until enrollment looked a little better . . ."

"Then . . . what?" I asked.

"It makes me nervous as hell to have a faction of the Board operating behind my back."

"The lawyer, Richard Wharton?"

"Right. Bodourian should have controlled him. And because he didn't, I'm worried that I won't be able to."

By the time my police and witness entourage reached the front door of our house I was so concerned about what pasty-faced Newkirk would try to make out of Rip's problems with Richard Wharton, I dropped my house keys on my foot.

In the glare of the porchlight the young cop who retrieved them took the opportunity to look hard into my eyes.

❀ Chapter 7 ❀

"*M*om," Chelsea ambushed me the minute I opened the door. "A reporter called. He thought I was you. He said somebody was killed!"

While I pulled my daughter in for a hug, people jostled into the living room around us, Rip and Newkirk included. Chelsea held fast, like she hasn't clung to me in several years.

Reporters. Inhuman leeches. Very few, of course. But a few too many. My mother-in-law learned that her father's car crash had been fatal when a reporter calling her for information asked, "How old *was* Mr. Fitzsimmons anyway?" Infuriating to think such callousness exists. Intolerable that my children had just been exposed to it.

"I'll answer the phone from now on," I told Chelsea. From my tone she knew exactly how I intended to respond, and the idea comforted her. The Barnes fortress was once again armed; she could climb down from the wall.

Garry stood close by his sister. The two were within eight inches of the same height, and now their identical fear enhanced the family resemblance despite their differences in coloring. Rip shepherded them both into the dining room for a whispered conversation, which I saw them absorb with wide eyes and open-mouthed glances toward the crowd in our living room.

"Freezing over there," Newkirk addressed me. "You got anywhere private?"

"Downstairs? No." The kitchen was standing-room-only, the laundry a narrow cubicle leading to the side yard. The dining room offered seating, but opened widely to the crowded living room.

The phone rang. I gave Newkirk a fiery glance, reached around the corner for the kitchen-wall extension, lifted the receiver, then pressed the plunger to disconnect. Then I dropped the receiver into a drawer and closed it. The phone would squawk for a while, but that would soon stop. Verbally frying reporters would be more satisfying without an audience, and at the moment I had a house full of witnesses and police.

"I'll see if our bedroom is presentable," I told Newkirk, then left him fending off Barney's attempts to spit polish his shoe.

Mercifully, the bed was made, and a ninety-second sweep of underwear and used towels took care of the main embarrassments. The ceiling repair still hadn't been repainted, the blue drapes from the old house didn't match the new yellow, white, and green flowered bedspread, and the hunter-green carpet I chose attracted lint the way white blouses attract mustard. However, there was an empty slipper chair and the bed to sit on, and the conversations could not be overheard downstairs.

Newkirk chose to finish with Rip first, which left the kids cowering alone at the far end of the dining room table. I went to them as if the aftermath of a murder was just another curve the Main Line had chosen to throw our way, one that I intended to take in my stride. "You eat anything?" I asked them.

Chelsea shook her head no, while Garry admitted he had some pretzels.

"I'll fix something," I said, tousling Garry's hair on my way behind them into the kitchen. His neck was stiff and his skin a little cool. "Feed the dog?" I asked.

"Yeah," he sneered with approximately the same disgust the question usually generated.

"Get me two packages of English muffins from the laundry room freezer," I suggested.

"Pul-eeze," he mocked.

"Please," I added dutifully. Garry was fine. Chelsea's eyes were a little shiny, but if the run-off was between "fear" and "titillation" now, my vote went for the latter. I left her feigning interest in the map of Europe spread under her arms, knowing she was memorizing every word within hearing, every gesture, every expression. She was, after all, my daughter.

From the kitchen I surveyed the gathering around our naked Christmas tree. We had misjudged the tree's size, and it bit into the social space considerably. With a brick fireplace consuming the shorter far wall and the TV and one chair filling the near wall by the kitchen, that left our sofa facing the tree and what little could be seen of the tall, broad front window.

Presently everyone was staring past the tree out the window. I looked out myself and saw Richard Wharton's body being loaded into the coroner's van. I moved toward the cord that closed the burlap drapes, glanced at the gathering for permission, received one nod from Joanne, and closed the sight off from the grim faces.

Pamela Washington and Sophia Mawby, two of the teachers from Rip's office, began a quiet conversation on the sofa. Danny Vega, the other, resumed pacing. Joanne sat primly on the chair by the TV, and Kevin Seitz rocked on his feet with his hands in his back pockets glaring at the drapes with x-ray vision. Two uniformed cops leaned against the walls.

Perhaps the grimmest face belonged to Kevin. His family had lived two doors from mine when he was little, and on Friday nights I often came home from dates to find the adults playing poker and Kevin and his younger brother slumbering softly in my parents' bed. Eventually the boys and their blankets would be slung over our fathers' shoulders and carried down the street to their own bunks.

After the Seitzes moved, I heard news of their family through my mother. Until this summer I hadn't spoken to Kevin as an adult except at his father's funeral.

"Help me make coffee?" I suggested. He needed to expel some energy before his turn with Newkirk. His furtive nervousness made him look guilty as hell.

"Did you know Richard Wharton?" I asked while I handed him the coffee can and showed him where we kept the pot.

"Indirectly," he answered. Adrenaline kicked my heart into high gear.

Garry plunked the frozen muffins on the counter. Kevin and I waited while he escaped. Ten seconds later my son was flopped in front of the TV treating questionees and cops alike to a Cosby re-run.

"What do you mean, 'indirectly'?" I prompted Kevin, softly so no one heard over the television laughter.

Kevin's efficiency with a coffee pot did bachelorhood proud, although my patience wore thin while he counted scoops.

Finally Bryn Derwyn's young business manager turned his college-boy face toward me and admitted, "Wharton helped my father fight the lawsuit." The one in which an employee sued over a scratch from a rusty nail and won.

"Oh," I said heavily. My mother had delivered that

story and the rest of the saga in installments, the final
episode with tears smeared down her face. While Arlen
Seitz bluffed his family and friends, his building-supply
business dwindled with the recession until it reached a
critical low. Kevin, not long out of Tulane, gave up an
impressive corporate job to apply his M.B.A. where he
thought it would do the most good—helping with the
family business. He pruned and regrouped and refi-
nanced but it was too little too late. His father filed for
bankruptcy. That night Arlen Seitz waited for his wife to
fall asleep, slipped back to his warehouse, sat down in a
pile of sawdust, and fired a bullet into his brain. Kevin's
mother told mine that Arlen blamed excessive attorney
fees for the beginning of the end.

"You blame Wharton?" I asked Kevin. I had been
thawing batches of muffins in the microwave, but I
paused to hear his reply. In the muted kitchen light he
looked almost childlike again. His straight honey-blond
hair fell over one eyebrow, his moonstone-blue eyes
blinked with fatigue, even his wrinkled white collar was
partly in and partly out of his patterned sweater. I
wanted to brush his hair into place, tidy his collar, and
smooth away the worry lines on his brow with my hands;
but the whim passed, and I was just me and nobody's
fairy godmother.

Kevin shook his head out of a trance. "No," he said
sadly. "Wharton was a callous bastard, but he didn't
cause Dad's problems."

The unspoken "just hurried them along," hung in the
air between us.

"So where were you when it happened?"

Kevin gaped at me. "I don't know."

"In your office?"

"Probably."

"Hear anything?"

He stared at my elbow. "No."

I widened my eyes and tilted my head. "Too bad."

"Pour that when it's ready, will you?" I said with a nod toward the perking coffeepot.

"Sure," Kevin agreed, his head hung low.

I gathered the two dozen muffins onto two cookie sheets, grabbed three forks, and left Kevin to collect himself in private. While Garry, Chelsea, and I separated muffin halves in preparation for assembling a bunch of impromptu pizzas, I mentally kicked myself for the offhand comment that brought Kevin to Bryn Derwyn and now exposed him to this nerve-wracking situation.

"I wonder if the school could afford Kevin Seitz." That's what I said, and that was why he was here.

As Rip had become immersed in the financial mires of Bryn Derwyn Academy, he came to believe that a business manager would pay for him- or herself and also relieve the headmaster of several messy chores. By August he had begun to shake the grapevine for a candidate.

As it turned out, the school could indeed afford Kevin, because at twenty-seven the up-and-coming business whiz already needed an upbeat enterprise to put some purpose back into his life. Interviewing cooks, managing a health insurance plan, streamlining the payroll, shopping for everything from paper clips to a better mortgage—in short, making sure Bryn Derwyn met its financial obligations in every way—suited the young man's needs. Kids would benefit from it all, either directly or indirectly, and Kevin liked the way that felt. He allowed the job to consume him. Recently, I'd begun to think he needed a woman in his life, and I introduced him to a couple prospects without much luck.

"Kevin Seitz!" Lt. Newkirk called from the top of the steps as Rip trotted down from the second half of his interview. "Could I see you, please?"

On his way by, Kevin glanced into the dining room where I was sitting with the kids. I felt a chill of apprehension when our eyes met.

The family who was delinquent with their tuition had probably departed in a hurry. That would have left Kevin and Richard Wharton alone in the Community Room minutes before Richard's death. One word from Kevin about his father's bankruptcy, one snide retort from the arrogant attorney—who wouldn't want to reach for a shovel?

When I shuddered, five muffin halves fell off the cookie sheet I was carrying back to the kitchen. Fortunately, Barney was always hungry.

Chapter 8

*I*n the midst of the people waiting in our living room, Rip donned his plaid wool jacket and pulled on some gloves. We met at the kitchen doorway.

"Jacob went home," he explained, "so I have to lock up the school after the specialists finish with the crime scene." He kissed my bangs, squeezed my shoulders and left, shutting the front door tight behind him. The house felt quite a bit lonelier.

From her chair by the TV, Joanne, the consummate caffeine addict, smelled the coffee and eased into the kitchen.

"You're not fooling me," I said in an attempt at normal banter.

She shrugged. "Where are the cups?"

I indicated a cabinet door with my elbow, since my hands were sticky with the spaghetti sauce I was spooning onto the muffins.

"You okay?" I asked.

"No. Are you?"

"Not really."

"Don't talk to reporters," she said, as if it was foremost on her mind and she hadn't wanted to wait for an opening.

I glanced at the phone I'd shut into a drawer and thought of the scathing remarks I'd been preparing in my head. "Why?" I asked.

"It's a PR thing. Let Rip do it." Joanne emphasized her words with a somber look in the eye, then poured coffee and turned tail on me. She walked stiffly, like a much older woman.

I stared after her with my mouth open. The kitchen had tilted somehow, and I reached out to steady myself.

I had wanted Joanne to keep me company in the kitchen, to watch me sprinkle cheese and oregano and maybe calm me with an inconsequential argument over the temperature of the oven. I had not expected her to verbally punch me in the stomach and then leave.

With both sticky hands on the edge of the counter I stared at the portion of school property I could see through the window beyond my own silhouette.

Word of mouth generated by his summer networking lunches had netted Bryn Derwyn thirty students by September, yet to me the process had simply amounted to cold cuts and iced tea. When Joanne looked me in the eye, I finally got it. Goodwill was not just part of the private school business, it was the currency that paid the bills. Education just happened to be the product.

Which meant that if the press decided to sensationalize Richard's murder, public opinion could diminish Bryn Derwyn's reputation until the actual institution became extinct.

My neck went rigid. Quite suddenly I realized I didn't want to leave this place.

True, we'd only been here half a year—six exhausting months—but those months had committed Rip to the school, and to my surprise—me, too. Bryn Derwyn had become the Barnes' family business. Every evening when Rip related the details of his day, I took every word to heart. This was personal. We lived here. Even this leaky, drafty, cramped, unreliable house suddenly seemed worth fighting for.

Until Joanne's remark I saw Richard as the only victim, felt compassion and anger and fear only as they related to him. Now I feared for anybody who depended on Bryn Derwyn Academy.

And nobody, I realized, depended on it more than Rip, me, and the kids.

If Bryn Derwyn closed, the current students would be absorbed by other schools. The alumni might or might not notice that their mailings stopped, and the Board members would probably cross a time-consuming chore off their lists with much relief and very little regret.

Yes, the teachers would be in quite a bind—several months away from similar permanent employment.

But as soon as the bank caught on that the school's mortgage was no longer being paid, we Barneses would also be out on the street.

Even worse, beyond all reasoning, Rip would consider the school's failure to be his fault. My instincts yearned to prevent any of those possibilities from happening.

Burdened with frustrated resolve, I shouted, "Coffee's ready," and served the pizza rounds after the cops and "witnesses" helped themselves to the dark brew. My attitude was grim, militant. I could feel it in my muscles and see it reflected on the faces of my reluctant guests.

Joanne refilled her mug and waved the food away. She forced a breath into her lungs and wiped a tear from her cheek.

"I won't say anything," I promised. She was right with her advice; I was much too forthcoming with information, much too honest and blunt. I would sink Rip's ship with my first sentence.

"Probably doesn't matter," she said.

"Oh, Joanne," I moaned. "Is it really that bad?" She knew everything about everybody. She had been Bill Bodourian's assistant for years.

"Joanne Henry," Lt. Newkirk called.

I poured a mug of coffee for her to carry up to Newkirk. If he didn't drink it black—tough.

The school's pivotal employee wiped both eyes with her cuff and finally responded to my question. "Maybe not. We'll see."

That's when it occurred to me to wonder exactly what Joanne would be telling the police.

Kevin Seitz danced down the stairs from his session with Newkirk like an athlete thrilled by an open field. His face was flushed with relief. He could scarcely refrain from grinning. He had been up there a mere five or six minutes.

When he retrieved his coat from the pile on a dining room chair, Newkirk bent down from his position on the stairs and saw him. "Not just yet, if you don't mind, Mr. Seitz. I may have a few more questions later."

Kevin simply deflated. If a dining room chair hadn't been two feet from his rear, he'd have slumped to the floor.

I put some food in front of his face. "Eat this," I ordered in grandmotherly fashion. "Then I have something for you to do."

Kevin looked through me as if he wondered where my voice had come from, then he looked at the pizzas as if they were yak dung. I hooked his arm and said, "C'mere. Our Christmas tree lights need untangling. I promised the kids we'd do it tonight."

He glanced around for somebody to delegate the chore to but found no one even slightly interested. "You're the man," I said, clapping him on the shoulder,

"There they are." Garry had deposited the boxes of lights and ornaments under the tree.

When the kids saw Kevin open the box and peek inside, they were beside him in a flash, grabbing handfuls of green wire strung with tiny clear bulbs. Some of the bulbs would be burned out, so none of them would light. I'd given Kevin an annoying time-consuming job just determining how to begin. Exactly the distraction he needed.

Someone had shut the TV off, and an uncomfortable silence permeated the room. Music? We usually played our ancient Christmas albums while we decorated, the only time I could stand listening to them. Soon the radio and mall public address systems would sicken me with the repetition. Yet hearing the carols for the first time after a long hiatus always cheered me with the promise of the season. Soon enough we would all become cynical, resentful, irritable, and tired.

Chelsea ended my internal debate by switching on the radio—to her station. Bump bumpy bump, la la la. I could never quite get behind the new music, couldn't quite imagine Chelsea becoming nostalgic over any of it thirty years from now, turning up a favorite, singing along. But who'd have guessed that "I Want to Hold Your Hand" would linger. Chelsea strung wire through her fingers looking for burned out bulbs, bouncing and swaying and whispering song lyrics as she worked, tactfully though, just being herself. I wanted to cry. It was perfect, precisely what everybody needed.

Okay, so I did cry. Just a little, and in the kitchen. Danny Vega, humming along, brought in debris from the impromptu meal. A stick of a guy with a beaky nose and sloped shoulders who always wore short-sleeved permanent press shirts he probably bought from a catalog, he ignored me, dumped the trash and left. Danny taught civics, and I knew of no connection between him and Richard Wharton except that he'd been in the building when Richard was killed. In Rip's office to be exact.

He flipped the lid off the ornament box and began to examine a light blue, wooden airplane on a thin red string. He stuck it on the tree, extracted a styrofoam snowman, peered at it quizzically. "My mother only did red balls and tinsel," he explained when he caught me watching. We shared a smile. What was it about celebrating holidays the same way year after year that comforted us and at the same time made our families feel unique?

The hostess in me surveyed the room. The two cops still leaned against the walls apart from the others—professional, unapproachable, and alert. If I walked up to the nearest one and said, "How's the wife," he'd have gawked as if I had said something rude in Swedish.

On the far end of the couch Pamela Washington and Sophia Mawby conversed softly under the music and tried not to glance at the cops. Both women had pressed their knees close together as if for warmth. Warmth?

"Danny!" I called to the storky civics teacher. "How about lighting the fire? It's ready to go, just open the flue." I walked in and handed him some matches.

Pamela was a compact African-American woman of about twenty-six with large, prominent bones covered with firm muscle. As an artist's creation her title would have been "The Elegance of Pride." She taught fifth grade, an especially good time to introduce that concept. She also managed to express herself with a minimum of effort. For example, right now she was conveying sorrow, discomfort, and impatience with a simple, graceful frown.

Her companion was an amorphous white woman of fifty-five who taught middle school math. Her shoes were scuffed brown lace ups, her stockings washed to a shade paler than her skin. She wore a softly pleated brown skirt, a brown belt, and a tan blouse with pearl buttons. Her hair was fine and as washed out as her stockings. Glasses dangled down her bodice on a thin silver chain, leaving naked dark eyes of a formidable clarity.

Within Sophia Mawby's vision the world was strictly ordered, a paint-by-the-numbers formula that scorned deviation. She chaired the Social Concern Committee of which Pamela, Dan, and Rip were members. I later learned that at the time of Richard's death, Joanne had been in Rip's office getting instructions from them for a general mailing about an evening program on teenage promiscuity and AIDS.

No doubt Lt. Newkirk had already determined the validity of their mutual alibi, but these people had also been closest to the main entrance of the school. They might have seen the murderer enter or leave, a possibility Newkirk was surely pursuing.

However, I doubted that it was taking Joanne half an hour to describe what little she saw. My guess was that the lieutenant was pressing her for dirt—who hated Richard Wharton, to be exact.

Which meant she was probably relating what she told me about Jeremy Philbin back in September, the night Bryn Derwyn's veteran algebra teacher ruined my inaugural faculty party all by himself.

Philbin's story was a humbling one because although he could be a reactionary pain in the butt and was potentially alcoholic, he was also a rather ordinary guy, like all of us either living with his flaws or in spite of them.

I settled into Joanne's former seat by the TV, sipped some bitter black coffee, and tuned into my own thoughts.

If Jeremy Philbin killed Richard Wharton, I decided

half the population of the world was probably in danger from the other half.

Which, it chilled me to realize, has never been far from the truth.

❈ *Chapter 9* ❈

Once when I was fairly young, my father, a some-times musician, took me to watch an open re-hearsal of the Philadelphia Orchestra. The tickets were a bonus for donating $100 or more, and someone who Dad knew had done that and passed the tickets on to him. For the second half we sat where we could watch all the players, but initially we chose the first row.

The guest conductor was Russian, a thin, elegant man wearing a pale gray, three-piece suit of a fine, light-weight wool. His shirt was white, and I could see that the points of his collar were stiff with starch. His me-dium-brown hair puffed high with waves. His shoes were a plain shiny black, and I thought to myself as he stood in the wings, holding himself still, waiting: How is he going to do this? He doesn't speak English!

Suddenly he burst onto the stage, and with long strides across the pale, clean floor quickly arrived front and center. He ripped his arms free of his suit coat and threw it onto an empty chair. He tore loose the knot of his tie, rolled up his sleeves, and stood, hands on hips, while he made eye contact with every orchestra member seated before him, every last one of them sitting at at-tention. I was ten years old with no musical training whatsoever, but *I* sat on the edge of my seat ready to get to work.

Our first summer at Bryn Derwyn I was so new, so full of optimism and pride, that I believed Rip's and my first faculty party could do for Bryn Derwyn what that conductor had done with the orchestra: set the tone for their entire performance together. What an idiot I was.

All summer long Rip had preached his family atmosphere theme to anyone who would sit still and listen. Less pressure with more personal attention. Extracurriculars for balance. His spiel enumerated the educational techniques the teachers would use to accomplish these ideals.

The party would manifest the theme with a casual elegance. I would serve make-them-yourself hoagies and put up the badminton net. There would be mint for the iced tea, twists of lemon, wedges of lime, and summer games to entice new friendships. A gold-plated idiot.

That was obvious the minute three teachers broke free of their all-day meeting and wandered across the front of the school toward our new beer cooler under the tree.

For my outfit I had shopped five stores, finally choosing a short, tailored golf-style skirt and top in grassy green to contrast with my tan. My white canvas slip-ons were pristine, rescued countless times throughout the summer from muddy paws, filthy car carpets, and ketchup.

The teachers who straggled over from the school wore assorted flip-flops, cut-off jeans, a T-shirt advertising fitness equipment in one case, and in another a striped shirt that resembled some of Rip's pajamas. The two young men and one woman walked like marathoners the morning after. They were sweaty and inclined to rub their eyes. They looked like they might stay awake just long enough for a quick beer and a sandwich, if the sandwich didn't take too long.

"Hi. I'm Gin Barnes," I said, sticking out my hand when they wandered within range.

"'Lo," said the first male. He mumbled a name I didn't catch.

"Hi," and "Hi," said the other two. They sipped beer from the cans and looked at each other for a clue what to say.

"How'd the meeting go?" I asked.

"Fine, fine."

"Well, we've got horseshoes, badminton, darts," I said. "If the mood strikes you."

"Maybe later," said the woman sympathetically. Her eyes scouted around for seating. The school's single picnic table waited under a second tree, and she went over and sat on the bench facing the yard.

"You catch the Phillies last night?" said one male to another, permission for me to leave if ever I heard it.

Rip then arrived with a larger batch of people and others close behind. He introduced me around, but I must have been nervous because the names refused to stick. Then Rip directed everyone to the bar and the cooler. Clumps of three and four fell into conversations. Everybody had drinks. More people came. And that was it, thirty-five weary guests. I brought out the pretzels.

Joanne Henry stood alone near a card table I had centered on the grass in front of the house, away from the bar to allow for traffic flow. After I deposited cheese and crackers and leaned against the table, she said, "Too bad your kids aren't here."

"Why?" I asked with alarm. I had gone out of my way to give them movie money and deposit them at the nearest mall.

"Somebody to start those games," Joanne elaborated. She bit a cracker without blinking. The stare came off a bit frigid for the circumstances, reminding me of an overzealous border guard. Since my husband worked inside her territory eleven hours a day, I decided I'd better befriend the gatekeeper.

"Care for some wine?" I asked my nemesis with the fine, beige hair.

"Chardonnay?" she inquired with an accompanying raised eyebrow.

"I believe that can be arranged."

I lifted the large green bottle from the ice cooler and filled two seven-ounce cups just short of the brim. Then I crooked a finger to indicate the two sunbathing lounge chairs in front of the bushes beneath the living room window. Joanne followed, easing herself onto the yellow-and-white striped one and leaving the orange-and-white one for me. She crossed her legs, which were clad in a navy blue cotton print, and rested her heels on the chair's extension. The tumbler of white wine was received with a solemn nod. After a long dip into it, she leaned back and sighed.

We drank in silence to within an inch of the bottom of our cups. Then I said, "Who the hell are all these people?"

Joanne widened her eyes and blinked. "You don't know anyone?"

"I know you."

"Oh dear," she observed, obviously realizing that if she was my best friend there, I was a virtual stranger at my own party.

"Well, the stork with the short sleeves is Danny Vega," she began. "Civics. And with him are . . ." and so it went. Fortunately we were out of earshot of them all.

After my tutoring session was over, I went to refill Joanne's cup, neglecting my own since I still had hostess chores. While I stood at the bar, I noticed an older man

downing vodkas neat, two cups while I watched out of
the corner of my eye. He was tall, with a square jaw and
sallow skin and white/blond straight hair disturbed by
the breeze. The puffy flesh around his bloodshot blue
eyes was further narrowed by his calculating squint. He
had placed his left hand between his bottom and the
coarse bark of the oak tree that sheltered the cooler. He
could have chosen one of the folding chairs, but they
were positioned several paces away from the liquor.

I stuck out my hand and said, "Hi, I'm Gin."

"Wonderful," he said, "I'll have a double." Then he
croaked out a little laugh.

"Gin Barnes?" I hinted.

He immediately stood erect and saluted. "Aha," he
told me. "Jeremy Philbin, algebra. Pleased to meetcha."

"Is anything wrong?" I asked.

He pawed my forearm with his narrow hand. I could
still feel the indentations made by the tree bark. "All
good ideas, I'm sure," he said. "On paper. Of course,
it's me and you have to implement them."

Warning him with my last name had been useless; he
thought I was a new teacher. Also, he pronounced "implement" with the greatest of care. This guy was going
to need a ride home.

"Excuse me," I told him. "I have to get out the food."

"You do that," he called after me.

He stepped away, and I heard him ask the first group
he infiltrated, "What is this six-day rotation shit?"

"I believe it's to . . ." a mild young man began to
reply, only to be interrupted by Philbin. "Shit. That's
what it is. How the hell will we know where to
be . . . ?"

"Read the schedule?" Pamela Washington replied
only half in jest.

"You seen your schedule?" Philbin pressed. When
Pamela, who taught fifth grade and therefore didn't use

the new schedule, stood mute, he turned to the others in the group. "Have you? Have you?"

One of the men accepted Philbin's invitation to gripe. "Yeah, and it's a bear . . ."

I stopped listening and proceeded to deliver Joanne's drink.

Before I went inside I noticed that Philbin had joined yet another group and was remarking loudly, "Only thing he did right was hire that shrink, '. . . to answer any questions we have regarding our students,'" he quoted Rip in a singsong whine. "Hell, he should have hired thirty shrinks—one for each of us!"

Shaken, I took a few extra minutes arranging the food on the dining room table where the starving September yellow jackets couldn't out-eat the guests. First was the tray of ham, cappicola, cooked salami, and provolone from the Bryn Mawr Deli. Then I placed long rolls from the Conshohocken Italian Bakery into a huge basket. (They offered a discount to schools.) Next I uncovered bowls of sliced onions, shredded lettuce, and sliced tomatoes, all from a farm stand way on the other side of Ludwig near Didi's Beverage Barn, where I had also picked up the beer and soda. I put out a cruet of olive oil and a shaker of oregano, potato chips, and pickles. In all I'd probably driven a hundred miles to make the food appear simple, family style, warm. With Jeremy Philbin out there scorching the earth, I felt warm all right, bordering on torrid.

Outside I began wending my way among the guests announcing that dinner was served. It was five PM. They had only been there half an hour, but it was time. All my instincts said so.

My route more or less followed the path used by Jeremy Philbin. I could tell by the conversations.

". . . goddamn yearbook. When in the hell am I go-

ing to find time to do that? I've got four preps this
year!"

"Pardon me. Dinner is served."

". . . first thing the soccer team's going to have to do
Monday is pick rocks off the field . . ."

"Dinner's in the dining room. Please help yourself."

"She's directing the chorus? Can she sing?"

"Community service? You mean like offering rides to
drunks? Stuff like that?"

"You seen my schedule?"

"You seen mine?"

"Don't trip over the badminton pole, Georgie."

"My ass aches. How do the kids sit on those chairs all
day?"

"Those miserable Phillies lost again. You believe
that?"

I put two fingers in my mouth and did my police whis-
tle. Then I blushed daintily when every face turned to
gawk.

"Excuse me," I said in my normal voice. "Dinner is in
the dining room. Please help yourselves."

Enough people responded to my announcement to
clear the bar for me. I repeated the seven-ounce pour
for Joanne and myself and returned to the lawn chair at
her side.

"What a rotten apple," I remarked, certain she knew
who I meant. A few clouds had moved overhead simu-
lating an early twilight. Most everyone, except two men
who were actually playing horseshoes and a group talking earnestly around the picnic table with Rip, had wandered inside to collect their dinner.

Rip's secretary and I watched the clouds and drank. I
felt curiously detached from my tense, weary body, immune from the consequences of my thoughts and state-
ments. So I said, very thoughtfully, à la Jeremy Philbin,
"Joanne Henry, kind of a marshmallowy name for

somebody as competent as you, don't you think? Mind if I call you Hank?"

Joanne choked on a sip of Chardonnay, scowled at me earnestly for three seconds, then replied, "Okay. If you want to," except it came out "ookay," and "wantoo."

"Never had a nickname," she added.

We clinked plastic cups. "Mine used to be 'Tink,' " I confided, "because I liked watching my father fix things. Except kids started calling me 'Tinklebell,' and stuff like that so . . ."

From my side came a gurgling sound that might have been 7-Up boiling or Joanne Henry laughing. Suddenly I felt as if I had seltzer in my nose, too. I began to giggle. Joanne riposted. I guffawed. She barked. And we were off on a tear, laughing at the sound of our own laughter until our ears rang and our eyes leaked and our stomachs were sore.

Bunches of people were eating now, sitting around on the folding chairs and the grass. Rip's group had gone inside. Jeremy Philbin had gravitated back to the oak tree by the bar.

Soon Rip emerged from the house carrying a plate. He looked serious but not uncomfortable, as if he had been casually talking business.

Jeremy Philbin stood up and treated us to his stage voice, the one that reached the rafters, "Ah, the eminent Robert Ripley Barnes," he intoned. Then under his breath, but quite audibly, he muttered, "Where the hell is Bill Boudourian when you need 'im?"

The crowd held its breath—the very air held its breath. Then Danny Vega, the stork in the cheap shirts, put down his plate and his napkin, and eying Rip all the while, moved quickly to Jeremy Philbin's side. He grabbed the totally blitzed algebra teacher by the elbow and said gently, "C'mon now, Jer. Let's get you home. I think you've had a bit too much."

"A bit too much for one day. Yesss," Philbin agreed. Miraculously he allowed Vega to lift his elbow high, poke his head down under his armpit and come up supporting him with his shoulders. They walked this way, like newborn colts, across the expanse of grass to the parking lot in front of the school, where Vega deposited the old lush into the back seat of a faded blue Buick trimmed with rust. A pudgy woman who hadn't been far from Vega all afternoon had scooped up Danny's plate and trotted along behind the men. She set the plate down on the front seat of her friend's car through an open window. Danny nodded his thanks while we all watched. Then he slammed the driver's door shut, started his car, backed swiftly out of his slot and drove away. At the main driveway fifty feet later he signaled a left turn, which was how I determined that he was more rattled by Jeremy's behavior than he let on.

Rip twirled a racquet through his fingers. "Badminton anyone?" he asked, and the tableau dissolved as we all began to breathe again.

At some point I put out the brownies, date-nut bars, and coffee. Twilight had settled in for real by then, and Joanne asked to borrow a sweater. By seven-thirty it was her and me on the lounge chairs and Rip drinking black coffee on a folding chair at our feet.

He patted my shoe, which I noticed was now smeared with either chocolate or mud. "I'll go get the kids," he said. He still looked composed, but his eyes seemed a little pinched.

"Oh, I can . . ." I offered from pure guilt. He had just conducted his first all-day faculty meeting and endured a scathing insult from a drunken employee—he shouldn't have had to drive to the mall.

"No," he said, pointedly staring at my cup of white wine, "I'll go."

He was right, of course. My reflexes were impaired.

After he left, Joanne and I resumed staring at the sky. Night was nearly total, and we saw each other as the only positive images left on an overexposed film.

"He's not alcoholic," Joanne said as if I had asked. "He's always sober when he teaches. He just . . ."

"Hates Rip?"

Joanne, herself sobered by food and time and Philbin's inexcusable performance, glanced my way in alarm. "No. No, I'm sure that's not it."

She sat back in her lounge chair and watched the clouds reform. "Bill hired him ages ago. He has seniority over everybody by at least ten years. He and Bill were never really friends, but over time they developed into what they are together, and that made them allies."

"What are they?"

"A couple of old men who loathe change." She seemed to consider that for a moment. "Jeremy can do it though. He's survived a lot."

"Like what?" I had to ask. At the moment it was difficult for me to sympathize with the old sot without names, dates, and places. Or maybe I wanted to gloat over his past misfortunes because he'd driven a bulldozer through my party.

"His marriage was long and . . . awful. His wife had, she was, she . . ."

"Just spit it out, Joanne. We're both adults."

"She had kinky tastes. She liked stuff most women don't. Domination, things like that—okay?"

"Yikes." I took a big gulp of wine for the feel of cold reality. This was much more than I expected, more than I wanted. But how did I turn off the spigot now?

"How'd you find that out?" I blurted.

"I've been here a long time, too. Remember? Around

the time of his worst trouble, Jerry and I . . . he just got drunk and told me. Okay?"

"Okay."

"So he's finally fed up with her cheating, with whatever, and he's ready to get a divorce. So who does he decide to confide in? The only lawyer he knows—Richard Wharton. Young guy, hip. Smooth. Philbin figures he's got an in with him because of the school connection. Figures Wharton'll be discreet, maybe cut him a break on his fee. So he makes an appointment. Goes to the office at the end of the day. Stammers his way through his story. Sober, you understand. Probably the hardest thing Jerry ever did.

"So Richard Wharton sits there, sort of on the front edge of his big desk with Jerry down in this cushy low chair squirming like a bug on a pin. But he gets through it. Confides every embarrassing detail. Evidence for the divorce, you see. Jerry figures Wharton needs to know it *all.*

"And Wharton just lets him talk, spill the whole megillah. And then he just stands up, his face looking all concerned in that way that's indifferent as hell, and he crosses his arms and walks around his desk and puts his hands down on his blotter, leaning over toward Jeremy like he's really sorry to say this in that way that isn't really sorry about anything, and he says, 'Gee, Jer, that's tough. But you see, I don't handle divorces.' "

My mouth dropped open. "That's right," Joanne told me. "That's exactly how Jeremy reacted only worse. He hates Richard Wharton, and with good reason."

"What a jerk," I remarked, referring of course to Wharton. And then I realized Joanne had done it, swung me like a pendulum until I came upon Jeremy Philbin from the other direction.

"Hey," I said, realizing I was contemplating sympathy

for the guy. "That doesn't mean he can turn around and treat other people like that."

"No," Joanne agreed. "But it sure explains why he tries."

We talked a little more around the subject. I wanted to know how she knew about the meeting, how Wharton looked and sounded. When she had described it, I had been there, too.

She shrugged. "Oh," I said, catching on. "He got drunk and told you."

"I'm going home," she said. "School tomorrow."

"You okay to drive?" I asked with genuine concern.

In perfect balance she tip-toed a pretend tightrope along our brick sidewalk, the hems of her slacks waving back and forth in the now-harsh porchlight.

"Goodnight, Hank," I called after her.

The day following the faculty party, Rip met with his veteran algebra teacher for an hour and a half, no phone calls thank-you, Joanne.

It isn't widely known, but conditional to keeping his job, the volatile algebra teacher was talked into meeting weekly with the psychologist he so sarcastically praised Rip for hiring. She has managed to work wonders with Philbin's public persona.

The man carries himself proudly now, like an elephant trained to dance for the public. I thought about all this and more while Joanne was detained talking to Lt. Newkirk.

I thought about it; and I decided that it's best to remember—trained or not, elephants can be extremely dangerous animals.

✵ *Chapter 10* ✵

On Saturday morning, December 4, the morning after Richard Wharton's murder, Rip went over to
his school office about seven-thirty.

In keeping with his open-door, I'm-here-for-you policy, our home telephone number was listed. Conse-
quently, the instrument began ringing the moment Rip
stepped out into the frosty dew and continued to give
me and the kids collective headaches until I changed the
tape on the answering machine. "Mr. Barnes is taking
business calls at the school today. If you have a personal
message for Rip, Gin, or one of the children, please wait
for the beep and we'll get back to you."

Didi was the only person I called back.

"My God, Gin," she yelped. "What have you gotten
yourselves into over there?" Obviously, she'd seen the
network news.

"No idea." Didi was from Ludwig, too, and at that
point neither of us claimed to know much about behavior over here on the Main Line, although it was looking
less and less different from what I'd seen anywhere else.

"The kids freaked?"

"Chelsea and Garry?" I hopped onto the kitchen

counter myself, bouncing my sneakers harmlessly against the cabinets.

"Who else?"

"Didi, we've got a whole school full of who else. Rip is busy as we speak dealing with their parents." Plus all the alumni, the Board, and the press, but it wasn't worthwhile to divert Didi's attention too far from the original subject. "He's hiring two extra psychologists for Monday to deal with who else."

"I'm sure that's a wonderful idea," Didi assured me. "I'll look forward to meeting them all." The holiday program. Didi was revamping the whole production and she only had eight days to do it. Correction. Seven days.

"Sorry, Didi. Not on Monday you won't."

"I won't?"

"All after-school activities are canceled out of respect for Richard Wharton. There'll be an open meeting and a short memorial on Monday night. You can come to that if you want."

"Nooo, thank you."

"Tuesday then. Stay for dinner."

"Thanks. Be delighted. Are you going to answer my question now?"

Question. "What question?"

"How are Chelsea and Garry?"

I made a fist in my bangs, a gesture Didi couldn't see but probably sensed. Most likely she also knew my face had flushed. "Sorry, kid. I'm a little tense. Chelsea and Garry are okay. Shaken."

"Shaken, but not stirred?" The opposite of a James Bond martini, Didi's little way with words.

"Early to tell."

Satisfied, my best friend's mind moved on. "Was Wharton a good guy?" she asked.

"Sometimes."

"He the creep who put his hand on your knee?"

"The same." I swear there was a hum on the line from the intensity of Didi's thoughts. After a pause she said, "Well, that's different anyway."

"What is?"

"Over here we mostly bump off the regular working stiffs."

I was so slow coming up with a suitable reply that Didi said, "See ya Tuesday. Don't have eggplant," and hung up.

I hopped down and stared at the receiver before hanging it up. True, Wharton had been an attorney, no regular worker by Ludwig standards. But in this fifteen or twenty-mile strip of comfortable homes for the comfortably off, lawyers pretty much were the regular folks.

Yet Didi's "good riddance" implication made me think of how dogs were regarded in Ocean City, New Jersey, the "family resort" where we usually went for vacation. Down there people either had a dog or they hated them. From the sound of it, lawyers got similar treatment on the Main Line. Of course, in Ocean City you had to clean up after your dog; with attorneys it was the other way around.

Didi's comment also suggested that "our" victim was more judiciously chosen, as opposed to the straightforward, heat-of-the-moment violence perpetrated elsewhere. Had she forgotten that Richard Wharton had been hit with a shovel? What could be more straightforward than that?

"You're wrong," I told Didi in absentia. "Somebody was just plain flat-out furious. Same as anywhere else." I believed that, too. Meanwhile, my mind had seized upon a nasty irony.

I moaned and sank onto the chair by the TV. I also swore mildly, and a couple tears sprang into my eyes.

"What is it, Mom?" Garry said with touching con-

cern. He had padded into the living room wearing pajamas and socks.

"Just something totally awful I did." Unwittingly awful, but no less embarrassing. To kick off the Christmas
break, in two and a half weeks on Wednesday evening,
December 22, Rip and I would be entertaining the
faculty again. Hoping to project a more jovial spirit than
our first fiasco, I had dubbed the event the "Barnes'
Holiday Bash" on an invitation of my own design. To my
extreme mortification, they were already mailed.

I groaned. Garry put his hand delicately on my shoulder.

"Chelsea says the shower's cold."

I winced. "Totally cold?"

"Totally," Garry confirmed.

Suppressing another colorful response, I hurried into
the laundry room to check the hot water heater. A rust-
ing white cylinder with a blue top and bottom like an
enormous cold capsule, it now stood in a small lake of
its own making. Some of the floor tiles curled at the
edges in evil vinyl smiles.

"Get dressed," I told Garry. "We'll shower at the
school later."

The phone rang. I sat down by the TV again, around
the corner from the phone. Garry lingered, watching me
curiously.

"You going to answer that?" he asked.

"I don't think so."

Soon the answering machine on the kitchen counter
allowed us to hear the voice. "This is Sylvia Smith. I've
got a son in second grade . . ." she told our tape and
us. Sylvia's son was traumatized, it seemed, which might
or might not explain why Sylvia hadn't listened to my
message very well.

My son, at about four feet tall, looked down at me
from a slightly higher angle. His beautiful green eyes

met mine with more maturity than I'd ever before noticed. His hand reached out, but didn't quite touch my arm.

"Poor Dad," he said. Then he dropped his hand and turned toward the stairs. The phone rang again.

"We've got to get out of here," I called up the stairs.

Chelsea, Garry, and I delivered Rip a packed lunch, hugs, and much sympathy. Sitting behind his broad desk, he looked dwarfed by adversity, a grown-up Dutch boy with little hope of saving the dike.

"Give it up," I suggested.

"Pretty soon," he replied.

First the kids and I stopped at my favorite discount appliance store to buy a hot water heater. Then we cruised for a parking spot at the King of Prussia Mall. Ten minutes later a van left me a slot between a scrawny pin oak full of dead leaves and a certain corner of a certain department store. Luckily, despite the Saturday bustle inside, the place was familiar enough that I didn't have to think too much about where to find what.

Chelsea took forever choosing pierced earrings for her girlfriends while Garry and I did the comic book rack at a newsstand. In JCPenney's I found a tie for Rip and, in a stroke of brilliance, paid for it at the customer service counter rather than growing moss with the others lined up at the regular checkout.

Waiting for the kids to come back from a "private" side trip, I spent fifteen minutes people-watching at the feet of an especially aloof mannequin. It felt quite peculiar, really, buying meaningless pretty things for the kids to give as gifts while my husband was struggling to preserve a school and, by extension, our new home. Uncharitably, I imagined the everyday concerns of the other shoppers to be trivial and foolish. Of course, I immediately realized I was being unfair, that I knew nothing of their concerns except that in spite of them these people were living their lives.

Well, so were we.

When we got home, the answering machine had run out of tape, but Rip had taken the phone off the hook anyway. He and Barney were asleep on the living room sofa in front of a Boston College football game.

I turned off the sound and put on a tape of Dvorak's "New World" symphony. Personally, I find classical music pretentious and annoying, which is why it suited my mood. But mostly I thought it might give Rip a smile when he woke up. Two weeks ago I caught him rattling the windows with Rachmaninoff and conducting a football game with a Bic. Two weeks ago. Might as well have been last year.

On Sunday Rip activated the "phone chain," the prepared list of who called who in case the school was closed for snow, except this information was a bit less welcome. Rip firmly recommended that at least one parent accompany each student to school Monday morning and remain for a brief meeting. He also announced that a second meeting open to all parents and friends of Richard Wharton would begin at 7:30 PM in the auditorium. Questions would be answered by Rip and also by the school psychologist, followed by a brief memorial service for the deceased.

The actual funeral was being held on Tuesday out in Pittsburgh, where Wharton still had some family; but it was eminently clear that many people connected to Bryn Derwyn needed some more accessible closure. Perhaps no one more than Rip.

Sunday, Chelsea and Garry woke up bickering like they usually do, so I determined that it was safe to leave them with Rip and do a bit of shopping on my own. Since I was so far from being in the spirit of the season, naturally I had tremendously good luck finding gifts. By four-thirty, both exhausted and refreshed with optimism, I drove home, locked my booty in the gardening shed, and staggered inside to fix dinner.

"Whoo," I said, rubbing my hands and blowing steam. "Feels like Alaska out there."

Rip looked at me and blinked. There were dark bags under his eyes I'd never seen before and a hardness to his expression. "What'd you say, babe?"

"Dinner in an hour."

He nodded and ambled into the dining room where he'd set up a temporary workstation. As I cooked, I could hear his computer click and beep. When Garry put on MTV to watch music videos, Rip shouted, "Read a book," and when silence didn't come quite quickly enough, he yelled, "Dammit, I said turn that off."

My kitchen seemed to chill. This was not the man I married. My Robert Ripley Barnes was fun and happy and polite to his kids, even when they behaved abominably. His smile brightened rooms and his touch magnetized me. This new stranger sounded like a bitter, frightened man, and I hated whoever was responsible for creating him.

While I stir-fried chicken, I mused about to the oblivious days when we shook the contents of our wallets onto the table to see if we had money for a six-pack. Rip's biggest problem had been making Shakespeare palatable to the eleventh grade. Mine were morning sickness and toilet training a two-year-old daughter with a demonic smile and the disposition of a terrier.

Later that night, when Rip and I were in bed with the lights out, the covers pulled up, our breathing just easing down toward sleep, I referred to those salad years. "Do you miss . . . before?" I asked.

"Yes," he said with a heavy sigh. Then he rolled away from me.

The lump thickened in my throat, and tears trickled into my pillowcase; yet I resisted voicing the habitual, "I'm sorry." I didn't say anything, just rubbed the crook of my husband's neck with my hand, then pulled it away and tried to go to sleep to my new mantra: It'll get better. It'll get better. It'll get better.

Monday morning Rip showered and dressed with energetic resolve, wrapped an English muffin in a napkin, stuffed it in his overcoat pocket and gave me a lingering hug. He was behind his desk by 6:50 AM.

I packed lunches as usual and saw the kids off to their bus, which stopped for them at the end of Bryn Derwyn's driveway. From my vantage point at our front door, I could see that the school's lots were full; Jacob had begun to direct cars onto the lawn. I considered standing in on Rip's delicate and difficult morning assembly, showing my support, listening to what the psychologist had to say.

Instead I poured a mug of coffee and sat down in my silent living room. Barney lay with his paws across my feet and I absentmindedly scratched his ears. This was the first privacy I'd had since the murder. Rip would never miss me. I had delicate and difficult things of my own to face. Things I had been putting off.

Last year an airline crashed into a mountain in western Pennsylvania. Along with all the sordid details, newscasters mentioned that a team of psychologists had been dispatched to the scene. Odd, I thought. What could they possibly do to help?

"Counsel the bereaved," Rip had pointed out. But that wasn't all. According to the newspaper, when the searchers could no longer tolerate the horror of collecting body parts, they would stop and get themselves some counseling. Then, presumably, they could return to their gruesome job.

The notion offended me. "I don't think I'd listen to anybody who hadn't done the work themselves," I remarked.

Rip shook his head. "The psychologists aren't allowed to go," he explained. "If they did, they'd be useless to anyone else."

Strange animals, we humans.

Perhaps—eventually—I would benefit from being with a group, sharing my feelings with caring friends. Maybe even tonight. But for now I wanted to stare down the visions of bone shards and brain matter until they ceased to sicken me, until they became simply another by-product of life. I wanted to name every fear that threatened to gray my hair or sour my stomach or cause my hands to tremble. So I sat with my cold coffee and my warm dog and stared and shook and hugged myself tight. I rocked and whimpered and cried. I pounded my fist on the sofa cushion until Barney gave up on me and trotted away.

I swore. I prayed. And finally I sobbed myself to sleep.

Naturally, the phone rang. Thinking of the weekend, I nearly let the machine pick up, but no. I was revived now, emotionally bandaged and ready to return to that gruesome mountain.

Rip's ragged voice made my arms feel hollow. "Okay if I come home for lunch?"

"Sure. Absolutely." Since school had opened in September, he had not once been home for lunch.

"Thanks, babe. I really need a break."

I heated frozen Welsh rarebit and tossed a green salad. I even frosted some glass mugs for some non-alcoholic beer and arranged our best green dishes on bright red place mats. Winter clouds had shadowed the dining room despite my cheerful wallpaper, so I put out candles. Then I put them away and set the chandelier at a gentle level. You'd have thought I was preparing for a heavy date.

Rip ate mechanically, unaware of my presence; he was scarcely aware of the food. As quality time went, a total bust.

"How'd the morning session go?" I asked.

My husband lifted his head. "I'm here, aren't I?"

"Oh."

Someone pounded on the door, and I automatically stood. Barney barked the deep threatening roar he reserved for sudden noises and twirled in a frustrated circle.

"Don't answer it," Rip advised.

The pounding repeated, louder than before. Barney became frantic.

"But . . ."

"Oh, go ahead. This day couldn't get any worse."

Lt. Newkirk stood on the front step wearing a limp, London Fog raincoat. His reddish mustache twitched and his eyes bore into mine.

"Your husband is here," he informed me.

"Yes, I know."

"Speak to him, please."

"Come in, Lieutenant," Rip called. "I want to talk to you, too."

When Rip returned from shutting Barney in the laundry room, the two men stood ten feet apart on the living room carpet and locked eyes. Their arms hung loosely at their sides like Wild West gunfighters. Both appeared to be exhausted, and the day was scarcely half over.

Rip fired first. "What was the idea of placing uniformed officers in the lobby this morning? I never gave permission for that."

"They were there to help me. And I don't need your permission. I happen to be investigating a homicide."

"And I'm responsible for the welfare of two hundred and thirty-nine students. Your men frightened the younger kids so much that several burst into tears. We'll be weeks settling them down thanks to your thoughtlessness."

"You ever think that some of the kids might have been *reassured* by the uniforms?"

"No I didn't. And if they were reassured, how do you explain them lining up halfway down the hall to meet with our psychologists? Hell, I already asked the extra two to stay all week. I might as well offer them a contract."

Pacing, Rip raised a finger to forestall interruption. "Forty families were so upset they kept their kids home today." He stopped to point the finger at Newkirk. "And some of those may never come back. We already lost five permanently. Permanently, Lieutenant. Parents pulled them right out." The finger wagged. "You keep on scaring everybody, we won't have a school left. Do you have any idea where that leaves all the people who depend on it?"

"You done?" Newkirk asked. "Cause if you're done, I got a bone to pick with you."

Rip stepped back, hands on hips, an irritated expression on his face.

"I been talking to that fifth grade teacher again, the one was here the other night?"

"Pamela Washington."

"Yeah. You mind telling me why you didn't mention George Kelly?" Newkirk asked, shifting a foot. His hands flapped from thumbs tucked into his coat pockets.

Rip's eyebrows raised and his mouth opened. His annoyance had diminished, but not his intensity.

"I'm sorry, Lieutenant. I just plain forgot."

"You report an abusive father, he storms the school coming after his son and his wife, and you forgot?"

"All sorts of things like that go on around here. It's a school, for chrissake. What I forgot is that Richard Wharton was involved."

Newkirk sucked his teeth and frowned. "So now that I reminded you, you want to tell me *how* Wharton was involved?"

Rip sighed and gestured for Newkirk to sit down on the sofa. He took an opposite chair, and I took its twin.

"From the beginning?"

"From the beginning," Newkirk agreed.

"Susan Kelly brought Christopher in for an interview this summer. He was a quiet kid, and we felt he was overwhelmed by the size of his current school. Four hundred students in one grade can bury a kid like him. So we accepted Chris for fifth grade, keeping him back a year to catch him up a bit, a common practice for boys transferring into private school. The idea is he's not going to feel a stigma because so many others stay back. Okay?"

"Okay," said Newkirk.

"But young Christopher didn't adapt quite as well as we hoped; and his teacher, Pamela Washington, began to keep an eye on him. One morning she caught Chris walking the wrong direction after assembly, just zoned out, not paying attention. So she hooked his arm to wake him up and sort of spin him to face the right way. Chris cried out in pain. Since just catching his arm like that shouldn't have hurt, Pamela took the boy straight to the nurse to get him examined. The kid was covered with bruises. You could even see the spacing of the father's fingers.

"We hated the possibility of making matters worse, but we hated what the father was doing even more. So we reported it."

"As you must by law."

"Right, but as we feared, we knocked over the whole row of dominoes. The wife, Susan, left Kelly because after we reported him, he was furious and became even more violent. Of course, once an incident is reported, the child is automatically protected by the county; but the mother's another matter. She had to seek her own legal protection.

"So one morning Kelly parked his car out front and waited for Susan to bring Christopher to school. He 'stormed' up to her, as you said, causing quite a scene. Wharton was in my office, and we saw what was going on through the window. Richard ran out, physically intimidated Kelly—there was quite a size difference, and Kelly had already drawn a crowd, something I don't think he expected—anyway, he shook his fist and yelled a few threats and left.

"Wharton shepherded Chris into school, counseled with the mother, and in about half an hour I saw them drive off in Wharton's car. Turns out Wharton talked her into a restraining order, and off they went to get one. Next thing I heard, Susan and the boy had moved to an unknown address and taken an unlisted number. She had to give me and my secretary the address—in confidence—in case there's ever a problem at school with Chris. But her husband no longer knew how to find them, and if he showed up here looking for either his son or his wife, he would have been arrested."

"So Kelly blamed Wharton for the break-up of his family."

"That's about it."

"They never blame themselves, do they?" Newkirk mused.

"Not in my experience."

"So Wharton was the logical target."

"Guess so."

Newkirk lifted himself off the sofa with effort.

"Pardon me, folks. I got to go question another suspect." Before he turned toward the door he paused to inspect our dirty plates. "Whatcha got here? Cheese sandwiches?"

"Sort of. Want some?"

"Nah," he said. "Cheese don't agree with me."

After he left, Rip placed his hands on his hips and reflected bitterly. "He doesn't give a damn about the school."

Since my husband was swimming too hard to see the water, I mentioned the obvious. "That's not his job."

"You got that right," Rip agreed. Then he armored himself with his overcoat and set off to do his.

❊ *Chapter 11* ❊

Nothing could have deterred the crowd that collected at Bryn Derwyn Monday night. Overhead
clouds clamped us under a dome of black relieved only
by cones of misty light dropped by the school's spotlights. Vehicles of all sorts overflowed the lots and littered the gloomy practice field like a junkyard on
Halloween. Because of the planned memorial service,
television crews were barred from entering the building,
so representatives from the two opposing networks who
chose to come huddled in separate dispirited clumps,
occasionally stepping forward to pester the most agi-
tated-appearing parents.

Inside, the gently sloped auditorium contained few
empty seats. Lighting was kept respectfully moderate
except for the podium centered in front of the stage,
which was little more than a platform. The speakers
would be eye level with most of the gathering.

Soon after eight, Rip tapped the microphone and
said, "Ladies and gentlemen, we should get started. If
you'll be seated, please?" A small flurry of activity en-
sued as people complied.

Around the periphery I noticed a few print reporters
poised over their notebooks. Also, Lt. Newkirk stood off

by himself smoking a cigarette until one of the teachers
scolded him and he temporarily stepped outside to dis-
pose of it.

"Can we sit down there?" Garry asked, gesturing to a
couple of empty seats halfway down the right side.

I shrugged. "Sure, but I think I'll stay back here.
Okay?" I was too nervous to sit still.

Bringing our children had been a risky choice, one no
other parents had elected that night. But then no other
parents were quite in our situation. Since we lived on
campus, Garry and Chelsea had the option to stay home
and wonder what was going on virtually in front of their
noses; or they could come over and hear for themselves.
True, they might have to endure some heavy, worrisome
information, but the evening was meant to promote rational thinking. On balance, I thought our kids could
tolerate reality better than they could their imaginations.

Also, it wouldn't hurt for them to see firsthand how
their father handled a sensitive situation, something I
knew Rip would accomplish with self-control and tact.
Of course, the kids might have to dismiss the bad exam-
ples to learn from the good.

A man twelve rows back rose and began without preamble. Around him people hastily settled down and
faced forward. "Mr. Barnes," he said, "how can you assure us that this school is safe for our children?"

The thin blond hair on the back of the man's head
made him look vulnerable. Suddenly I realized I was
looking at the backs of three hundred heads, so I eased
slightly down the right wall nearer my children where
my view was of profiles.

Rip spoke into a microphone. His unbuttoned brown
tweed jacket revealed a blue oxford shirt and a crooked
brown tie. The hand holding a folded page of notes
appeared steady.

"There is no indication that what happened had anything to do with Bryn Derwyn Academy, John, or with any of its students. The police agree that the only reason the crime occurred here is because Richard Wharton happened to be here. It's extremely unfortunate, but there is no reason to think the school is any less safe than it ever was.

"Nevertheless, all of us who work at Bryn Derwyn have become acutely sensitized to the safety of your children. Two teachers, rather than one, will supervise any outdoor activities. We've begun issuing visitors' passes"—he held up a large white card in a clip-on plastic envelope—"and anyone from the outside will first sign in with the receptionist before doing business inside the building. The badge must be worn until the visitor is ready to leave the premises."

"I heard that someone who works here did it," a woman called from her seat. Murmurs of agreement erupted from around the room.

"I'm glad you mentioned that, Carolyn. I've heard the rumors, too. But surely you realize that if there were any truth to those speculations, the police would have made an arrest; and all of us would be informed by now. The news media, who are well represented here tonight, will see to that."

"I don't hear you saying it *wasn't* a Bryn Derwyn employee who did it."

"In my heart I don't believe any of our staff would do such a thing, but what I feel has no substantive bearing on the investigation. It's best if people like you and me leave the burden of proving who committed the crime to the professionals."

"What are the police doing?"

Rip scanned the back of the room until his eyes found Newkirk. "Lieutenant, perhaps you would be kind enough to enlighten these folks."

Newkirk filled his lungs, rocked on his heels and blushed. Obviously, he thought of himself as an observer protected by anonymity, but that role was no longer possible. He cleared his throat, hung his thumbs on his overcoat pockets, the better to nervously flap his hands, then mumbled beneath his moustache, "We're pursuing several leads. Nothing I can discuss just now." Judging by the finality injected into his last words, he thought he had said enough.

Yet more heads had swiveled to skewer him, not fewer. He tucked his chin like a tortoise trying to hide. Rip crooked his finger to draw the man forward.

"Not everyone can hear you, Lieutenant. Perhaps you'd be good enough to use the microphone."

So Newkirk plodded toward the low stage, chin down, eyebrows pinched, and hands flapping. To speak into the microphone, he simply leaned forward.

"I said we're pursuing several leads. I can't tell you more."

"What can you tell us about the crime itself?" someone shouted from the far side.

"Oh, yes. All right. White male caucasian, subsequently identified as Richard J. Wharton, a local attorney with the firm of Dodsworth, Evans, Pinckney and Wharton, was dealt a fatal blow to the head in the Community Room of Bryn Derwyn Academy sometime between three and four PM last Friday, December third."

"Was the weapon really a shovel?"

"Yessir."

"Is there some significance to the shovel?"

"No significance that we're aware of."

"What was Richard Wharton doing here?"

"He was working with the business manager, but he and the people they were talking to left early, and their whereabouts between three and four were accounted for."

"So you're saying it could have been anybody?"

"Not quite anybody. We're pursuing several leads—"

"Okay, Lieutenant." Rip clapped Newkirk on the shoulder to dismiss him. "Thank you for your help." It was difficult to guess which man was more relieved to have the policeman headed back toward his inconspicuous corner. However, a father I knew to be a bulldog of an attorney had left his seat in order to ambush him. Too bad for Newkirk.

Rip hastily continued. "We will now hear from Mindy Cosnosky, our full-time psychologist. Mindy will explain what steps have been taken to help your children cope with this situation. Mindy?"

Mindy was slender, just short of bony, a mere four-foot-eleven with kind hazel eyes, fluffy brown hair and a no-nonsense demeanor. She wore a knit, two-piece combination of rust and black that would have blended into a boardroom, a funeral, or one of those cocktail parties where you don't expect to have fun.

"What we did today was a sort of emotional triage," she began with a soft, clear voice. "By teacher referral, we interviewed any students who, who didn't seem to be themselves. If a child was despondent, refused to do work, became quite obstinate or hard to reach, we tried to talk to them to gauge how affected they were by, by Richard Wharton's death. And I urge you parents, if you notice this sort of behavior in your son or daughter, don't get angry—get help!"

A mother shouted from the back, "My daughter said she was put into some sort of play group. What was that all about?"

"When children from kindergarten through third grade seemed to warrant further observation, we organized some informal play therapy, in which they were given an opportunity to express their fears by playing with dolls. What they did with them helped us to determine if they were perhaps fantasizing about death."

While I watched Mindy's somber professional face, I tried to envision how the fear of death would manifest itself in play. All in all, it sounded like a tough day for the therapy dolls.

"So then what do you do?" another mother asked.

"We try to normalize the situation, to take their fears apart and put things back into perspective."

A father spoke without standing. "My son's in seventh grade. Surely you didn't have him playing with dolls."

"No, we didn't. At that age they're usually embarrassed about expressing their fears, so the therapist does the pretending. It's called 'modeling,' and it's a way to teach the students coping techniques.

"For the oldest students, we set up some role-playing scenarios that allowed them to express themselves comfortably. All these techniques are designed to alleviate their tension and also indicate to us any children who might need further evaluation. As yet, no one appears to be seriously traumatized, but it's a little early to say that with complete certainty. That's why I'd like you as parents to keep an eye on your children. With the younger ones there may be some regression—thumb-sucking, wetting their pants. You should also watch for bed-wetting, nightmares, and something we call night terrors, which are different. With night terrors a child sits up screaming then a second later falls right back to sleep.

"But I hasten to repeat that I haven't seen any students who appear upset enough to require private counseling. Neither have my colleagues. So far, your children appear to be reacting as we might expect them to react to a very distressing situation. If you as parents keep your perspective, your children should return to normal very quickly."

"How can you say that? A man was murdered . . . !"

Which, I realized, was a perfect example of what Mindy meant. Scarcely a student at Bryn Derwyn had any idea who Richard Wharton was and, therefore, responded to his death only as far as their imaginations took them—unless they were reflecting their parents' paranoia. And that was probably the real agenda for the evening, to teach the parents how to behave in front of their kids. I wondered if anybody ever did a study of that success rate!

Rip nodded to Mindy and took her place at the microphone. "It's getting late, folks, and you'll all be wanting to get home soon. For those of you with specific questions, I'll be available for a short while after the memorial service. If anyone cares to leave now, please go right ahead. For those of you who wish to remain for our brief service, we'll get started in about five minutes." He stepped back while most of the gathering dispersed, leaving perhaps thirty interested in mourning the deceased attorney, Bryn Derwyn people who knew him plus a few strangers I assumed were from his law firm but had not made the trip to Pittsburgh.

After the interval, Rip told the remaining group, "We're conducting this service using a Quaker format. Some of Richard's family were Quaker, and for those of us who may be of another religious persuasion, I think you'll find their approach accommodates us all. The idea is, if the spirit moves you and you have something you'd like to share, a special memory perhaps, please stand up and express it. If no one is moved to speak, then we will all simply meditate in silence. When it comes time to dismiss, I'll just stand up. Okay?"

He took a chair beside Mindy, and the silence lasted scarcely a minute.

Quivering with nervousness, Susan Kelly, soon to be ex-wife of abusive George Kelly, stood and addressed Rip.

"Richard Wharton . . . was . . . very nice to me. And to my son, Chris. Is that what you meant, Mr. Barnes?" Rip smiled and nodded. Susan Kelly fluttered back into her seat, and I had my first uncharitable thought. It was the same thought I had right after Richard intimidated George Kelly in the school driveway and subsequently sped away with Susan in the passenger seat of his Jaguar.

My thought was that Susan Kelly was a very beautiful woman.

A rear door opened and shut via its compressor. Unaware that Jeremy Philbin was stumbling down the left side of the room, one of the attorneys who had worked with Richard began a reminiscence about fishing. The story seemed to be headed toward a warm and clever punch line, but Jeremy Philbin interrupted before we got to hear it.

"Yeah, yeah, yeah," Philbin said, leaning against the wall, hand on chest, booming with his hear-me-in-the-last-row voice. "Very heartwarming, I'm sure. But now it's my turn, thank you very much, and I'm here to tell you that Richard J. Wharton was a horse's ass. Would anyone care to know why?"

Rip had begun moving the minute Philbin opened his mouth, arriving beside the embittered algebra teacher just in time. Before Philbin could impart any embarrassing details, Rip grabbed him by the lapel and shoved him up the aisle toward the exit. Lt. Newkirk joined Rip on Philbin's far side and together they effectively ejected the man.

"Is Mr. Philbin drunk?" Garry asked.

"As a skunk," Chelsea confirmed.

An awkward minute later Rip returned to the podium, slightly breathless and disheveled. "Thank you all for coming," he said. "This concludes our evening."

Thus ended the lesson.

❋ *Chapter 12* ❋

I waited while a few people spoke briefly with Rip, parents in need of one more reassurance, maybe a polite person or two expressing sympathy over how the evening ended. For all the squeaky wheels, it was good to remember that not all concerned people were antagonistic. When the problems piled up, it just felt that way.

"C'mon. I'll walk you and the kids home," Rip told me.

Outside, the footsteps of the exiting parents crunched on the rock salt Jacob had spread while everyone was inside. The mist hovering over the school's lawn and the slick blackness of the driveway suggested the possibility of ice before morning.

His back to us, Lt. Newkirk spoke with Susan Kelly on the sidewalk just outside the front door. The poor lighting under the overhang made Susan's brown overcoat appear dingy and limp, her normally beautiful face ordinary. Her breath dispersed in short bursts as she nodded to emphasize her answers to Newkirk's questions. When she finished, she waited for a response she apparently did not get.

Finally, the investigator grunted and scowled at his

shoes. Susan shook her lovely blonde head with annoyance and stalked toward her car.

We Barneses had drawn close enough for Newkirk to accost Rip. "Hey, you leavin'?" he asked.

Indicating Newkirk with my chin, I suggested that Rip stay and finish up. "We'll be fine. He can help you lock up."

Rip glanced at me hard, startled by my implied precaution. But after all, he was male. Most women acquire a certain wariness at a young age, but some men never learn; and, unfortunately, some learn too late.

"Okay," he said dubiously.

The children had gone to bed and I was nearly ready myself before Rip stumbled up the stairs to our room. He said good night to the kids before he joined me.

"What did Newkirk want?" I asked. Rip's face seemed all creases and sags, more worn than I'd ever seen him.

"Nothing important," he answered evasively. It seemed he would step no further down that path, so I chose another.

"What was Susan Kelly saying that made him so unhappy?"

Rip dropped his shirt on the floor. "Just that her estranged husband was with her during the time of the murder."

"Really? I thought she had a court order to keep him away."

"She does."

"And she alibis him for the time of the murder?" Odd, to say the least. Had George Kelly's intimidation of his wife continued despite all the steps she'd taken to escape?

Rip simultaneously yawned and sighed. "I was really hoping he was guilty."

"Why?"

"Because all Newkirk's other suspects work for the school."

"That's not good." Since the very nature of an attorney's work was adversarial, I had expected the suspect pool to be vast. Now I realized that few, if any, of Richard's possible enemies outside the school would have known how to find him at Bryn Derwyn.

"You're not kidding," Rip agreed, "because that means there might be a school-related motive for the murder."

"Would Bryn Derwyn survive that?" I wondered aloud.

Rip made a wry face, which I took to mean, "I don't know, and I don't want to find out." Then he kicked away his trousers and tumbled into bed. A minute later he was snoring.

Me, I lay in the dark with my eyes wide open, working jagged questions around and around as if they were stones I could worry smooth just by caring.

By morning I looked every bit as haggard as Rip. Garry even did a double-take when he saw me. But he said nothing, just snared his toast and swilled his orange juice as if everyday routine constituted the backbone of life.

"Jeez, Mom," Chelsea remarked. "Do yourself a favor. Buy some new makeup."

She was partly right—I needed to do something. Why had I taken on cleaning the school damn near by myself? Because for PR purposes it needed doing. The fool who always rushed in? Me. Demurely hold down the homefront while my husband fought the war? No thanks, I don't need a coronary.

My father was happiest when he was trying to repair something. "So what can happen if you fail?" he philosophized. "Is the gadget going to get more broke? And you just might fix it, Tink. You just might fix it, and then what?"

I took his grin to mean success, pride, confidence—wonderful things to own according to that grin. Things I wanted, if only to prove I was his daughter. Standing in my boxy, prefabricated kitchen, feeling attacked and ineffective, I saw my father lean down in my memory, saw his smile broaden to the limits as he answered his own question. "Then you have your gadget back, and even better: you learned something you didn't know." About how the gadget worked. About yourself.

I kissed the kids, promised Chelsea I'd fix my face, and waved them off to their bus.

Then I leaned against the back of the door and wondered exactly what it would take to do that.

"Start easy," Dad always advised. "Work up to hard."

That made Susan Kelly first. If I could satisfy myself that she was telling the truth about George, I could rub that question off my list.

To find out where she lived, I wrapped two chocolate donuts in a napkin to bribe Joanne, who, along with Rip, knew where to reach Susan in case of an emergency.

Although it was only 7:40 AM, Lt. Newkirk strolled up beside me just as I reached the school's front door.

"Morning," he remarked.

"Long time no see," I replied. Both of us were too tired to put much camaraderie into the exchange. Silently we turned left together into Joanne's territory outside Rip's office, me first, Newkirk right behind, although the detective passed me in the open on his way toward Rip.

Joanne was away from her desk, so I gravitated toward my husband's open doorway, wondering what was on Newkirk's mind this time.

"Guess you ought to know," the detective told Rip.

"Your algebra teacher, that Philbin fellow from last night . . ."

"Yes," Rip replied warily.

"Gave the cop drove him home something of an earful."

"Yes."

"About you and Richard Wharton. Have to check it out, of course." The detective glanced around behind me, for discretion's sake.

"What did he say, Lieutenant?"

Newkirk scratched his ear and scowled. "Well now that's the shame of it," he told Rip. "He heard this argument between you and the Wharton fellow. Back in September?"

Rip reddened slightly, turned and parked himself in his swivel chair.

"Ring a bit of a bell, does it? Know the conversation I mean?"

Rip leaned toward the policeman and took a deep breath. "Richard and I had a disagreement about that time. What I don't understand is how Jeremy learned about it."

Newkirk hitched a visitor's chair up under his rump. "Oh, that one's easy. Says he heard it himself—every word."

Rip squeezed his brows low as he gave me a blank glance. An offhand remark of mine had instigated the confrontation with Wharton, as perhaps my husband's subconscious reminded him.

"I don't see how."

"Oh sure. Philbin says he was digging around in the supply closet right back here." He reached behind his chair and tapped on the wall. A closet on the other side of the wall opened into the classroom hallway. Theoretically, the closet served as a buffer to keep private conversations private.

"You want to give me your version of it?"

"Certainly, Lieutenant." Rip sighed and looked over at me meaningfully this time, now apparently remembering my comment and what it had instigated.

While I was refurbishing the lobby I was around the school quite a lot—and so was Richard Wharton. At that time I had no idea how his services were being used, only that he seemed quite . . . available. So I made a joke. I said I thought Bryn Derwyn ought to issue Richard Wharton a locker.

Rip had became thoughtful, even concerned. What he heard me saying was that the school's attorney spent far too much time visiting one of his smallest clients. Having drawn his attention to that fact, Rip's question was why.

"He's not charging you to drink coffee, is he?" I had asked.

"Damn, Gin. Sometimes I think I'm wearing a sign that says, 'Kick Me.' "

It turned out that Wharton's invoices were so padded the man could have stuffed a Santa suit with the fluff. His excuse was that Bryn Derwyn was on the way to his office, making it ever so convenient to stop in and keep on top of things.

"You argued," Newkirk prompted.

It had been an argument all right. Rip's investigation revealed that every one of the attorney's visits had been on the clock. Revising previous bills would have been tricky business, so they compromised.

Now my husband spread his hands. "Wharton had been overcharging us. As a Board member and fund-raising chair, much of his time was supposed to be gratis."

"Yes?" Newkirk encouraged patiently.

"I told him we needed itemized bills from then on

and that his volunteer work was to be strictly that—volunteer."

Newkirk smiled. "You called him an underhanded son of a bitch."

Rip tilted his head and smirked. "I called him worse than that."

Newkirk nodded with satisfaction. "So I heard."

"That was the end of it, Lieutenant. I got no further trouble from him."

Newkirk sighed like a chagrined uncle. "Yes, Mr. Barnes. I believe you. Except I don't suppose you were real fond of each other after that. Were you? I mean Richard Wharton wouldn't have exactly been on your side the next time something came up. You see what I mean? You want to hire a reading teacher or something like that and the Board needs to vote. I figure Mr. Wharton was maybe the type to vote the other way sort of as punishment, if you see what I mean. Anything like that happen, Mr. Barnes?"

"The board doesn't vote on hiring teachers, Lieutenant."

"But don't they approve the budget that gives you the money to hire the teacher? It's just a hypothetical example, Mr. Barnes. I'm sure you take my meaning."

"Oh yes. You're telling me that Jeremy Philbin—and you—think I had a motive to kill Richard Wharton. But don't forget that Philbin's trying to get his own ass off the hot seat, and despite what I thought of Wharton, I was in a meeting with three other people when he died."

"Yeah, probably. Except the death occurred between three and four, and part of that time you were busy firing your parttime music teacher. Then you were alone for at least a couple minutes."

"No," I said impulsively. "We walked out of the auditorium together." How could this bozo possibly think

Rip was capable of murder? It was my initial fear coming true.

"Did you actually see him come into the office?"

I said nothing, just scowled, but Newkirk read my mind. "Didn't think so."

I flushed with fury.

Meanwhile, my husband slowly shook his head. Then he shrugged apologetically at the detective. "I didn't do it, Lieutenant," Rip said simply. "I might have been alone a minute between the time Nora left—she quit, by the way—and when the teachers joined me here for our meeting; but I didn't even know Wharton was in the building. And even if I had known, there wasn't enough time for me to have killed him."

Newkirk nodded in earnest now. "I hear you, Mr. Barnes. And between you and me, I believe you. For now. The reason why is you could have fired him. Right? So I believe you. But that's not the same as the facts. And right now I got to go get me some more facts." He stood and tossed Rip a "Have a nice day."

He stopped at the doorway because I was still there. "Those donuts?" he asked.

"Yes." Stale chocolate donuts melted into the napkin where my fingers had been squeezing them. "You want them?" I asked sarcastically.

"Don't mind if I do," he replied.

After he turned left out of Joanne's area for a destination somewhere within the building, Rip flopped back against his chair. The impact swiveled him away from me. I dropped into Newkirk's former seat.

After a moment, I asked Rip what he intended to do.

He swiveled back, his hands resting on top of his head. "About what?" He had mentally moved on. Since Newkirk had not arrested him, he was free to attack a real problem. That was how his mind worked.

Me, I'm not nearly so bottom line oriented. I've noticed that sometimes if you don't steer in the right direction early enough, you skid into a tree.

I told Rip I'd see him later and set off to find Joanne.

I found her perfecting her hairdo right around the corner in the women's room. Even without chocolate donuts, she was happy to direct me to Susan Kelly's apartment. She wanted George Kelly to be guilty just as much as Rip and I.

❈ *Chapter 13* ❈

I appreciated Jacob's foresight with the rock salt as I walked out to my car. Pennsylvania doesn't do its serious freezing until January, but it calls for turtlenecks and sweaters, and maybe some boots on the chillier December days. This was one of them: twenty-eight degrees this morning and scheduled to drop tonight.

If Susan had been among the more ostentatious parents, I'd have dressed a bit more formally just to stay on even ground, but I knew she wasn't overly concerned about appearances. Fortunately, I could get away with looking very "Ludwig," as Rip described my casual everyday clothes.

Even then, I was overdressed. When I found Susan's apartment, a tiny thing over a car repair shop in the outskirts of King of Prussia, Susan still wore a bathrobe and slippers.

She had peeked under the window shade half covering the door, gaped with surprise, and reluctantly let me in. The smell of grease and hot solder pervaded the place, and startlingly loud car repair noises made sleeping late an unlikely luxury.

"Is Chris all right?" She nervously clutched her robe closed at the throat.

"Oh yes. As far as I know. That's not why I'm here."

"Thank goodness," she said, forgetting modesty and slumping into a bentwood kitchen chair. The whole apartment scarcely consisted of more, just the table and chairs, a sofa and TV, and a green braided rug. A kitchen unit took up eight feet of the right-hand wall. A narrow hall door led to the rest, probably two small bedrooms and a bath. No, Susan Kelly was definitely not one of Bryn Derwyn's wealthy contingency.

"Then why . . . ?" Her mind went out the window.

". . . am I here? Something very personal—to me." Taking off my jacket or sitting down would have been presumptuous, so I simply waited.

Susan's soft brown eyes studied me with curiosity until another fear intruded. "How did you find me?"

"Joanne Henry. She brought Christopher home once when you went on that job interview, remember?"

Susan Kelly shrugged with resignation. "It doesn't matter," she said. "George knows about this place already." She laughed humorlessly, encompassed the room with a wave of her hand. "Lovely, isn't it? I thought it was perfect. Hard to find. Totally opposite from what George would expect me to pick. Cheap. He found me within a week."

"What about the restraining order?" I asked.

She looked me in the eye. "Any cops out there when you came in?"

I shook my head no. Susan huffed and glanced away.

I finally pulled out a chair and sat next to her, a friendly, non-threatening distance. "Then George really was here at the time of the murder." The realization made me feel deflated and foolish. Had I actually believed that protecting the school and Rip's job would be so easy?

She snorted. "Yeah. Too bad, isn't it?"

I stared across the room at a clown print, one of those

teary-eyed men with a painted-on smile. It seemed to be off center, but Susan Kelly's whole life had slipped off center. Why should her artwork be different?

"He didn't hurt you, did he?" My very being there constituted an intrusion; a few blunt questions couldn't matter.

Susan's face relaxed as if she was pleased by my concern. "No. It was just his weekly attempt to get me back."

I shuddered inwardly, shocked by her life, surprised by how completely I empathized.

"You won't go back?"

She shook her head and smiled at the hand she had resting on the table, amused, but not wishing to embarrass me with it. "No, I won't. Thanks to Richard. He explained how I was strong, and my strength was the reason I was able to stay with George as long as I did. He was right, too. I am strong." Her eyes seemed to summon a private memory of Richard, because her expression contained a wistful trace of awe.

"Richard is sort of the reason why I'm here," I admitted.

Susan's glance was sharp.

"But then if you say George was here during the murder, I'm already wrong."

"About what?" Susan asked.

"Remember that morning when you left Bryn Derwyn with Richard, when you were going for the restraining order? I remember having the nasty suspicion that all Richard wanted was . . . you."

Susan's face colored slightly, as a woman's face does to flattery. "That was what he wanted."

My own face flushed for a different reason. "Oh," I said.

"What's this really about? Were you and Richard lovers, too?"

What? Where did that come from? "No," I answered, perhaps too hastily. "No. I was just thinking that if George came to the same conclusion, it might have angered him enough to . . . to . . ."

"To commit murder. Well, he was *here* that afternoon. How many times do I have to say it? And why the hell would I lie? To protect a piece of slime who beat me and my son every payday like clockwork?" She stood up, folded her arms across her chest and began to pace.

"I'm sorry." Suddenly my reasons for insinuating myself into this woman's privacy seemed shallow, despite all the people who might suffer if Bryn Derwyn closed.

"Frankly, I was damn glad Richard was interested in me," Susan continued. "Do you have any idea what lawyers charge these days? Maybe I did lead him on a little. So what? He was no saint. I'd say we both got what we wanted."

I resumed normal breathing; my motives held up to comparison better than I had originally thought.

I stood and eased toward the door. "You're right. I was wrong. I was just afraid you still loved George, and somehow he persuaded you to cover for him. Foolishly, very foolishly, I thought I could convince you to tell the police the truth. Dumb idea."

Susan did not contradict me.

Just before opening the door, I paused. One other thing bothered me. It was an irrelevant detail, but it bothered me. I wondered how a woman who couldn't protect herself from her husband over a long period of time, years actually, suddenly managed to remain unscathed after he tracked her down and confronted her.

What the hell. I asked.

Susan took a handgun from her bathrobe pocket and set it on the table for my inspection.

Probably because I've read a few newspaper accounts

of weapons being used against their female owners, my enthusiasm was forced.

The lack of confidence implied by my hesitation irritated Susan. Scowling, she walked across the room and tilted the clown print away from a hole in the plaster.

"George didn't think I would shoot either."

I shuffled a foot. "Glad I'm not the only one who was wrong," I said. "Sorry to·have wasted your time."

When I returned home, a tow truck was hauling Bryn Derwyn's one and only full-sized yellow school bus down the driveway. Jacob watched from the service parking area, hands on hips, scowling venomously.

Chapter 14

Naturally, a school bus breaking down merited some irritation from the man responsible for its maintenance, but Jacob Greene was clearly furious. Dark and balding, standing at only five-foot-eight, he appeared formidable enough to defeat George Foreman.

I stopped my Nissan at the edge of the service lot and walked over to find out why. Recent events had made me suspicious and edgy. If something else odd had happened, I wanted to know about it now.

"Bus broke down?" I asked, giving Jacob the opening he craved. "Goddamn," he cursed and more until I pointed to the classroom windows thirty feet away.

"Sorry, Gin," he said, subduing himself with effort, "but this is too much."

"What happened?"

He paced left then right before he stood squarely before me. "Water in the gas tank. Froze overnight. You have any idea how much it'll cost to fix that?"

"Plenty?"

"You betcha, plenty. Damn little vandals. This is really too much."

"How do you know it was kids?"

"It's a school full of kids. Who else could it be?"

I could name one or two possibilities, but I chose not to name them to Jacob. "You sure about the water?"

"Yeah, I'm sure. I was going out for gas and the damn bus quit fifty feet down the driveway. Just had it serviced, too."

"So what did you do?"

Hands back on his hips, Jacob paced and wagged his head, a toreador lamenting the cowardice of the bull. "I checked the gas gauge, checked for a spark, finally found drops of water in the filter and looked in the tank. Gas was floating on the stuff, sure enough. Damn kids," he muttered. "My budget is down the tubes. Your husband won't be happy about this." His breath huffed frosty clouds of disgust.

"Insurance?" I asked.

"Maybe. Yeah, maybe. But still." The deductible, the future rates. I wondered how long the destructive pranks had been going on. Joanne's computer keyboard and now this—if other incidents had occurred before Rip took over, maybe Richard Wharton knew about them. Maybe he even knew which vicious, vengeful mind was responsible.

Jeremy Philbin immediately came to mind. The veteran algebra teacher had been at the school last night and could have sabotaged the bus while he was still sober enough to unscrew the gas cap. Then he could have proceeded into the auditorium for his embarrassing display of hatred.

Unfortunately, I had difficulty imagining him doing both, but only because the two behaviors were juvenile and vengeful in different ways—one sneaky, the other quite public. If kids had really sabotaged that school bus as Jacob believed, maybe it wouldn't be necessary to mention this development to the police. Bryn Derwyn's reputation could do without any more gossip.

Also, to possibly rule out Philbin, I thought a conversation with his ex-wife might give me a clearer notion of what the man might and might not do.

Since I now had my own reason for wanting to go to the office, I told Jacob I would give Rip the bad news about the bus. He nodded curtly, then turned back toward the building, focused once again on his anger.

I drove my soon-to-be-discontinued Nissan wagon to its accustomed spot near our house and walked back to the school.

After greeting the receptionist in the lobby and paying my respects to Joanne, I checked that Rip was alone and available before entering his inner sanctum.

"Saw you talking to Jacob," he said. "What's up?"

"Water in the gas tank of the bus," I told him. "Jacob's furious. He thinks it was kids, but . . ." I shrugged and let the sentence hang. Rip knew as well as I that during the meeting and memorial service an adult vandal could have blended into the crowd in half a second.

Rip muttered a few curses of his own, quietly. At her desk just outside his door Joanne couldn't have heard him.

Suddenly my attention was fixed by a new distraction. Looking beyond Rip, who stood with his back to his tall, wide windows, I had a clear view of the school's moderately long driveway. Three police cars crept along it. When they arrived at the front circle, they deployed themselves like Patton's troops positioning for an attack.

My husband noticed the widening of my eyes and turned to see what had caused my surprise. He got to see Newkirk emerge from the passenger side of the middle car and carefully shut his door.

Rip threw some papers he had been holding onto his desk and rushed from the room. I won't say he ran, but he managed to intercept the police when they entered the lobby.

My body had tensed from head to foot. Adrenaline sharpened my senses. Three squad cars probably meant an invasive search or maybe even an arrest. Like Joanne I was strongly drawn to the doorway to watch. I, too, wanted to be among the first to learn what was happening. But whatever it was, my presence wouldn't stop it, and my curiosity could wait. The distraction was an opportunity too perfect to ignore.

I shut the door on the commotion. Alone in Rip's office, I snatched my husband's big ring of school keys out of his desk drawer. Then, fumbling through them with shaking fingers I chose the smallest keys, the possible file drawer keys, and painstakingly tried each one on the locked personnel file drawer in the credenza under Rip's window. The third one fit. The button popped at the corner of the drawer, and I was in. Elation and dread fought for my soul.

"P" for personnel. "P" for Philbin. My heart hammered. There was no movement outside at the circle, just two cops leaning against their cars watching the front door. I scanned the few sheets of paper in Jeremy's folder looking for his ex-wife's name, hoping with a little luck to also learn her address.

Nothing. Not one word about her. I replaced the folder, re-locked the drawer, wiped the sweat off my brow with the cuff of my jacket.

I hefted Rip's bunch of keys in my hand. They opened lots of doors, lots of drawers. Where else could I find information about Jeremy Philbin?

Health insurance. Next of kin. Philbin and his wife had divorced, but it was possible he named her beneficiary of the small life insurance policy that was one of the school's benefits. The policy probably wasn't on file, but most likely the application was.

In the past Joanne doled out all the health insurance forms. I considered asking for her help again, but my instincts told me not to involve her in this. Joanne had always defended Jeremy; if I asked her to betray his privacy and she refused, I might never get the information. That went double for my husband, whose ethics were the cornerstone of his career. And hurray for that.

My own ethics would have to be examined later. The opportunity clock was ticking.

Trouble was, I had no idea if the insurance files had been transferred to the business manager's office after Kevin Seitz was hired. All I could do was check where the files used to be.

The lobby remained quiet. A glance assured me that Rip's secretary was busy rubbernecking with the receptionist and a few others who had gathered there. The police were nowhere in sight and neither was my husband.

Closing Joanne's door would be too suspicious. If I got caught, I would have to lie my way clear. I hated what I was doing, but my concern for the school was too deep, my need to act too great. "What you do may not work," my father always admitted, "but doing nothing doesn't work for sure."

So I took a bracing breath and opened the bottom left drawer of Joanne's three file cabinets lined up behind her desk.

Relief. The files were still there.

Again "P" for Philbin. Again a few sheets of paper, forms this time, and finally an application for life insurance. "Emily Philbin beneficiary. 419 Elm Drive, St. Davids, PA."

I shut the drawer and slumped from my crouch to a yoga squat on the floor. My face was sweating worse than before. I wiped it again with the sleeve of my jacket.

Out in the lobby a group of people moved swiftly into view. Four policemen, Rip, and Bryn Derwyn's Director of Development, Randy Webb.

Damp clumps of wavy, blond hair bounced against Randy's waxen forehead. Gone was his trademark leggy stride, replaced with mincing steps that appeared to be all pointy knees and not much progress. Understandable, considering that his hands were cuffed behind his back and a policeman maintained a firm grip on his arm.

❈ *Chapter 15* ❈

The three police cars took turns backing up and pulling away as if they had jammed many a school
driveway and were showing off their efficiency. An ominous quiet remained.

Standing on the sidewalk with Rip and Joanne and a
few others watching the aftermath of Randy Webb's arrest, I felt stunned stiff and inexplicably frightened.

"Is he charged with murder?" I asked just to be sure.
Rip had been present during the arrest; he would know.

"Oh yeah. What else?"

I shook my head. "Sudden," I said, voicing the worst
part of my fear. "Too sudden."

How could Newkirk act so precipitously? He must
have uncovered new evidence—damning evidence—of
Randy's guilt. But what? And how convincing could it
be? I'd discovered the body I knew how little there was
to go on. Even if they found traces of Randy's clothing
stuck to the shovel or his hair on the floor, how did that
help? He regularly worked in that room. Furthermore,
the shovel was his responsibility. In fact, he probably
bought it and put the bow on himself. When the fund-
raising for the gym was completed and the construction
was about to begin, Randy would probably be the one to

hand the ceremonial shovel to the Chairman of the Board!

Behind us, more staff members had infiltrated the lobby, chattering like children. To comfort us both, I wanted to grab Rip's hand, but I made do with a longing look. My husband stared unblinking down the driveway. A multitude of students and faculty members would have seen the police remove Randy, and those who hadn't witnessed the arrest would know about it within seconds. Soon Rip would be contending with panic and rampant rumors and who knew what else. I touched his arm. "See you at home," I said.

He looked down, but not at me, nodded and finally gave me an unnerving glance. Then he strode back into the school. The slow-closing door effectively shut me out.

I ordered my legs to walk to our house, ordered my hands to work the key.

Inside I drank decaf and ate something, I'm not sure what, and listened to gibberish on the TV until about ten-thirty when the phone rang.

"Got anything for sandwiches?" Rip asked without preamble. I sighed with relief, ignoring the bad, concentrating on the good. He was turning to me.

"Sure," I answered.

"Valley Forge Park about twelve?" he suggested.

"I'll pick you up," I said, knowing the tension must be unbearable if he wanted to flee so badly.

At exactly twelve I pulled my car up to the front door of the school. Then, reluctant to let anyone in on Rip's temporary escape, I walked across the grass and tapped on his office window. Two mid-sized girls gawked at me like goldfish, pointed at the window, and hastily finished whatever they were saying.

Rip stood, retrieved his coat from his closet, and ushered the students into the lobby. Through the door, I could see the two girls, heads bowed, their friendship galvanized by the brave act of actually speaking to The Headmaster together.

With a heavy sigh, Rip climbed into the car beside me. I put the Nissan into gear and fed it gas. Rip and I said nothing for a mile, but I could sense my husband's tension by his breathing, the twitching inside his clothes, the way he held himself.

We left stoplights behind. Rip held my right hand when I wasn't shifting. Large homes close together gave way to larger homes farther apart, their yards sculpted with perfectly proportioned shrubs and trees. Most of the fallen leaves had been relegated to back yard mulch piles. Overhead the sky was muted blue, softened with thin winter cumulus clouds. Tree trunks were dark with dampness, bricks deep red, white siding a gentle pearl gray. Rip watched the scenery as his thoughts slid by, and soon his breathing slowed, his back curved into the bucket seat, his head tilted, and I relaxed.

I found one of the back ways into the vast national park I'd recently learned, then wound around past bunkers made of dirt, past small clusters of short, squat log cabins caulked with mud and straw, up to an empty, U-shaped parking area with a huge bronze statue of a guy on a horse overlooking a distant sloping field ending with woods. To our right a portion of park was reserved for flying remote control airplanes, but none of the hand-built toys were up today. No buzz, scarcely any sound at all but a bit of breeze against the car windows and the *ffff* of the Nissan's heater. I parked facing the long view and kept the engine running.

"It's Pearl Harbor Day," Rip remarked. December 7. So it was. I laughed briefly at his little joke in order not to cry.

After a silence he said, "Newkirk came back again."

"Oh? I don't suppose he told you why he arrested Randy."

Rip turned toward me. "Actually, he did. He said Elaine Wrigley saw Randy rushing out the back."

I inhaled an especially deep breath before I asked, "Fifth grade? Ten years old going on forty?"

"That's the one. She finally told her mother what she saw, and her mother called the police. But—this is the best part—the kid was positive Randy was wiping blood off his hands."

I shivered. Elaine Wrigley made me shiver even when she wasn't accusing adults of murder. "This is bad," I said aloud.

"No shit," Rip agreed.

"What else did Newkirk say?"

"He said Randy's prints were on the shovel—big surprise—but put all that together with public pressure and Newkirk felt he had no choice."

"You think Randy's guilty?"

Rip shook his head slowly. "I really don't know. But I can tell you one thing. Something weird is going on with him."

"Why do you say that?"

"Because the reason Newkirk came back was to pump me about something Randy said. The *only* thing he said without his lawyer. He told Newkirk that Richard found a new donor to replace D'Avanzo, mainly so the school didn't have to use Longmeier Construction. Randy wants Newkirk to check out Eddie Longmeier."

I stared at the wintergreen grass interwoven with thatch. On one of the farms we passed, horses had been grazing.

"What did you say?"

"That it was news to me. Then Newkirk, the sonova-bitch tells me, 'That's what D'Avanzo claimed, too.' "

"He spoke to Michael D'Avanzo?" I was truly

shocked. Donors of D'Avanzo's generosity were few and far between. They were also highly mercurial. Being questioned by the police regarding a murder investigation was more than enough to turn Randy's story into reality. Just the possibility of Newkirk costing the school $750,000 spiked my temperature.

"What I can't figure out," Rip continued, "is why Randy pointed a finger at Eddie Longmeier. What possible connection could there be between him and Richard?"

"His wife," I blurted.

Rip shifted to face me square on. "Where the hell did that come from?" he asked.

"When we first got here, I used to practice remembering the names of people out in the parking lot."

"So?"

"So one morning I was looking out the kitchen window and I saw Randy and Richard talking to an absolutely gorgeous woman. Long black hair, short-shorts, orange T-shirt, and no bra. I found out later she was Tina Longmeier, and she'd been delivering some blueprints to Randy. Anyway, she was flirting with both men like, well, let's just say she was very suggestive. And the men! The gleams in their eyes could have lighted New York."

"So?"

"So what if it wasn't just play? What if Tina delivered?"

"I'm not sure I'm following you."

I huffed with exasperation. "What if Randy wanted the police to pick up on Richard and Tina without implicating himself? He'd suggest they check out Eddie Longmeier, right?"

"I don't know, Gin. Where are you going with this?"

I played my trump. "I saw Randy and Tina pulling away from a clinch. In the copier room."

"What were you . . . what . . . Are you sure that's what you saw?"

I thought it through again and realized, again, that my conclusion was more intuition-based than fact-based. "I saw a couple of people moving away from each other and blushing. I had the impression they'd been . . . close."

Rip shook his head. "Doesn't mean a damn thing."

I shrugged. "It could. Especially now that Randy is accusing Eddie Longmeier of having a motive to kill Richard. What if Randy tried to cash in on Tina's offer and failed, but Richard succeeded?"

"What kind of sandwiches you got?" Rip asked.

Pierced, I said, "Liverwurst." Privately, I was glad to see him wince.

We ate in silence, Rip's the brooding kind, mine the slow burn. When it was time to mollify each other, I asked, "What about Randy's work?"

"Oh, shit," Rip exclaimed. "He was doing a mailing, going after tax-deductible donations before the end of the year. Damn. Now they'll be late."

"Anything I can do?" another of my blind offers. I really ought to curb that habit.

"Yeah," Rip replied, his own eyes sparkling for the first time in ages. "You can do the mailing."

Yippee, I thought. Stuffing envelopes.

"You need to hand-write messages on about a thousand solicitations. Thanks, babe. You're a lifesaver."

"No problem," I mumbled through a mouthful of liverwurst.

Rip finished eating first and resumed brooding wherever he'd left off.

"Penny for your thoughts," I pressed.

He gazed through the windshield far into the distance. "Just wondering," he said.

"About?"

"Richard Wharton and another donor. Whether what Randy said could possibly be true."

"How could it be true? D'Avanzo denied it." Although . . . D'Avanzo might lie to deflect suspicion from his son-in-law regardless of whatever unpleasant politics were involved, even if it cost him a $750,000 donation he no longer wished to give.

"I don't know, babe. I just have this prickly feeling that Wharton was scheming behind my back again."

Valley Forge was the most famous encampment in the world, where George Washington's ragged troops were drilled into a cohesive unit capable of defeating the British. I looked into my husband's green eyes, eyes no longer idealistic, no longer naive, eyes committed for the duration regardless of the possibility of defeat. I looked back at those eyes and felt my resolve tighten into a fist.

I knew several things I could *discreetly* do to help, provided I did them in a hurry.

Only one of them involved stuffing envelopes.

❈ *Chapter 16* ❈

After I dropped Rip off, I stopped into the school only long enough to wash some mustard off my fingers. Then I was back in the car headed for the nearby village called St. David's.

Emily Philbin's address was a little difficult to find until I noticed some reflective house numbers attached to a split-rail fencepost. Apparently, she lived in a tidy square gatehouse with burgundy shutters parked in front of a similarly trimmed stone monster with a creek and plenty of trees. The two-lane road running in front of the property dropped off steeply on both sides, so there was no place to pull over. Also, the driveways amounted to private roads where small, foreign station wagons would be suspiciously conspicuous.

While I crept along at twenty miles an hour, irritating the Type A personality in a red Honda just behind me, a woman emerged from the gatehouse and climbed into a blue car with peculiar round headlights. Emily Philbin was on her way out.

Further infuriating the Honda driver, I whipped left into the first driveway a hundred yards down the road. Then I backed out and headed back toward Emily's place. If she intended to run errands, and early afternoon was a lovely time for that, I was in position to follow her toward town. If not, I was up a creek.

Emily dutifully turned left directly in front of me. I celebrated by putting in a Fats Domino tape.

At the light on Lancaster Avenue, Emily steered her little roadster, or whatever it was, left toward Wayne. I followed.

The elderly man shuffling diagonally across the intersection of Wayne and Lancaster walked across my left lane before Emily's right. Not wishing to outdistance her by much, I hastily eased right and slowed as if contemplating a turn into Main Line Federal Bank. Emily scooted around me.

I soon rejoined her lane because of the traffic mess at the Farmer's Market, which was open today. Then I waited two cars behind while a Volvo tried to cross the other two oncoming lanes into McDonald's. When Emily impatiently stepped on it, I prayed that the driver in between us was vegetarian.

"Yes," I cheered while Fats lamented something about jumping overboard.

We continued past Spread Eagle Village, a lovely shopping complex I can't afford; past Braxton's in Strafford, my favorite dog supply store; on past Lancaster Avenue's bunch of car dealers and the place where I got our mower fixed. A sign proclaimed that we were now on "Lincoln Highway." Same road, new name—the Main Line shell game.

At the Dalesford Station traffic light, Philbin's ex remained centermost in front of a large white appliance truck. I hastily calculated that a hatchback with a "Kids on Board" sign might be marginally faster pulling out than a truck full of refrigerators, so I lined up behind Mom. Bad guess. The truck managed to tailgate Emily off to the right within three car lengths, while "Kids on

Board" slowed to ogle a man across the street leaning against a telephone pole. He appeared to be asleep standing up while waiting for a ride.

Finally, it was a sprint parallel to the railroad tracks into Paoli. Once there, Emily Philbin immediately turned into an Acme shopping center and parked around the corner from the grocery store at the end of a row of shops. With no extra slots available, I simply stopped behind her car and watched to see where she went.

She locked up, snapped her keys into a dark brown handbag, and walked rather regally into a hairdresser's. She wore a gray wool coat over a muted plaid skirt; I could tell because the coat didn't quite cover the skirt. While I drove, I had been reflecting that her appearance was at odds with what I knew about her, which was that she had given her ex-husband far more trouble than he could handle. Evidently, even hellions get old, for that's all Emily Philbin looked like to me—an elderly woman in an overcoat purchased during a previous decade.

When I was certain about her destination, I found a parking spot two rows over and zigzagged through the rows to the hairdresser's.

The reception area contained a boy of about four scribbling into a coloring book, also a woman behind one of those tall desks hairdressers provide for writing checks while standing up. The woman's hair was shiny and black and about two inches longer on the right than on the left. On her it looked interesting.

"Help you?" she asked.

"I don't have an appointment," I admitted. "I just want to speak with Emily Philbin if I may. She just came in."

"You must mean Emily Walker. She doesn't use Philbin anymore."

"Yes, of course." My insides squirmed. This wasn't my usual approach—to anything.

"Right around the corner," The receptionist, who outweighed me by thirty pounds, directed me with a graceful handful of long, dark red nails. Her black V-neck dress revealed an alluring amount of pale white flesh. I thanked her and glanced around the rosy room at each of three occupied work stations. Straight ahead lay a blue manicure area containing a few sinks with reclining chairs. Emily Walker was nowhere in sight.

"Around *there,*" insisted the receptionist.

Through an alcove on the right another room contained two customer chairs, a row of hair dryers, and one sink. Mirrors doubled the bountiful flower arrangements and gave the place the aura of a stuffy, backstage dressing room.

Emily sat in a customer chair while a woman in a stylish taupe outfit and comfortable shoes tucked a towel around her collar.

"Are you Emily Philbin?" I asked discreetly, as if I didn't want the hairdresser to hear. "I mean Emily Walker?"

Emily glared at me. "Why do you ask?"

I fluttered a little. "It's just that I need some information about your ex-husband, and you're really the only one who can help."

Emily's glare became more heated. "Who exactly are you?"

The hairdresser fluffed a dark blue plastic drape around her client's shoulders while casting me a few sharp glances.

"I'm Ginger Struve Barnes. Jeremy works with my husband."

"Works *for* your husband, don't you mean?"

"Well, yes."

"And what exactly is it you want from me?"

The hairdresser seemed to be considering calling for a bouncer, perhaps the receptionist, who would have been quite effective. I met her eyes with as much innocence as possible while I answered Emily Walker. "Just a couple questions really. Jeremy caused a scene the other night . . ."

"Do you have to do this now?" the hairdresser interrupted. She was a slender, pretty thing with honey-blonde hair twisted high and wispy tendrils flattering her neck. Her eyes were brown and skillfully made up, but no amount of mascara could disguise their hostility.

"Yes, I do," I stated with extra volume. "This happens to be extremely important."

The hairdresser saw my raise and called my hand. "I am giving Mrs. Walker a permanent here, and I don't need you interfering with my schedule. Why don't you make an appointment to speak with the lady some other time?"

A permanent, as I recalled, involved sitting for about twenty minutes with stinky solution on your head. "Emily," I addressed my target, "do you mind if I come back for a few minutes after you get your curlers in?"

Emily's mouth twitched beneath hard, old eyes that didn't often smile. An age spot darkened her left jaw, and her nose flared wide around its unusually round tip. With a face like that a permanent was mostly for morale. Yet the eyes caught and held your attention. Sensual, wily, and fascinating, they conjured up visions of gypsy campfires.

"Kelly, it's all right," she mollified the younger woman. "I'd just as soon get it over with myself."

Kelly had drawn out a flat band of Emily's gray hair. As she tapped her customer's shoulder to demand one of the square tissues Emily held in her hand, she fixed her eyes on mine Clint Eastwood style. "Come back in half an hour." Somehow she managed to make reaching for a pink plastic spindle to clamp on another woman's head look arrogant.

I checked my watch. "Thank you," I told Emily, who grunted and offered Kelly another tissue square.

Since I didn't especially want to wait in the reception area, I bought myself some hazelnut-flavored coffee and a croissant in a French bakery across the way. There were tiny round tables, uncomfortable wire chairs, and wide store windows for watching the parking lot traffic. Not particularly enthralling, but my mind was on the prospective interview with Emily anyway.

What exactly did I need to ask? What approach would get me my answers? I focused on the image of Randy Webb being led to the squad car in handcuffs. I reminded myself of the many absent students at Bryn Derwyn and of Richard Wharton sprawled across the Community Room table. By the time the caffeine kicked in my nervous system was at least equal to Clint Eastwood and probably equal to Kelly the Hairdresser.

"Now what's this all about?" Emily greeted me bluntly. Her head was swathed in a white towel with pungent permanent solution fumes escaping around the edges. Between the dark blue drape and the head wrap, her old woman's face appeared to float in midair like a hologram I'd seen in the Disney World haunted house.

From the second chair another customer leaned forward to eavesdrop on my answer. Similarly draped and wrapped, her face resembled a friendly, eager Pekinese.

"It's really rather private," I murmured to Emily.

"No it's not," she disagreed. "Everybody knows I think Jeremy is a drunken son of a bitch."

A hand with four gold-and-diamond rings emerged from under the Pekinese's drape and squeezed Emily's arm, or what was probably her arm. "Oh, sweetie. I had one of those, too. My second, may he rest in Hades."

Emily shrugged off the ringed fingers.

This wasn't going well, but what choice did I have except to proceed? "Would you say Jeremy is well-balanced? By that I mean when he's distraught, would he be inclined to take action or just . . . just talk?"

Emily scowled thoughtfully at me. In a few seconds when it became clear that she had no intention of answering my question, I asked another. "Was he very handy around the house?"

"Not really."

"Oh, honey, you can be glad for that. My first fancied himself a handyman, and it cost me a fortune in repair bills."

Simultaneously, Emily and I gave the eavesdropper a do-you-mind? stare. Pouting, she reached a claw out from under to grab her purse off the counter, stood up, and shouted, "Diane, dear. I'm coming out there ready or not."

After Emily and I gratefully watched her go, I said, "Naturally you're aware of the problem Jeremy had with Richard Wharton . . ." I was mentally into the part about whether she thought Jeremy was capable of murder, so her interruption brought me up short.

"Who?"

"Richard Wharton. The school's attorney. He was murdered last Friday."

"At the school. Of course. I just didn't remember the name."

"Do you mean you forgot the name? Or do you mean you never heard of him before?"

"I suppose I read it in the paper; but since I was unfamiliar with the man, I ignored his name."

"Oh." I had to reorganize my thoughts. "So you didn't know about Jeremy's problem with him."

Emily was growing a little testy. "No I didn't. What problem?"

My cheeks had grown warm. I had not expected to have to explain. "When he was . . . was contemplating getting a divorce . . . Jeremy spoke with Richard Wharton . . . and . . . and . . ."

"And what?"

"And told him all about your marriage."

Emily surprised me with a bark of laughter. "And you think Jeremy killed him over that! Ha!" She exercised her imagination some more before adding a few more ha's.

I inhaled a deep breath of permanent-wave solution, coughed, and finally asked, "So how about that first question?"

Emily sobered. "What question was that?"

"Is Jeremy all talk, or does he sometimes act?"

"Act like what?"

"In your opinion, is your ex-husband capable of violence?"

The older woman fixed me in her gypsy stare. I returned it unblinking, emphasizing the seriousness of my question. The white kitchen timer on the hairdresser's counter rattled double-time, gobbling up the silence.

"Jeremy Philbin wouldn't hurt a fly." A slightly peeved expression crossed Emily's face when she said that, as if she regretted that her ex-husband was incapable of such behavior. For a second her disappointment confused me. Was she actually sorry that Jeremy was incapable of murder? Why? To my knowledge, Richard Wharton had done nothing to her.

Then, much to my own regret, I remembered Joanne's story about Emily's reputed sexual preferences, which, if Jeremy was to be believed, ran toward domination and who knew what else. Until that moment I thought Joanne had exaggerated.

"Jeremy Philbin wouldn't hurt a fly," Emily Walker said

with chagrin, causing the hazelnut-coffee and croissant to churn in my stomach.

As soon as I turned on the Nissan's engine, Fats Domino tried to sing me out of it.

I told him to shut up.

❈ *Chapter 17* ❈

Trying to forget Emily Walker's sexual preferences—
and believe me, I was trying to forget—I realized
that Philbin's ex-wife had given me some useful information. But did it apply to Richard Wharton's murder?
Who knew? Could a man who was disinclined to work
with his hands make an exception and put water in the
gas tank of a school bus? Sure, why not? Would a man
whose wife made him feel less than masculine in the
bedroom go to violent extremes to prove himself?
Tough call. I decided to let my speculations simmer
overnight.

Meanwhile, cooking dinner was next—anything but
eggplant, considering that Dolores "Didi" Martin would
be joining us. My own appetite was non-existent, but I
didn't want the others to suffer; therefore, I prepared a
pot roast with carrots and potatoes, even threw together
a cherry pie.

My visit with Emily Walker had reminded me how
much I valued my oldest friend. More than just our long
history, we offered each other a huge inventory of simi-
larities and differences. Maybe I happened to be physically braver, formerly with sports and now with my
ladder-climbing, nail-hammering activities; but Didi

much more easily risked her feelings. If I was behaving like a jerk, a glance from Didi told me so—and vice versa. If she needed grounding after an emotional upheaval, she came over to play with my kids. Just knowing she would be there for dinner, I felt more like myself than I had in days.

She arrived just after I set the pie on a cooling rack. She hugged me hello, then shed her fringed shawl overcoat onto a living room chair. Underneath she wore a silk gym suit in pastel blues and greens with a matching blue turtleneck. Today her blonde hair formed a variegated French braid down the back of her head. I assumed the getup was chosen for dancing with kids who still expected her to look grown up. Didi thought of those things.

"Frozen crust, canned filling?" she asked as she sniffed the pie.

"Of course," I replied, and my best friend nodded her approval. We had discussed this before. Maybe we were what we ate, but Didi and I agreed that life was not conducted inside a kitchen. Not if we could help it.

"How's it going?" Didi asked as she hitched her bottom onto our blah tan counter-top. Behind her the square kitchen sported equally blah blond cabinets with stainless-steel handles. Their interior design could efficiently accommodate anything from auto parts to shoes and socks.

Across from Didi in the work square the motor of our elderly refrigerator shuddered to a stop. That left the music videos Chelsea and Garry were watching on MTV for background noise, so I answered truthfully, "Awful, thank you."

"That's what I figured. The rehearsal wasn't normal."

"How so?"

"The kids threw themselves into learning the songs and dances as if they were desperate to be kids."

"That's not normal?" Didi's selections would be nothing if not fun, no pious eyes to the skies for her.

"What would you say?"

I summoned up a picture of the concert rehearsal just before Nora quit. Despite my preoccupation with Rip's anger, I realized the kids had tried to be mature, for the audience, or for Nora, or maybe just for themselves. That was one of the reasons the non-singers stood out; they appeared to be speaking volumes about discrimination, just by keeping their mouths shut.

"Not normal," I agreed. "Although it could be the new songs. What are they?"

"Ordinary stuff, although I do have ten boys doing the 'Skater's Waltz,' "

"Boys? In seven days? That I have to see."

"There is a small logistics problem."

I imagined boys cavorting every which way like bumper cars.

Didi chewed her lip as if the difficulty approximated her disappointment over a new nail polish color. "It'll work out," she decided. "Your turn. Tell me everything."

I did. While we set the dining room table, I told her about Randy's arrest and what that probably meant to the school. Then I described my conversations with Susan Kelly, and Emily Walker, formerly Philbin. Naturally, I stressed Jeremy's incriminating behavior, but I also mentioned Kevin Seitz's grudge against Richard Wharton regarding his father's suicide.

While I sliced the roast, Didi returned to her perch and, deep in thought, nibbled pinches off a dry roll.

"So?" I prompted. "What do you think?"

"I think you better not tell Rip what you're up to."

My arm flew up so fast that meat juice from the knife splashed the ceiling.

"Put that down," Didi said, referring to the knife. "And close your mouth. I merely said . . ."

"I know what you said, and I assumed it was understood. Rip has no idea what I'm doing."

"Good."

"Not good. Not good at all, but necessary."

"Of course."

I rolled my shoulders and tried some normal breathing. I even picked up the knife and went back to work on the roast while Didi brought in a chair and wiped my ceiling.

If anyone knew anything about the male psyche, it should have been her. To Didi, dating was a science, men the curriculum of a lifetime. Her errors in judgment only served to rededicate her to her studies. Yet it was those errors in judgment that usually prompted me to state the obvious to her; such as, "Don't tell Rip anything." For her to reach that conclusion by herself shocked me and underscored just how delicate my situation was. Bryn Derwyn was Rip's domain. I'd better not forget it.

Our "understanding" made for a very stilted dinner. Didi behaved like the perfect guest, avoiding controversial topics, letting others speak. When she complimented the pot roast, I glared at her.

She rolled her eyes and addressed Chelsea. "What's up, kid? You look glum."

Chelsea gave Didi her now-that-you-asked stare and related her complaint about a discrepancy on her latest English test. "I had the essay right," she groused. "Mrs. Hoffman really has it in for me. I bet it's because of the murder."

Rip and I simultaneously exclaimed, "What!" and "No way," while Didi nodded noncommittally and continued to chew her food. She had become the perfect guest again, vanishing at the first sign of friction like the

Cheshire cat. Also, something about this new topic bothered Garry, but I could not guess what.

My husband and I looked at each other, and Rip gave me the chin signal to handle our daughter; he gets enough juvenile problems at work.

"Chelsea," I opened, securing her attention over any other distraction. "What's happening at Bryn Derwyn has absolutely nothing to do with whether you got an answer right on an English test. Mrs. Hoffman is an adult. She's much too mature to think that way."

"But you always say that teachers are people. And people aren't always fair. Other kids look at me funny now and then, too, and I know it's because they're wondering what's going on at Bryn Derwyn. Why couldn't a teacher be wondering the same thing?"

I set down my coffee mug. "Maybe kids are curious about our problems, maybe they're even a little excited by what they've heard, kind of the way people are fascinated by some sensational movies. But if you think you got marked down on a test because of all this, you're crazy."

Chelsea stared at a forkful of meat, then stared at me. "I got the answer right," she insisted. "So why did Mrs. Hoffman mark me wrong?"

I curbed the temptation to joke our daughter into a better mood; this was a real dilemma to her. It deserved a real answer. "Perhaps Mrs. Hoffman made a mistake. Or maybe you don't understand *how* the answer was incorrect. Either way, you've got two choices. Go to Mrs. Hoffman and ask her to explain what was wrong with your answer . . ."

"Nothing was wrong with my answer."

"And if nothing was wrong, she'll have a chance to see that for herself and fix your grade—or else she'll explain what she really was after."

"But . . ."

"But if you go to her all angry and confrontational, she'll get angry and confrontational, and the odds are you'd get no satisfaction whatsoever. Which brings me to your other choice. Let it alone and figure it evens out with all the times you got marked right when you didn't have a clue."

"Yeah, sure."

"Up to you."

Didi's thoughts still appeared to be elsewhere. Rip was smiling around a mouthful of carrot, but his eyes were weary. When they rested on Garry's lowered head, he asked, "How about you, Gar? The kids at school giving you any trouble?"

A shrug.

Rip looked at me with the sorrow of the ages. Children shouldn't have to pay for their parents, but they do. All our lives; sometimes all their lives.

Rip put a hand on Garry's shoulder. "I'm sorry, son." Both Rip and I were imagining jeers and jokes and possibly even threats. Nasty stuff. Honest stuff. Fear manifesting itself, separating itself from the source. "Truly sorry. Is there anything we can do to help?"

Garry shook his head. His face was wet with tears. At his age parental intervention was verboten, unless he wanted the jeers and jokes to escalate.

My chest had developed an ache. My throat was stiff with emotion. Speaking would have been difficult, eating impossible.

So naturally I jumped when Didi blurted, "I've got it."

The rest of us stared at her. "The 'Skater's Waltz.' I figured it out." She seemed surprised that she had to explain. Recovering quickly, she addressed Chelsea and Garry. "Tomorrow when the bus drops you guys off, can you come right over and help with rehearsal?"

The kids shrugged their halfhearted assent.

"Perfect," Didi proclaimed. "Knew I could count on you guys. You're the greatest." Then she pinched their cheeks like an old aunt and began to clear dishes as if two children feeling harassed by a situation totally beyond them was unimaginable and, therefore, impossible.

Minutes later Didi herded the kids back into the living room. Alone in the kitchen, Rip and I were now free to reveal our concern. We faced each other in silence, sharing most of what we had to say without words.

The evening paper lay on the counter, headline up. "Development Director Arrested for Murder," it reminded us and anyone with a subscription. The network news would inform the rest.

"Tomorrow should be a real winner," Rip remarked.

❀ *Chapter 18* ❀

Wednesday morning gave off a pale winter glare. The trees held still beneath a white sky, and I couldn't guess whether we would be in for sunshine or rain.

After seeing off the kids and cleaning up breakfast, I put on black boots, a tailored black skirt, and a fuzzy peach sweater, something I deemed appropriate for spending the day in the development office.

About nine, when the busy-ness of morning assembly was over and classes had begun, I walked over to Bryn Derwyn through what had broken into a cold, thin sunshine. Rip interrupted his work with Joanne to get me started on the mailing.

"Why does it seem so quiet?" I remarked as we strolled down the hall. Usually you could hear the squeak of sneakers on waxed flooring, basketballs bouncing in the gym around the corner, teachers' voices drifting through open doors, footsteps other than your own.

Rip stiffened painfully. "Attendance is down."

"To what?" I blurted.

"Half." His eyes flicked toward mine.

No response would have eased Rip's worry or his disappointment, so I made none, just grabbed his hand and squeezed. Taking solace in everyday details, as Garry instinctively had, seemed to be the only way to endure.

Rip unlocked Randy's door and ushered me inside. Judging by the moderate mess and the abandoned coffee mug, Bryn Derwyn's development director had been interrupted in the midst of a purposeful day.

Rip waved his hand across the clutter at two boxes of labeled envelopes, each holding 500. He knocked three inserts with his knuckles and reminded me of the fourth in the box on the floor of the Community Room. Noticing the distaste on my face, he offered to go get them. When he returned, he pointed to the alphabetical pile of computer-personalized letters and suggested that I hand write, "Your help will be greatly appreciated," under Randy's forged name.

As my husband turned to go, I asked, "Any news on Randy?"

Rip shook his head. "He's not saying a word."

Left alone with the mountainous, boring chore, I decided to do what everybody else does when they work in an office. I went for coffee. Not hazelnut-flavored and certainly not the pot in the Community Room. Joanne's.

I found her putting memos into the teachers' mail slots in the utilitarian inner room next to the offices.

"Morning, Hank," I said.

Her chin had been tilted up for reading names through her bifocals. Now she leveled it at me.

"What's good about it?"

"I didn't say it was 'good.' I merely said it was 'morning.' "

She capitulated. "You're right. No point in grousing. I'm just sick of smoothing feathers. Bunch of ninnies."

"The kids?"

"The parents. You'd think we harbored Jack the Ripper if you listened to them. And the attorneys. The attorneys are the worst. They all want to give Rip advice —all want to replace Richard Wharton more likely— and poor Rip has to placate every last one the best he can. It's no wonder we're out of aspirin."

I stirred sugar into my borrowed mug while Joanne stuffed a few more mail slots.

"Joanne," I began carefully. "The reception desk has a good view of the front circle. You notice anything unusual Friday afternoon? People, cars? Anything?"

"As if I haven't asked myself the same question a thousand times. No unusual people. Newkirk covered that one, believe me."

"Cars?"

"He asked that, too. None that stood out. None I haven't seen fifty times before.

I wished Joanne luck with the phones and returned to my boring chore. "Your help will be greatly appreciated," I wrote over and over until I could stand it no longer and finally picked up the phone.

Whoever answered for Longmeier Construction was genial and, best of all, trusting. I told her I was from Bryn Derwyn and asked where I might find Mr. Longmeier.

"He calls in regularly," she offered helpfully. "I can ask him to phone you."

"Thanks, but there's a question about a change Mr. Barnes needs answered right away," I lied. "He wants me to take the blueprints over to Mr. Longmeier this morning." Just the annoying sort of thing a semi-large client might do. Apparently his secretary agreed; she told me exactly how to find her boss.

Comprising the corner of a busy intersection, a huge white sign proclaimed a flattened lot to be the future location of a bank. Facing corners contained a gas station, a five-store strip mall and a veterinarian's office inside a former white clapboard house. What had once been yard was now asphalt, edged with over-fertilized weeds.

I borrowed the vet's lot, tiptoed through weeds damp with what I hoped was sun-melted frost, then hastily crossed between traffic to the bulldozed expanse of mud and tree roots. A gusty breeze mussed my short hair, and I smoothed it down with my fingers.

Eddie Longmeier and the employee with whom he was speaking spared me a glance, but Longmeier finished what he was saying before waving the guy off.

"Mrs. Barnes, what brings you all the way out here?"

Michael D'Avanzo's son-in-law wore dusty twill pants and work boots, a blue chambray shirt with a black knit tie, and a red-and-black buffalo plaid hunting jacket. Under the obligatory white hard hat his pale eyes exuded a neutral amount of social warmth. He was of average height for a man, perhaps five-foot-nine. Beard stubble and weathered skin made him look worn rather than handsome.

"Can we sit down for a minute?" Glancing around I noticed only one available spot, a pile of cement blocks waiting to become foundation. Today's project, apparently. Three rows aligned with string already stood about three feet tall on concrete footings. Beyond the bank's rudimentary outline a backhoe was poised to unearth an enormous tree stump. Everything remained moist from the overnight frost. Like a row of denim birds, four workers sat on a tree trunk eating out of lunch boxes.

I tried the lumpy blocks, being careful not to rough up my wool skirt. Longmeier chose to fold his arms and stand between me and the distant men.

"Something tells me this isn't about the gym." So far I

was an interesting interruption to his day, one he would cut short if I took too much time.

"Yes and no." I answered, resting my chin on my fist the better to gaze up at him.

"The police been here yet?" I asked.

"Yeah." He wagged his head as if the visit still puzzled him. "Is that what this is about?"

"They ask you about your wife?" I had given a lot of thought to my approach, and now I fervently hoped I had made the right choice.

Longmeier's eyes sharpened their focus and his body braced. "No . . ." he said tentatively. "Why should they?"

So Newkirk had pursued Randy Webb's fairy tale and nothing more—so far.

"What's Tina have to do with this?"

"In a way, that's what I'm trying to find out."

"Go on."

I hesitated. If Eddie was truly ignorant about his wife's behavior, what I was about to say might embarrass, infuriate, or even devastate him. I became gratefully conscious of the distant row of witnesses.

"I'm pretty sure I know why Randy Webb tried to throw suspicion on you," I said, "but before I mention anything to the police, I'd like to hear your opinion."

"Of what?"

I tilted my head and looked up at him. "Have you ever noticed your wife flirting with other men?"

"You're out of line, Mrs. Barnes. Way, way out."

"Am I?"

The contractor glared, huffing slightly, visibly fighting for control. His men noticed his stance, watched a moment, then looked away. For perhaps a minute Longmeier continued to stare at me, pushing hard for me to back down.

Eventually, he hooked his thumbs into his jeans pockets and crushed a lump of dirt with his boot. "Yeah, okay. You're right. Tina was a slut before I married her, and she didn't change. So what?"

Reluctantly, I said, "I saw her flirting with both Randy Webb and Richard Wharton."

To my surprise, Longmeier laughed. It was a dry, humorless sound directed at himself. "Good ol' Tina. No wonder Webb's anxious to make me look bad. Webb and Wharton. Wow. She really stuck her nose in the bees' nest this time, didn't she?" his next laugh contained some pleasure.

"You don't sound particularly upset."

"Why should I? I haven't given a damn about Tina for more than a year. Just woke up one day and didn't give a damn. Told her that, too. We more or less ignore each other."

I frowned, remembering my first meeting with Michael D'Avanzo. "Your father-in-law know that?" I asked.

"Oh hell no. Why should we tell him?" I suspected no one needed to tell Tina's father, unless the couple deliberately hid their feelings to delude him.

I shrugged. "No reason. So, if you don't mind my asking, why do you and Tina stay together?"

He took a breath while his eyes strayed over the wasteland that would eventually become a bank. "Business hasn't exactly been booming recently. Perhaps you've watched the news?"

I had, for years. "You can't afford to break up."

"Got it in one."

At least now I understood why both Tina and her husband kept her father in the dark. If he knew, he would have had little incentive to throw 1.5 million dollars' worth of business Longmeier's way, and both the Longmeiers obviously welcomed that money.

"You won't tell Michael? No, of course not. Without Michael D'Avanzo, you don't get your gym."

I neither agreed nor disagreed, although I knew of no reason to involve myself in their family politics.

Longmeier's stare seemed to penetrate my skin. "Why are you really here?" he asked.

I was happy to give him an honest answer. "Because I think Newkirk has it wrong, and while he's stumbling around in the dark, he's ruining the school."

"I see." The contractor's smile was smug and not particularly attractive. "Not very different are we?"

He meant we were both whores when it came to D'Avanzo's money, and I resented the implication just as much as he intended me to. Yet trying to clarify the differences in our motives would be tantamount to acknowledging their similarity.

"It depends," I said instead. "Did you kill Richard Wharton?"

That surprised a snort out of him. "Over Tina? That's good. Really good."

I stood up, ready to leave.

"Hey, wait," Longmeier delayed me. He stepped closer and brushed my arm, looked into my eyes. "Just to put your inquiring mind to rest—I did not kill Richard Wharton. Not over the gym, and not over Tina. So I would appreciate it if you didn't give the police any more ideas."

"What if they find out about Richard Wharton and your wife?" I asked.

The contractor looked straight into my eyes. "If I thought Wharton and my wife were having an affair, which I had no reason to suspect until now, I wouldn't have done anything."

I raised an eyebrow.

"Why?" He snorted again. "Because Tina D'Avanzo-

Longmeier is punishment enough for any man. And now, Mrs. Barnes, I suggest you be careful crossing the street." He swept his arm toward the humming traffic.

I assumed he meant that literally.

❈ *Chapter 19* ❈

*B*illie Holiday wasn't among the tapes in the glove compartment; and after speaking with Eddie Longmeier, everybody else seemed too damn cheerful. I drove back to Bryn Derwyn in silence.

My main reason for confronting Edwin Longmeier had been to gauge whether he knew if anything more than flirting was going on between Tina and Webb or Tina and Richard Wharton. Although he admitted that his wife fooled around, he denied knowing anything about either her and the school's development director or her and the murdered attorney. But what else would he say? And what, if anything, had I learned?

If Eddie had been truthful—a rather big *if*—he didn't care at all about his wife, which definitely tilted the scale toward her having an affair with somebody. Why not Webb or Wharton? Why not both? Her husband practically gave her permission. Unless, as he suggested, she gave herself permission long before Eddie quit caring.

In that context Randy's ploy to cast suspicion on Longmeier made a bit more sense.

I parked near the house and walked back to the school, intending to return to the development office.

Did Longmeier kill Wharton over his wife or the gym contract? Maybe, maybe not.

Like Newkirk, I needed more information. That's why when I saw Jeremy Philbin emerge from his classroom into the busy hallway, I changed directions and asked for a minute of his time.

He carried an armload of stapled papers. Beneath his gray-blond hair his skin looked pasty, and his eyes darted like flies anticipating a swat. He stepped into the flow of teenagers changing classes.

"I'm not volunteering to clean any more latrines," he announced over his shoulder, his lips lifting with amusement he didn't expect me to share.

"Oh? Did you clean some in the army?" Philbin certainly hadn't scrubbed anything at Bryn Derwyn when I asked, not even his own classroom.

The patronizing smile disappeared. We zigzagged around a corner, and I dodged a boy with a backpack running straight toward me. Behind us a locker slammed shut.

"Listen, Gin dear," Philbin said, "I've got tests to finish grading and a splitting headache. Could we do this some other time?"

We paused just outside the Faculty Room, that haven of soft seats and hot coffee tucked into a quiet corner. Through the door's window I could see that only Sophia Mawby had been using the long mahogany table, and she appeared to be leaving.

I held the door open for Jeremy. "Now suits me best," I said cordially.

Long, long ago Jeremy probably had been an obedient child. With abject resignation he went inside and threw down his papers. He poured himself black coffee from the table on the right, then settled into a blue sofa next to the window. The pinch of pain between his eyebrows looked quite genuine.

I turned the wooden chair vacated by the now-departed Sophia so that Philbin and I sat knee to knee.

"Got my hair done yesterday," I fibbed. "Like the color?" My hair was the same golden red it always was; but if Philbin was a typical man, he would not realize that.

"Lovely," he said without sincerity. So I was right—he probably thought his former wife's hair was naturally curly.

"And guess who I ran into at the hairdresser's."

"Eliza Doolittle?"

I smiled tolerantly. "No. Emily Walker."

Philbin squeezed his eyes closed.

"We had a nice little chat. She says you weren't especially good at fixing things around the house. I could teach you a few basics. Sink washers. Weather stripping. Simple stuff. Maybe you could give me a call next time you need a socket replaced."

Philbin cleared his throat. "Is there a point to all this?"

"Yes indeedy. I was wondering if you strayed out of character the other night and put water in the gas tank of the school bus. Not too original, but effective in its way. I understand it's costing Bryn Derwyn about a thousand dollars if you include renting a replacement bus and disposing of the contaminated fuel."

The algebra teacher glared. "Why would I do a thing like that?" He spat each word at me like a lead pellet.

"Oh, I don't know. Because you want to punish my husband? The school? You tell me."

"I would never do any such thing, Mrs. Barnes. Even a dimwit should be able to figure out why."

Stepping delicately into the insult, I said, "Why?"

"Because, Mrs. Barnes, I happen to like this job."

For an older man who drank, *need this job* was probably a more accurate answer, although neither reason prevented him from becoming vindictive. Yet his sizeable satisfaction at my expense forestalled the many retorts I might have made.

Instead, I crossed my boots and locked my hands over the knee of my black skirt. After his glow dimmed some, I cocked my head and asked, "Except for that day when you consulted him about your wife, did Richard Wharton ever do anything to hurt you?"

"I beg your pardon?"

I waved a hand. "What I'm trying to understand is specifically why you hated him. Did he broadcast your private life all over town? Did he tell a specific person who told the whole town? Do you see what I'm getting at here?"

Philbin stood. He was quite tall, and his gray trousers and bright white shirt made him look huge. I felt like a student huddled down there on my hard chair.

"You've no right to ask this," he said. "I've a mind to speak to your husband about your impertinence."

I stood. "Please do. I'm sure he'd love an opportunity to discuss your behavior at the memorial service."

Philbin's square face scowled at the floor while his cheeks colored.

"Also, Rip might like to thank you for telling the cops you thought he murdered Richard."

The teacher's mouth opened to protest then snapped shut after he reconsidered. His bloodshot eyes narrowed with furious concentration.

"Don't bother, Jeremy," I counseled the man. "If I behaved as badly as you did, I'd block it out, too. But you did give the cop who took you home quite an earful. Rip regrets that you don't like him very much, but of course he realizes that it isn't necessary.

"By the way, what's your alibi for the afternoon of the murder?"

Now Philbin's cheeks went deathly gray. Two matching veins pulsed visibly across his temples. His mouth trembled while his wounded eyes all but bled.

"The police questioned me at great length yesterday and dismissed me," he managed at last. "Am I to take it you have not?"

"I have a different agenda from the police."

He gave me a swift glance. "Oh?"

Behind him, something across the room caught my eye.

Once when I was doing some Mop Squad work, I came into the Faculty Room to use the soda machine. While I drank my Diet Coke I idly perused the bulletin board.

All of Rip's memos had been doctored up with sarcasm. Funny, nasty remarks. Same wit, same pen. I stormed into Rips' office to report that his memos had been defaced, also to ask if I could take them down.

"Leave them," Rip told me. "It's their room, their bulletin board."

Another sarcastic barb hung there now. I walked over and yanked the offensive message off its pin, then I compared it to a comment Philbin had penned on one of his student's papers. The teacher merely rubbed his chin and watched.

"You," I said. In part, my previous anger had been calculated. Now it was entirely real.

Philbin wrinkled his nose as if something had tickled it.

"Really, Mrs. Barnes," he patronized me. "I have tests to grade."

"And you have a headache."

"Yess," he hissed, pleased as the snake that he was.

It occurred to me that I had just received the answer to my Wharton question.

Rip's initial changes to the school had been minor, with scarcely any tangible effect on the teachers. Since

Philbin seemed to have initiated a propaganda campaign roughly because Rip added Computer Club to his after-school schedule, I realized that it didn't matter whether or not Richard Wharton had spread gossip about Philbin's personal life. The man was perfectly capable of distorting reality to suit the warped needs of his ego.

He jammed his hands into his pockets and rocked on his heels. "Go home, Ginger Struve Barnes," he said mockingly. "Fix a toilet or something. I'm sure you're very good at that."

My hackles raised, just as Philbin intended. I wanted to shout and hammer his chest with my fists, to beat him down, to win.

Poor Emily. He really *was* a slimy, infuriating, son of a bitch. If Jeremy had been my husband, I would have battled with him regularly, too—pick a reason. Any reason. He made me want to . . . to do what I'd just done.

I deflated. Just like that. It came to me that how I felt didn't matter. How Emily felt didn't matter either, except to her.

What mattered was Jeremy Philbin's response to it all. Somebody was going to have to examine his feelings and what he did about them. Rip, a psychologist, Newkirk—somebody other than me.

"Have a nice day," I told the upper-school algebra teacher as I departed for the development office.

I deserved to write, "Your help will be greatly appreciated," a few hundred times, like the blackboard punishment teachers used to assign.

Maybe if I wrote it enough times, it would become true.

✦ *Chapter 20* ✦

Working in someone else's office is an intimate thing. Sitting in another person's chair you learn how he orders his environment, maybe even see a portion of daily life through his eyes. You smell the brown residue left in his "Virginia is for Lovers" coffee mug, the pencil shavings in the waste basket, the lingering scent of his clothes, possibly even the soap he used to bathe.

Randy Webb's office spoke of a solid Main Line upbringing. Parental expectations oozed forth from the Colby diploma nailed, no doubt with difficulty, to the otherwise empty off-white cement block wall. Male hormones, tastefully in check, pulsed inside the brass bookends depicting skiis leaned against an immovable mountain. Inhibitions ordered the paper clips and rubber bands inside his drawer. Chewing gum and breath mints waited upon private vices, whether an occasional martini lunch or a hasty afternoon tryst. The wife and kiddies were nowhere to be seen. This was Randy's space.

The desk had been centered to face the corridor with a table under the window at its back. My coat hung on a hook screwed into the doorjamb near the hinges because that was the only available wood. Immersed in Randy's situation, sitting in his spot, I could imagine him asking Wilson Flagg for the hook. I could even hear the old maintenance man's probable response. When he first arrived, Wilson made Rip wait two months for a shelf in his closet, so Randy probably had screwed in the hook himself. The quiet engendered such thoughts, unless Randy's situation was so integral to my life that I fancied myself inside his head.

I cleared the one long table under the broad, drafty window so I could stuff the envelopes standing up. The hamburger I had eaten while driving bulged against my waistband when I sat down anyway.

With a total of four enclosures I developed a left, right, left, right pattern that allowed me to collate and stuff with maximum efficiency. There wasn't much mental stimulation after I worked that out, so I reverted to the stupor writing the note on the letters had induced.

"I just can't believe it," a voice behind me remarked.

I wheeled toward the sound so quickly I knocked a stack of finished envelopes to the floor.

"Sorry," Kevin Seitz told me. He hurried around the desk in the cramped quarters to help pick up the mess. Our proximity under the table made us both squirm, so he just as hastily returned to his doorjamb.

"What can't you believe?" I asked.

"Randy. Do you think he did it?"

"Not really. How about you?" It struck me that my response was based on instinct, that my facts were as skimpy as the ones that conjured up the history of the hook. Randy Webb remained a stranger to me, at best an acquaintance. I knew far more about the young man now standing in the doorway, and either man could have killed Richard Wharton for reasons well beyond my comprehension. I hugged my arms close to my body, scrunching my shoulders up to shield my neck.

Kevin shook his head the way he had in Little League when he missed a fly ball. The gesture both warmed me to him and woke me up.

"I don't know, Gin. He could have."

"Hell, you could have. But you didn't." Did he? The police had not worried much about his vague alibi, but it still worried me.

"Nope. But I sure hope it wasn't Randy either."

"Why?" Had they become friends working next door to each other?

"Because I'm not sure I have it in me to try to save another business." On the surface he sounded totally self-involved, but knowing his background I understood his perspective. He'd chosen to work at Bryn Derwyn because he needed an upbeat experience to offset his father's bankruptcy and subsequent suicide, events he had tried to prevent but could not. Now he was suddenly thrust into a comparable situation. If too many students withdrew, Bryn Derwyn would be as impossible to save as his father's business had been. Kevin's therapy could potentially turn into his problem all over again.

"You won't be doing it alone this time," I reminded him. No honest business manager could make or break a school single-handedly, and a dishonest one was probably fairly easy to catch.

Kevin shrugged his beach boy shoulders and pouted until his dimple showed. Then he backed out the door and slipped into his office. I knew because I heard the door shut.

I wagged my head and sighed. I could do without Kevin's pessimism; my own was quite enough, thank you. It was after one-thirty. If I worked a little faster, maybe I could finish my chore and go home.

To be certain Kevin and I had picked up all the fallen envelopes, I checked under the table once again. Back along the wall below the radiator cover was a page of white paper. Bumping my head in the process, I crawled under the table until I could reach it.

A receipt from a printer. Not knowing where it belonged, I set it on the desk. However, something about it piqued my curiosity. I picked it up and examined it again.

The receipt was from Audubon Offset Printers for 250 letterheads and envelopes, probably a minimal order for that sort of thing. Maybe it was for something special, a one-time school event, or stationery with Kevin's name and title that he didn't expect to use often. Normal enough stuff. Except something looked wrong. "Paid," it said. Then "$^{11}/_{14}$" and the year.

Suddenly I knew what was missing. The few times I had noticed invoices in the work Rip brought home, they always had a "Received" stamp and the date, plus the initials of the person responsible for approving the purchase. That seemed to be how Kevin knew to pay the bill. This invoice simply said "Paid." Also, old invoices belonged in Kevin's files, not Randy's.

I shut the door and picked up the phone. When the print shop answered I explained that I was calling from Bryn Derwyn and there was some confusion about invoice #10598. "Could you possibly describe that job to me?"

The third person the operator referred to me could. "Got a sample right here somewhere." A drawer rattled on its rollers, some papers were shuffled, and finally the woman came back on the line. I realized I was gripping the receiver like a hammer.

" 'Bryn Derwyn, Inc.' and a post office box number for Paoli, dark green lettering on white bond. Is that what you need to know?"

"Yes, thank you. We were confusing this with another order and didn't know which one we paid. You have been paid, haven't you?"

"Oh yes. You'd hear from us if we hadn't."

I thanked her for her trouble, hung up, and stared at the back of Randy's door. As far as I knew, there was no Bryn Derwyn, Incorporated. Private schools were considered non-profit organizations, so the "incorporated" part was just plain peculiar.

Ask Rip? The same reservations I had about confessing my other curiosity-satisfying excursions to my husband applied here, double. Even if he forgave me for interfering with his business, he would never approve of me breathing down the neck of a murderer. I admit I'd pitch a fit if he told me that was what he was doing.

However, this particular suspect happened to be in jail. What harm could it do to follow up on this one little oddity? For the next ten minutes I searched Randy's office looking for the letterhead and envelopes. No luck.

I decided to take a calculated risk and show the invoice to Kevin.

"You know anything about this?"

He studied the page for half a second. "We never deal with Audubon. Must be somebody's personal order." His attention returned to a spreadsheet printout he had been reading, all traces of his depression suppressed by the task at hand. Kevin would be all right, assuming that Bryn Derwyn survived.

Back in Randy's office I punched the automatic dial number marked "Anne" to phone his home. Answering machine—I should have expected that. Reporters were probably ushering Randy Webb's wife to a deeper level of hell.

Trying to sound natural, I left my message. "Annie, this is Gin Barnes. I'm doing a little of Randy's work and I have a question you might be able to answer. If you get home before three, will you please call me in his office? Thanks."

I'd stuffed about four envelopes before the phone rang.

"Gin, it's Annie." Her voice sounded old, as if she were speaking through a washcloth.

"Are you all right?" I asked. "Is there anything I can do?"

"No. No, you're already doing it. It's nice of you to help with Randy's work. I'm sure he'll appreciate it." Her voice broke when she said her husband's name, and I realized I needed to help her hold it together for her own sake as well as mine.

"Listen," I began as if asking something quite mundane. "I've been looking for some letterhead for a mailing, and I wondered if there's any chance Randy has it at home. A small box that says, 'Bryn Derwyn, Inc.' Have you seen anything like that around?"

"Why, yes, now that you mention it. I know just where it is. I noticed it in the hall closet the other day."

"Great. That's great. Would you mind terribly if I stopped over and picked it up?"

"No, of course not." She gave me directions to their home.

Randy and Annie Webb and their two children happened to live in nearby Paoli, Pennsylvania, which no doubt would be a reasonable distance from the Paoli post office, the post office where any replies addressed to Bryn Derwyn, Inc. would naturally go.

I tried. I really tried, but I could not think of one good reason why that post office box should be necessary. Bad reasons, yes. Incriminating reasons, certainly.

Legitimate reasons—no.

❈ *Chapter 21* ❈

Shortly after two I pulled into a parking space near the Webb's Paoli residence. It was an older home, a conglomerate consisting of stone foundation, white clapboard siding rising to the second story, and scalloped white shingles thereafter. A broad porch supported by thick wooden posts was crowned by an old tin roof painted green. The steeply pitched upper roof seemed to be slate, mildewed where an enormous maple tree shaded it in summer. Even now, the second week in December, tan leaves ground into crumbs littered the uneven cement sidewalk.

I crossed the porch and knocked. A skeptical black-and-white cat watched me from a front window sill.

"Oh, Ginger," Randy Webb's wife greeted me with ravaged eyes. The smell of home-baked bread wafted through the opened door.

My slight confusion over the contrast must have prompted her to explain. "Randy loves my fresh bread. I'm baking some for when he gets home." Since the date of his release was unknown, to say the least, his wife scarcely managed to complete the sentence.

"Have you heard something?" I asked hopefully.

Annie shook her head woefully as she closed the door after me.

"Has he been arraigned?" I asked with concern, going from one extreme to the other.

"I don't know. I think so. His lawyer said something about a Grand Jury hearing Friday afternoon."

So he must have been formally charged. The Grand Jury hearing would determine whether there was enough evidence to indict. If he was held over for trial, Randy's problems would begin in earnest.

I wanted to ask his wife much more, but pressing her to deal with those ramifications would have salted wounds already far too raw.

Instead, I told her, "That bread smells absolutely wonderful. What kind are you making?"

"Potato rolls. I tie them in knots and glaze them with egg. You want one?"

"You bet."

She led me down the hall, which ran along the left length of the house. Two tall windows viewing the side yard and two more viewing the back made the old-fashioned kitchen sunny and inviting.

I peeked through red-checked cafe curtains to the back. A swing set and a sandbox took up the only flat expanse behind the house in a yard that was perhaps double the square footage of the building but no more. Tangled honeysuckle covered the chain-link fencing between the Webbs and their neighbors to the right. A mess of azalea and forsythia bushes edged the other two boundaries.

Clearly this was a house of comfort rather than pride, the home of a young family whose priorities were child-proof furniture, clean clothes, and fresh bread rather than a showy decor to impress visitors. Or I should say those were Annie's priorities, for this was her environment just as totally as Randy's office was his.

"Kids asleep?" I asked as we settled across from each other at the formica kitchen table. The vinyl-and-chrome chairs could have been considered Art Deco except for the duct tape somebody used to mend one of the seats.

Annie nodded in answer to my question, and her eyes smiled, a maternal reflex prompted by the thought of her boys. Their ages were about one and three as I remembered, confirmed by the Palomino hobby horse on springs stabled in a corner. Beside it an open wooden crate overflowed with plastic blocks, action figures, a cowboy hat, and one of Randy's running shoes.

The floor seemed to be that imitation brick stuff that comes on a roll. The tall cabinets had honest-to-God windowpanes set into actual wood molding. They housed a set of Pfaltzgraff stoneware dishes, the gray-and-blue pattern.

The oven, behind me on the right side of the room, was the newest item there, a nice modern GE with a black glass door. The aroma of the rolls was overwhelming.

"Coffee?" Annie offered. My presence must have temporarily distracted her from her fears, for her movements seemed more at ease and her eyes appeared less haunted.

"Mmmm," I agreed. "Milk and sugar, I'm afraid."

My hostess hurried to fill two mugs and doctor mine to prescription.

"I drink mine black," she remarked. "Couldn't lose that baby fat after Eric was born. Guess I never will."

Since she wasn't noticeably plump, I could have said, "Oh, you look great," or something inane, but she'd have known better. The black bags under her eyes spoke of little or no sleep last night. Her hair was a dull brown growth brushed into a rubber band and forgotten, and her clothing consisted of jeans, sneakers and one of

Randy's striped oxford shirts with the cuffs rolled up.
Actually, it was my favorite Ludwig outfit, upgraded by
a professionally laundered shirt. I felt quite at home.

"Know what you mean," I remarked, alluding to my
own minor, yet chronic weight dissatisfaction. "But
think of it this way: we wouldn't be American women if
we weren't on a diet. Pass me one of those rolls, will
you?"

She laughed, a sound that surprised her, so she
laughed some more. She passed me a napkin and two
still-warm potato rolls from the cooling rack on the
counter behind her. I ripped into one as if I hadn't
eaten anything all day. Annie just held hers and watched
me eat. Eventually, she looked hers in the eye, sighed
and joined the feast.

"Comfort food," I told her. "Don't feel guilty. You
need it."

Her head dropped to her hand and quite suddenly
tears dripped to the table. She cried silently, like a
woman cries at night when she doesn't want her husband to hear. It can be done, but it takes practice—so
I'm told. Didi learned how during her brief marriage.

"You want to tell me about it?" I asked.

She shook her head no.

We ate in silence for a while, sipping the best coffee
I'd tasted in years. I would have complimented that,
except it was probably another skill Annie had culti-
vated for Randy, and Randy was currently a sensitive
subject.

"He's really a good husband," his wife told me at last.
"This whole mess is . . . unimaginable."

She meant the murder, and on that topic we agreed.
"Yes. I'm sure it's a nightmare for you. And if it's any
consolation, I don't think he did it." Those were my
feelings, and despite my admittedly flimsy basis for them
—mainly that other people had more apparent motives

—to voice even a slight doubt about Randy's innocence would have been to torture his wife.

"Thank you," she said, drawing herself up and wiping her face with Randy's shirt cuff.

"He bought the boys a sled for Christmas," she told me, apropos of nothing. "If we don't get enough snow here, he said we'll drive up to the Poconos some weekend so they can use it." Her gaze strayed out through the window to the back yard and beyond, possibly all the way to the mountains.

My heart ached to see her internal struggle. She was trapped by her love for Randy, trapped by the age of her children, desperate to believe she had chosen well and that these four walls were not confining at all, just the boundaries of her marriage.

"He sounds like a good father," I agreed.

She welcomed my remark as gratefully as a genuinely famished person might have accepted her cooking. "Oh yes. He is," she told me with conviction. "The boys adore him." Then her eyes dropped again as if the word "adore" applied to others as well. Rivals, real or imagined.

I squirmed in my chair, remembering Tina Longmeier flirting with both Richard Wharton and Randy the day I happened to be looking out my front window.

Silence settled around us. Annie's thoughts drifted out the window. I finished my rolls and coffee, contemplating the mess of bowls and covered dough and floured cutting board and thinking that Didi would never understand Annie Webb for a second.

Didi had refused to stay in a marriage that confined her. She was privately fanatical about her appearance, which, although unconventional, instantly announced her individuality, which, of course, was the point. Introducing her to an almost generic housewife would have been like introducing her to Cinderella, who my unconventional friend had dubbed "a drip," when she was five.

The contrast became especially painful because I realized I respected Didi and pitied Annie. When Didi escaped her marriage she learned how to sample a different flavor of life every day. As soon as she was free, Annie would hurry to offer another man homemade rolls and coffee; and she would plod through that marriage and any other wondering why her kitchens never had enough windows.

I hoped I was wrong. In fact, if the present mess escalated and ended the Webb's marriage, I would personally introduce the two women.

The oven timer buzzed, and Annie bustled over to save another batch of rolls from burning. I stood and watched her deftly scoop each one off the pan with a plastic spatula, her concentration on the task complete.

"Listen," I said. "I've got to get back to school. Did you say you knew where the letterhead was?"

"Oh yes. Just a second." She put the pan and spatula in the sink and proceeded to the doorway.

Then she turned back to ask, "Do you need the checkbook, too?"

☒ *Chapter 22* ☒

$\mathcal{A}$t the mention of a checkbook, my heart somer-saulted. I took a big breath to disguise my shock, and said, "Yes, I guess I do at that." Then I smiled, a weak smile, but sufficient under the circumstances.

While Randy Webb's wife proceeded upstairs to collect what might be incriminating evidence against her husband, I wandered into their living room to wait. Predictably childproof, the furniture included an indestructible tweed sofa with hardwood arms and legs, a matching recliner, and another basket of toys.

A white telephone was ajar on an end table, and I almost replaced the receiver until I realized the significance—Annie had given up on their answering machine and opted for complete silence. The signal telling her the phone was off the hook had already ceased.

Again my heart ached for this woman. Tears welled up in my eyes while self-doubt whispered in my ear. Maybe I should be playing Cinderella instead of Joan of Arc. Maybe I should learn how to bake bread and brew coffee.

The sentiment took less time to expire than the alarm beep on the phone. I was the Rosie the Riveter-type, like it or lump it, and deep down I knew I wouldn't change even if I could.

Annie's return caught me dabbing at my eyes with a tissue. She blinked with puzzlement before she was able to look past her own problem to see mine. "Things rough at school?" she guessed.

I nodded. "It'll work out," I told her lamely.

"One way or the other," she finished with a laugh I had to share. The boxes of envelopes and letterhead were in the way, but we shared a awkward hug.

"Let's do lunch sometime," I blurted.

Annie laughed at the obvious social kiss-off, just as I hoped she would. Then I told her I meant it, and her eyes widened.

"Sure," she said. "I'd like that."

As I struggled with the door and the boxes, she slapped a narrow black checkbook on top of the pile. "Don't forget this."

She held the door for me, friendliness warming her eyes.

Alone in the car I examined the items Annie had given me more closely.

The box of envelopes appeared to be full. One taped end of the paper-wrapped letterhead had been opened, either to check the quality of the printing or to use a sheet or two of the paper. Not very helpful.

The checkbook revealed just as little. It was the usual black plastic folder, personal size, not the taller book-type provided for some business accounts. The checks were ordinary blue beginning with number 100, and the account ledger didn't even show an opening balance. If Randy had some underhanded scheme in mind, maybe he had not yet implemented it.

A tiny optimism stepped forward for consideration but hastily withdrew. Even if the "incorporated" on the letterhead had been some sort of error, nothing honest explained away the checkbook. Whether or not Randy had carried out his intentions did not matter.

Saddened on Annie's behalf, I drove to the Paoli branch of the bank named on the checks. Only a few cars remained in the parking lot that spanned the front of the brick building. Evergreens lined up across the narrow front garden softened the bank's austere appearance, lending the warm this-isn't-really-a-business impression that Main Liners insist upon. Last summer one of the prettiest flower gardens along Lancaster Avenue beautified a car wash.

Only forty-five minutes remained before the bank would close, and already the pace had slowed. I was received with weary patience by a middle-aged woman with blunt cut reddish-brown hair, half-glasses, and a suit that couldn't decide whether to be pale purple or outright gray. Judging by the pink silk blouse the woman had chosen, matching anything to that suit color was a bitch.

"Good afternoon," she said. Her nameplate proclaimed that she was Diane Peale.

"Good afternoon, Ms. Peale," I agreed. "I hope you can help me."

"I'll try."

I sat in one of the two round swivel chairs in front of her desk. "This is a little awkward," I began.

An eyebrow rose slightly, but Ms. Peale remained patient.

"I'm from Bryn Derwyn Academy?" I used the questioning tone to see whether the eyebrow lifted any higher. It did, but only a twitch's worth.

"Yes?"

I passed the checkbook across the desk. The woman flipped it open but gave away nothing.

"Was this account opened here?" I asked.

"Yes." She could probably tell that by the account number.

"Well, the problem is I think only one person can sign the checks, and that person is . . . unavailable at this time. So the school can't use the account."

At last, Ms. Peale, reacted. So she had read a paper or listened to the news. Back straightened, she rapidly typed instructions into her computer. The screen, naturally, was turned her way and not mine.

Diane Peale peered through the half glasses and scowled. "I see," she said.

"See what?"

"Your problem."

"Can you solve it?"

"No, but you can."

"Beg pardon?"

She rummaged in the file drawer at her knee, extracted a few forms and handed them to me. "Get your Board to formally request a change—that's this form— then get the secretary to sign this, and finally, fill this out." She tapped a new signature card with a pen.

"I suggest that you authorize two people to sign this time instead of only one. That way if one person is temporarily . . . incapacitated, your corporation can still conduct business. Okay?"

"Okay. There's just one more thing," I said, fearful that I would be shuffled out the door without hearing her state the one fact I was there to confirm.

"Yes?"

"Do we need Randy Webb to sign a release or anything?"

"No."

"After we do all this, will he still be able to sign?" I waved the papers at her.

"No."

"But he *is* the only one who can sign now, isn't he?"

Ms. Peale shifted her bottom on her chair as if she were finally losing patience. Probably an intelligence snob, and she a woman who can match purple/gray with pink.

"I thought that was why you were here," she said accusingly.

"You're quite right." My smile must have been a little smug. "That was exactly why I was here. Thank you, Ms. Peale. You've been splendid."

She stiffened again, and I could see why she'd chosen the suit. Drawn up in full preparedness, she conveyed just enough suppressed femininity beneath the vault-like exterior bankers use to put us customers at ease if we're one of them, or ill-at-ease if we're not.

"Congratulations," I said extending my hand.

She shook it once, but only with her fingers.

❈ *Chapter 23* ❈

When I arrived back at Bryn Derwyn, the formality of the school day had slackened down to extra-curricular mode. The previously missed staccato of bouncing basketballs resounded into the lobby. Clusters of half-dozing students lounged on the soft furniture waiting for their parents to pick them up. Kindergarten children with late buses followed their teacher toward the rear pickup area like ducklings waddling after their mother.

Also, Garry and Chelsea scurried into sight. Both gaped with surprise to see me.

"Hi," I said. "I'm your mother. Remember?"

"Oh, Mom," Chelsea complained.

"Hi. What are you doing here?" Garry asked. Since I clutched the packages of letterhead and envelopes roughly at his eye level, he automatically stared at them.

"I'm doing a mailing for Dad," I replied. "And you?"

Both children scowled. "We're helping Aunt Didi." Chelsea's tone conveyed an implied, "Don't you re-member anything?" that bordered on an accusation of senility.

I shrugged. "I've been busy."

"Too busy to remember us?" Garry seemed incredulous.

I stroked his cheek. "You are never out of my mind. Now and then a detail or two may slip from my consciousness, but you yourself are always right up front."

Chelsea grimaced her distaste over my affectionate honesty. I think Garry's indifference meant he was pleased. Heck, Chelsea's disgust probably meant she was pleased—but I wasn't supposed to know for sure, because I *was* their mother. Magazines suggest such teenage behavior has to do with growing up and leaving the nest.

"See you at dinner," I said as they eased themselves loose to turn toward Rip's office.

Their father stepped into the lobby just then and they rushed toward him. Since I didn't want to be questioned about the packages, I wiggled my fingers hello from a distance and pointed my thumb toward the development office.

"Wait a minute," Rip called to me.

"Aunt Didi needs some chicken wire," Garry blurted. "Do you know where any is?"

Rip detoured briefly to ask Joanne, who manned the receptionist's desk at that hour, to beep Jacob so the kids could go wherever he was and actually get an answer for Didi.

"Here we go 'round the mulberry bush," I sang when Rip finally approached me.

"Huh?" he replied.

"You've become very good at delegating," I explained.

Pointing to himself, he asked reasonably, "Do I have any idea whether the school owns any chicken wire?"

"Of course not," I said. "What was I thinking?"

"Listen," he said, soberly focused on what he needed

to say. "The Board wants to have an emergency meeting tonight. I said they could come to our house."

"Of course," I said, acknowledging information received.

"We won't need any food or coffee or anything."

"Okay."

"Seven o'clock."

"Okay."

My concern had begun with the word "emergency" and grew considerably when Rip dispensed with the social amenities. Tonight's meeting would be confined to serious school business; and as I now understood, anything critical to Bryn Derwyn's fate was of vital interest to the Barnes family proper.

Did the Board intend to close the school? Or did they merely need to repair the damage caused by the murder? Would they be commending Rip or blaming him for the current situation? Although the latter seemed unlikely to occur in our home, I really couldn't guess what to expect. All my Struve instincts geared up for battle, even though I knew full well this campaign belonged to my husband.

"Do what you can do, and don't do what you can't," Cynthia Struve advised when she heard that Bryn Derwyn expected some form of participation from me. Remembering her deceptively wise advice, I mumbled a frustrated, "Yes, Mother," as I stalked down the hall into the development director's office and shut the door.

Sequestered in Randy Webb's cubicle, I hung my coat on his hook and parked myself behind his desk. The environment helped me refocus on my afternoon's inquiries.

If Randy was guilty of murder, whatever underhanded scheme he may have been planning would become public knowledge, especially if he killed to keep it secret. By association, Bryn Derwyn's reputation would suffer.

Even if the development director was innocent but went to trial, his covert activities would be scrutinized and could still undermine the school's credibility.

Which meant that if I could figure out exactly what Randy had done before his Grand Jury hearing, perhaps I could minimize the damage to the school and maybe even help Randy avoid indictment.

If I couldn't meet the Friday hearing deadline, the school's survival still depended on the public learning the facts as soon as possible. Then everyone could mentally move on. Unnamed fears always generate much more anxiety than the truth.

"Full steam ahead," I decided once again.

I proceeded to count every envelope and every page of paper Annie had given me. To my surprise, there were two hundred fifty-four letterheads and two hundred fifty-three envelopes. Although I tried, I couldn't decide what those figures meant, so I picked up the phone.

The first person who answered at Audubon Offset Printing got hit with my question.

"If I ordered 250 letterheads and envelopes, how many would I actually receive?"

As expected, a brief silence came over the line before the woman answered, "Two hundred and fifty." I didn't blame her a bit for sounding annoyed.

"Exactly?" I pressed. "I have a very good reason for asking."

The woman sighed, but her voice lost its edge. "No. Not exactly. Now and then the press misses a page so the counter isn't always accurate. That's why we usually print five extra, to make sure the customer gets his complete order. Is that what you wanted to know?"

"Yes. Thank you. You've been quite helpful."

I hung up thinking about the school's copier. Sometimes the gizmo that grabbed each blank page failed to grasp the paper, causing the count to be short by one. Apparently, that occasionally happened with printers, too, which was why Audubon compensated by automatically setting the machine to make extra copies.

So basically, I couldn't tell whether Randy had used any of the Bryn Derwyn, Inc. letterhead yet or not.

I locked the stuff in the desk drawer along with the breath mints, entertaining nasty suspicions about both.

Too preoccupied to deal with the solicitation mailing, I decided to go home and let my subconscious work while I made dinner and tidied up for the Board meeting.

I would have done it, too, except Nicky D'Avanzo happened to be sitting in the lobby staring dejectedly at his feet.

"Your aunt coming for you?" I asked without preamble.

Treating me as any ordinary meddling mother, the seventh grader shrugged. He was a beautiful young man with dark hair and pale skin and a tight jaw that suggested stubbornness or determination. Despite his multi-colored ski jacket, I could see he was large for his age and graceful in that athletic way boys have.

I glanced at the clock above the front doors. "Getting late," I remarked. "You sure she's coming?"

Another shrug.

"You call her yet?" Kids are usually pretty intolerant about any change in their routine.

"What's the point?" he asked. "She's always late."

Aha. Tina Longmeier's irresponsibility *was* the usual routine. "She ever forget?"

This time the shrug was pure dejection. I finally identified myself. Then I offered the young man a ride home.

Nicky D'Avanzo brightened instantly. "Sure," he told me. "That'd be great."

I brightened, too, pleased to have at least one teenager acknowledge me as a person today, even if we weren't related.

"Shall we try to call your aunt first?"

"Nah. We wouldn't get her." Normal kid that he was, Nicky cared little about his aunt's inconvenience as long as he got what he wanted, which at the moment was to leave. If Tina was as unreliable as she sounded, in this case, I sided with him.

Still, I took a moment to brief Joanne on the situation. That way if Tina happened to show up, Joanne could tell her Nicky was with me.

A psychologist would no doubt accuse me of rebellious behavior, choosing to do something—anything—more optimistic than preparing for that Board of Directors meeting. Assuming, of course, that driving a spoiled kid home to the man who intended to build him a gym qualified as an optimistic activity.

Rebellious or not, it was a good move.

❈ *Chapter 24* ❈

$\mathcal{N}$icky bounded out of my tiny Nissan, swung his backpack over his shoulder, and shouted for someone named Milly. With the early evening breeze chapping my cheeks, I leaned against my opened car door to see him safely indoors.

The circular drive lay approximately in the center of the D'Avanzo estate, which consisted of multiple acres secluded behind chain-link fencing lined with thick arborvitae. Inside, the property sprawled like a languid woman on a padded Roman lounge. At least the early dusk made the lawn appear padded, and the sheer slate-colored clouds edged in pink easily suggested a silk scarf. From my position near a marble fountain, dried and draped for winter, the house evoked thoughts of a romantic Italian movie.

"Whoa, there, my boy," Michael D'Avanzo himself stopped Nicky in the doorway. "Milly isn't ready for you. Go wash up." He slapped his grandson fondly on the shoulder and turned to regard me.

"Mrs. Barnes," the restaurateur greeted me. "Please come in and warm yourself a moment. Allow me to thank you for bringing Nicholas home."

My face felt raw and a shiver was imminent, so I allowed myself to be drawn into the foyer.

"I'm surprised you're not at your restaurant," I remarked in an attempt at casual conversation. Paying a spontaneous visit to a mansion was not my usual afternoon activity, but D'Avanzo didn't need to know that.

"Weekends I still do evenings, but Wednesday . . ." the older gentleman made a belittling "puh" sound. "I prefer to be home for Nicholas. However, do not tell that to my chef—he expects me at any moment." He winked to share the joke of his administrative ruse.

"Take your coat?" he asked, the consummate host. The courtesy surprised me, suggesting a lengthier visit than the few pleasant words I had expected. And still I allowed myself to be drawn further inside. Perhaps Michael D'Avanzo was a lonelier man than I first imagined, or a more flirtatious one, but more likely and most intriguing—perhaps he had something he wanted to speak to me about and was making use of an opportunity.

He waved his arm to direct me toward a study. "Second door on the left," he amplified. A gas fire hissed in a fireplace framed in black marble beneath a carved white mantle. Leather-bound books covered three walls of the intimate room.

Set between two wing-backed chairs upholstered in greens and burgundy was an opened bottle of Bordeaux. The fire sent rainbows to the ceiling through the accompanying faceted wine glass.

D'Avanzo opened a cherry cabinet and produced a duplicate glass. "Join me?" he suggested. "It's quite an exceptional vintage."

"Just a taste," I said. "I can't stay long." And I need to drive home sober. I had "tasted" an exceptional vintage once before in the company of comparative strangers. The wine had lighted my face like Times Square and forming complete sentences had become a neurological nightmare.

I slid into the chair on the right like a girl awkwardly preparing to socialize with her professor. The age difference was a thought, but a tantalizing one. Adding to the interest were D'Avanzo's prominence and wealth, not to mention his reputation. I felt a little as if the neighbor's pit bull was tolerating a scratch behind his ears.

My overstimulated imagination again. Probably I was just having a drink with the flirtatious grandfather of a Bryn Derwyn student.

D'Avanzo poured an inch and a half of dark wine into my glass and stood before me while I sipped it.

My eyes widened. I looked up at my host with appreciation. If my usual red table wine was one note, this was a symphony. All sorts of contrasting flavors seemed to be bouncing around in my mouth. I sipped again and focused on the experience, then widened my eyes once more in D'Avanzo's direction. If there were words to describe what was going on with my taste buds, I didn't know them.

D'Avanzo laughed, a deep warm sound that was both sensual and fatherly.

Tonight he was dressed in black slacks and polished black shoes, but a pale-gray cashmere cardigan hugged his white shirt instead of a suit coat. If there had been a tie, it had already been put away—neatly, I'm sure. The outfit flattered the man, causing my eyes to notice his hard-won waistline, dark eyebrows, and silvery hair. His lips were not too thin, not too thick. For a smile they held fairly straight, then curved abruptly upward.

The grin lingered while he sat down, crossed his legs toward me, leaned closer on the armrest, and asked, "Did you know that when Nicholas attended his previous school he became physically ill every morning?"

My mind snapped back from wherever it had been. "He did?"

D'Avanzo's wine remained on the beautifully polished table between us as if he preferred one activity at a time, perhaps in order to do each perfectly.

"Oh yes. Stress, of course. He hated that place. One of the teachers often tore his papers to shreds in front of his eyes. Poor Nicky. He had no idea what he was doing wrong, and still he lived in fear of making an error."

"That's terrible," I remarked, although the story had become familiar. As educators were ever more increasingly aware, Nicky had been born with a glitch in the information processing department of his brain. While his intelligence probably was quite adequate or even superior, an uninformed teacher could easily make the boy hate schoolwork and by inference, himself.

"Mrs. Aimes, your admission person when we interviewed, recognized Nicky's problem and recommended an extra class on learning techniques. Something about circumventing the problem?" Here D'Avanzo was less sure of his descriptions, but I knew exactly what had transpired. Testing had revealed the nature of Nicky's learning difficulty. Probably the problem was slight, because Bryn Derwyn could accommodate "learning differences" only so far. After that, a specialized school became more appropriate.

"And what do you suppose happened?" The boy's grandfather slapped his knees gleefully.

Although I knew what was coming, I shrugged, not wishing to deprive the man of his moment.

"Honor roll. Three times!" D'Avanzo made no effort to restrain his pride. His face glowed like mine would if I finished the wine. He giggled self-consciously. "A new boy. He runs out to the bus now like a young stallion feeling his oats. It is truly wonderful to see."

Then suddenly the man's face fell. As he scowled in the direction of his toes, I braced myself for the real reason I had been invited in.

"I am very sorry about my Tina," he said, referring surely to her forgetting to pick up her nephew. "Her mother and I spoiled her, as I mentioned, but that does not excuse her neglecting her responsibilities. So often I cannot understand."

The man's agenda was so ordinary I sighed with relief. Embarrassment over a child's behavior—so what else was new?

I took a calculated risk and said, "Perhaps she has a touch of Nicky's problem." Even hinting indirectly that the learning difficulty might have been passed along to Nicky from his mother's side of the family could have been misconstrued; some still consider that sort of problem a stigma rather than a blameless imperfection like nearsightedness or asthma. Fortunately, D'Avanzo correctly discerned my intention.

"No, no. You must not excuse Tina so easily. She thinks only of herself. That was why I made the arrangement to begin with, claiming I never knew when I would be free to leave my business. So I asked her as a favor to do this one thing, and you see how she behaves."

He stood and walked to a group of photographs, selected one and gazed at it a moment. Then he walked back and handed the silver-framed photo to me.

I had been thinking that D'Avanzo must possess some pretty powerful leverage in order to compel his daughter, a grown woman, to interrupt her day just to transport her nephew home from school. If he objected to Nicky riding the afternoon bus, why not pay for a taxi, or even a limousine? Yet speculate as I might about him holding his money just out of his daughter's reach, his need to check up on some bad habit, or even the simple compulsion to dominate his family—whatever was going on remained D'Avanzo's private business and none of mine.

The yellowing black and white photograph centered on a girl wearing a softball uniform. Below her cap two ragged black ponytails with pale-colored ribbons stuck out from behind her ears. Her smile lacked two front teeth. A bat rested on her left shoulder while her right arm leaned against another girl sitting on a bench. Similarly dressed but neater, there was enough family resemblance to require a clarification.

"Is the girl on the bench Nicky's mother?" I asked.

"What?" D'Avanzo had been daydreaming. "No, no. Tina is the one sitting. She hated sports, as you can see."

So the imp with the missing teeth was Nicky's deceased mother. And yes, I could indeed see that Tina was not a happy athlete, if glowering resentfully at the camera was any indication.

Despite an obvious affection for his daughter, Michael D'Avanzo still bristled at the challenge in the girl's dark eyes. What had been adorable defiance from a toddler became less endearing from the teen, intolerable coming from an adult. Much as he verbally excused his daughter's current rebellion, for that was the most likely reason for her negligence, he probably lorded his power over her like a guillotine blade.

D'Avanzo misread my chagrined expression. "Ah," he began in that soothing European manner. "How insensitive I am. You are troubled. That awful business at the school." He lowered himself into his chair, displaying gentlemanly sympathy with his whole body.

I blinked over at him, unable to respond. Funny. Now that he mentioned the school, I realized my throat was tight. For the second time this afternoon, my eyes also prickled with potential tears. Eddie Longmeier, Annie Webb, and the bogus checkbook, an emergency Board meeting after dinner—it had been a very long day and threatened to be an even longer evening. D'Avanzo patted my knee while I sipped wine to dissolve the lump in my throat. The day, the pat on the knee, the wine—my inhibitions went a bit lax.

"Why would Randy Webb say he had another donor for the gym if he didn't?" I asked.

D'Avanzo shrugged and pouted at his bookshelves. Then he met my eyes and said, "A man desperately trying to get out of jail?"

My chest tightened around something rigid, probably my fear. I nodded thoughtfully. "I guess I'd say whatever I thought would get me out, too."

"No, my dear," again the pat on the knee, "I believe you would only tell the truth." Then, longing to return to his daydream, he stood to dismiss me. The moment's privacy allowed me to wipe my eyes.

We walked to the door, the student having received both more and less than she expected from the professor.

Before leaving, I faced the man once more. "It isn't true, is it?"

D'Avanzo suddenly chilled, but not from the winter air. The stiffness of his posture made his silver hair and colorless clothes appear brittle.

"No," the patriarch answered from guillotine height. After his front door closed, I released my shudder.

❈ *Chapter 25* ❈

*A*gainst the now-completed darkness, spotlights illuminated D'Avanzo's driveway and every angle of the house. Heavy drapes had been drawn by an unseen hand to shield against the artificial brightness. At night the place looked very stagey, very intimidating.

With a music of pings and pops a motor worked at opening the tall halves of the chain-link gate I hadn't noticed earlier. Haunted now by D'Avanzo's range of moods, I managed to drive myself off the property within the minute.

Traffic remained sporadic along the narrow tributaries threading through D'Avanzo's generously spaced neighborhood but thickened as soon as I approached the Main Line's main artery, Lancaster Avenue.

My dashboard clock told me it was 5:10 PM—time to order pizza if the Barneses were to be ready for company by seven. The Board meeting could do without the clatter of me doing dishes anyway. Probably the kids should do their homework wearing headphones.

I pulled into a gas station to make the call, ordered a large pepperoni, and reassured the youth who answered the phone that their driver knew exactly how to find us.

For the next twenty-five minutes I devoted myself to the demanding protocol of rush-hour traffic, and with a sigh of relief followed the pizza delivery man into the school's driveway. I paid him off outside our door and swept into the living room feeling like Florence Nightingale, or at least Florence Henderson.

"Where have you been?" Chelsea quizzed. She was still a willowy five-foot-two, the size and shape fashion magazines have been using to push clothes for women who haven't been svelte since they were twelve. Fortunately, Chelsea's face was too innocent for modelling, and at the moment too angry. I thought briefly there might be some substance to Tina Longmeier's rebellion after all.

"Yeah," Garry echoed.

"Dad's been worried," Chelsea added.

"Yeah, me, too," echoed my son. Our dog twirled around under the pizza box.

"Dad? How long has he been home?" I asked.

"Twenty minutes. He's napping. We're supposed to call him for dinner."

Poor guy. Although if he was able to sleep, he couldn't be too worried about the meeting or about me.

"How long have you been home?" I asked the kids. My estimate was less than a hour; rehearsals usually lasted till four-thirty.

"Forever," Garry said. "That dinner?"

I handed him the box and addressed my daughter. "Chelsea," I said. "You're old enough to babysit other kids. You've been trained by the Red Cross to babysit other kids. Why the inquisition all of a sudden?"

"Somebody got *killed,* Mom. We were worried about you."

Damn. She was right. I had violated the first rule of adolescent freedom: call home.

"Sorry, Chel. I got held up taking a Bryn Derwyn student home. Won't happen again."

My fluff-topped pre-teen gave me a see-that-it-doesn't scowl, and arms-folded, turned into the kitchen to get glasses of milk for her and Garry.

"Cokes for Dad and me," I called after her.

I trotted upstairs and quietly approached my husband, who lay on his back snoring with his arms folded in imitation of his daughter. "Rip?" I whispered. "You want to wake up? Dinner's downstairs."

"Huh? Umm," he replied. "Oh, it's you. Where you been?"

I was going to have to re-educate my family, vary my schedule, alter expectations. All while keeping everybody scrupulously informed.

While Rip blinked himself awake, I thought of the woman I saw speaking into a cellular phone while pushing a grocery cart. I also remembered the teachers laughing about a kid who got a call on the phone in his book bag. He had been in class at the time. I decided my family didn't need to be quite that informed.

Rip had reached semi-consciousness, so I told him, "I took Nicky D'Avanzo home. His grandfather says there isn't another donor, that Randy just wants to get out of jail."

"Um. That was nice of you." Obviously, my husband wasn't totally awake.

"There's something you need to know about Randy," I tried again.

"Yeah?" Rip propped his fists behind him like the training wheels on a bicycle.

"He had some letterhead printed that says, 'Bryn Derwyn, Incorporated,' and there's a checking account using that name, too. Know anything about it?"

"Nope. I'll look into it. How'd you find out?"

"Found a receipt in his office." That seemed to be enough of an answer for now.

"Oh, right. You get that mailing done?"

"Not yet."

My husband patted my arm. "Hang in. What's for dinner?"

"Pepperoni."

Rip nodded. I couldn't tell if it was approval or acceptance of the inevitable.

A knock on the door interrupted the first bite of my second slice. My heart lurched and I almost choked. The clock on the living room VCR said 6:20.

"Early," I observed.

"Too early." Rip rose, probably to back me up in case it was a particularly rude reporter.

Lt. John Newkirk stood on the doorstep, peering with pseudo-shyness over his mustache. "Come in?" he asked.

I stepped back from the door. "We're eating," I said, just to say something.

"That's what I figured," he replied. Nodding to Rip, he said, "Sorry for the intrusion, but there's an oddity I need to discuss." Then he turned back toward me.

"You say you were in the Community Room to clean?"

From either side of the dining room table Chelsea and Garry watched Lt. Newkirk as if he were Columbo pacing back and forth on our television, except their eyes were wide with awe.

"So what I need to know is, how much cleaning did you actually do? Before you left, I mean."

I thought about it. "Not much at all. I unloaded a couple shelves, decided I needed to borrow a Dustbuster from Patrice and went to go get it."

"A Dustbuster." Newkirk rubbed his chin. His eyes danced with interest as lively as the kids'. "And where is that Dustbuster now?" he asked.

The question hit me like a brick. Where indeed? I'd forgotten about the hand vacuum in the easy way you forget something that isn't there.

"I have no idea," I answered. "When I first got back to the Community Room, Richard and Randy were meeting with that couple, so I set the Dustbuster outside the door and went to watch the chorus rehearse."

"Was the vacuum there when you went back the second time?" The time I found Richard's body.

Instinctively, I glanced toward Rip, my personal lifetime supply of moral support. His fingertips touched the tabletop in a loose mousetrap of tented fingers.

I shook my head. "No. I don't think it was."

The lieutenant nodded. Then he turned to Rip and asked, "Mind if we take a look around the school for that thing?"

"Sure," Rip agreed, reaching into his pocket for keys. "But there are five of them. Gin knows where to look." The purchase had been made to help the maintenance staff keep ahead of the creeping filth the Mop Squad had labored so long and hard to abolish. Quite a lot to ask of five small household appliances, yet they had already proven to be a brilliant investment, especially in the lunchroom.

I got my long wool coat out of the closet, took a final sip of Diet Coke from my favorite Phillies World Series plastic cup, buttoned up, and said, "I'm ready." Ordinarily, I knew Rip would have preferred to escort Newkirk around the school, but the Board was about to arrive.

At the last minute, I grabbed my nearly cold pizza slice. Rude or not, it was dinner; and I needed it.

Outdoors, cold humidity suffused the air with a distinctive prescience. The atmosphere possessed a uniform thickness, a certain chill, a certain smell. Most telling of all, the sky looked pink.

"Gonna snow," Newkirk remarked.

The effort to humanize himself warmed me toward the man. Yes, talking about the weather was feeble; but that's why I found it particularly touching. "Looks like rain," probably means, "We haven't got a damn thing in common except we're stuck right here right now and we need to speak to each other." "Hot enough for you?" translates to, "Isn't this the most awkward, saddest, scariest, and/or most embarrassing moment you've had all year?"

"Cold enough for you?" I asked Newkirk, and he snorted.

Just like that we became real to each other. Now we could search through a frigid, spooky-dark school building without being overly concerned about bumping a sleeve. If the dampness made our noses run, we could wipe them without feeling self-conscious.

Still, I felt sorry for Newkirk's social ineptitude. He must be a regular walking calculator. "You married?" I asked while I fitted the front door key into the lock with my mittens.

"Yeah," he said. "Twelve years. Four kids."

"Good for you," I complimented him as if he'd gotten A on an quiz, which wasn't very far off.

Only the safety lights illuminated the halls, so I went into the office, found the circuit box hidden around a corner, and threw the switch that brightened all the corridors like a circus. More than one person had sworn they saw ghosts roaming the school at night. Whether folklore or fabrication, with Richard Wharton already on my mind, I didn't care to encourage similar thoughts.

When we passed the squad car, Newkirk had reached into the back seat for some large evidence bags; and now he borrowed the carton Joanne used for recycling office paper.

The first Dustbuster resided behind Rip's secretary's desk. Black and Decker's current style amounted to a foot-long, flattened cone of gray plastic with a handle continuing off the top. You operated the thing with a thumb switch and emptied it by removing the cone to reveal a small, re-useable dust bag on a plastic frame that sealed the dirt away from the motor. With gloved hands Newkirk carefully lifted Joanne's out of its wall holder and delicately sealed it inside one of his paper bags. Then he labeled it with a tag, gently settled it in the box and rose with satisfaction.

Together we passed between the reception desk and underwear tree. Then as we juggled our way through the fire door leading to the hall on the left, I commented conversationally, "I take it your forensics people didn't find any evidence near the body."

"You could say that," the lieutenant agreed, although letting me say it was not quite the same as him saying it.

"I didn't clean the table or the floor at all, you know."

"So I gathered."

I stopped outside the faculty room. "Do you really think the murderer used my Dustbuster to clean up after himself? Wouldn't it make more sense that somebody connected to the school borrowed it back? Or maybe Jacob or Patrice saw their equipment lying out where it could get stolen and put it away?" I liked that theory. I liked it much better than an impulsive killer recovering quickly enough to vacuum up trace evidence.

Newkirk stared at me with a peeved expression. "Mind opening this door?" he asked. "I got four kids waiting at home, remember?"

"Oh, sure." And I have fifteen Board members coming to tea.

After bagging and tagging the one from the Faculty Room, we found two more just inside the door to the cafeteria. The fifth required quite a bit of hunting, and we finally found it on the science room desk. Scattered around the hardwood floor were little flakes of white paper, as if somebody had torn pages from a ring binder while ineffectively holding it over the wastebasket. Although someone had brought the vacuum to the mess, they hadn't gotten around to using it.

After all five appliances were gathered in the box, Newkirk asked if I had any idea which one I had borrowed from Patrice.

They all looked relatively new and interchangeable to my eye. Yet his question was important, so I peered at each one very carefully.

"None of them seems right," I admitted.

"Probably trying too hard," Newkirk sympathized. "Happens all the time."

We retraced our steps. I closed and locked doors behind us, shut off the brighter hall lights, tugged and rattled the front door to be certain it was secure.

When we emerged from the shelter of the entrance overhang, a chilling breeze of stinging snowflakes worked at my cheeks and the hem of my coat. Newkirk's eyes squinted protectively as we walked back to his two-tone squad car and deposited the now-heavy carton. Teeny snowflakes trickled down past the spotlights, illuminating the school's driveway. Elsewhere they were invisible except as a dullness on the windshields of the several vehicles gathered near our house.

"Sorry for the bother," the policeman told me as he shut himself into his driver's seat. He nodded good-bye, then proceeded to back around and pull away.

I stood at the end of the path to our house hugging

myself against the weather until he was too far into the darkness to glance back.

Then I scurried back through the tiny, biting flecks of ice and unlocked the door of the school for myself.

※ *Chapter 26* ※

This time I didn't bother with the brighter hall lights. Having just toured the school building with a policeman, I could afford to be brave.

And maybe I was testing my maturity, too, telling myself not to waste electricity when I could see perfectly well by the light of the exit signs. I passed muster, too, right up until I reached Kevin's door. Just the idea of betraying a friend made me sweat.

However, the thought of what was going on at my house forced me to use the key. As I saw it, Bryn Derwyn had a Friday deadline: Randy Webb's Grand Jury hearing.

Maybe there was nothing incriminating to find in Kevin's office, but even finding nothing would constitute a progress of sorts. If I was careful, Kevin would never know I had been there and would, therefore, never suspect my disloyal thoughts: mainly that he had an excellent motive to kill Richard Wharton.

Opportunity, too. Searching for the Dustbusters had reminded me how few people used this hallway after school.

I took a deep breath and flipped on the overhead light.

Kevin's cubicle revealed an entirely different persona than Randy's office next door. For decor he had robin's-egg blue walls, the same color as the kindergarten class-room, which told me that Kevin primarily worked inside his head.

Also, the condition of the room seemed to protect its tenant, all but shouting—go away, he's busy. Piles of stuff littered every available surface—the desk (especially the in/out tray), the credenza against the left-hand wall, the two file cabinets, under the computer desk, plus a couple piles on the floor in a corner, which was the only place they wouldn't have been kicked over on a regular basis. Even Kevin's briefcase, a nice-quality bur-gundy leather one, was opened in the middle of his desk, revealing folders and brochures of roof shingles, spreadsheets, colored pens, a calculator, and a Hershey bar.

My search of the briefcase did clarify one thing: catching a crooked business manager might be child's play for an auditor, but it was beyond me. It would re-quire weeks of observation for me to piece together Kevin's job description, never mind determining whether he was straight.

After fifteen minutes, the only oddities I came across were three easy-reader books in his deep, right-hand desk drawer: *Green Eggs and Ham,* an Encyclopedia Brown, and something about a goose. Puzzling, but scarcely incriminating.

Just as I bent to poke through one of the paper piles on the floor, I heard a sound that froze me and dis-solved me all at once—the school's front door closing.

At least that's what I thought I heard. Noise usually travels through the empty building like voices across a lake, but now there was nothing.

My ears could have been wrong, but my nervous sys-tem didn't believe that. The murderer had returned.

The lobby carpet was muffling any footsteps, that was all.

I turned off Kevin's light then decided I wanted a weapon. Nothing in the business manager's office came to mind except mess.

Leaving the door open, I rushed to Randy's door, frantically fitted keys into the lock, then stumbled through the dark to the shelf where I knew there were bookends, miniature skiis leaning against what I remembered to be very lumpy brass mountains. I hefted one of the weighty decorations in my hand and forced myself to think.

Who could be here, really? Rip looking for me? I doubted that he remembered my existence with the Board meeting going on; but if perchance he had come looking for me, he certainly would have shouted my name, if only to save me from the terror I was presently experiencing.

So who else? Not a student. No teachers had exterior door keys. It wasn't cold enough or snowy enough for Jacob to be checking the heater or his supply of rock salt.

If, as I was inclined to believe, the evening visit was related to Richard's death, I realized that now I was probably hiding in the intruder's destination. Randy was in jail. What better time to sneak into his office to plant incriminating evidence?

Too late for escape. The double door exit at the end of the hall had been chained for the night anyway. Clutching the bookend for dear life I scurried through the semi-dark hallway back to Kevin's mess.

The interior fire door creaked open just as I ducked out of sight. No time to shut the door. Hiding further out of reach risked making noise, so I merely huddled against the wall beside the doorjamb and tried to breathe silently.

Heavy heels clacked on the tile, a man's footsteps made with dress shoes. Not Jacob, who always wore rubber-soled work boots, even in summer. I wanted to groan, or possibly scream.

A hand reached around the corner next to my face and flipped the light switch.

I let out a guttural "arrugh" and raised the bookend high over my head.

"Hey!" Kevin said, jumping back. "Put that down."

I slumped to the floor.

He let out a nervous laugh and reeled back a little, as if he still feared a blow from a bookend. Then he settled down and asked, "What are you doing here?"

Honesty is the best policy, Mom always said. "I was collecting evidence with Lt. Newkirk. And you?"

"I don't see Lt. Newkirk anywhere, Gin. What's going on?"

I stood up. Probably Mom meant complete honesty, knowing her. "Okay. I did bring Newkirk over here, but after he left I decided it was a good time to search your office."

Kevin's college-boy face went stiff. His moonstone-blue eyes darkened into granite. He said nothing. He didn't have to.

"I'm sorry." Instinctively, I wanted to add his name to the apology, but to presume upon our family friendship would have come across as manipulative rather than sincere, and I certainly did not want to sound insincere. Kevin Seitz was no longer a sleeping, honey-blond boy slung over his father's shoulder. He stood before me a six-foot-tall adult at the peak of his strength, and part of me still wondered whether he had swung a shovel into Richard Wharton's head.

"I was getting desperate," I continued. "The Board is over at our house making 'contingency' plans. They're afraid the reason for Richard's death might be internal, especially now that Randy's been arrested."

"And you prefer the idea that I did it to avenge my father. Sweet, Gin. That's really sweet." He fell against the doorjamb.

"I said I'm desperate. I said I'm sorry."

He looked at me with disgust. Then he sighed. "Shit. I guess you really are desperate."

"Right," I was quick to agree.

"Gimme that," he said, referring to the bookend. "You're cutting off your circulation." He sounded like my big brother might have sounded, if I'd had one. He set the bookend on top of his in basket, while blood rushed painfully to my hand.

"So why are you here?" I asked, feeling myself blush at my own temerity. Much more of this and I would be wallpapered with blotches.

"I've got a 7:30 meeting with a roofer tomorrow morning and I'm not ready. Luckily, the snow reminded me."

"That doesn't sound like you."

"Yeah? Well, sneaking around behind my back doesn't sound like you either."

If possible, I blushed harder. "It hasn't exactly been business as usual around here," I replied, in an attempt to excuse us both.

"So did you find my secret game plan? The one with the diagram of the shovel?"

"No. But I would like to know who you were talking to on the phone the first time I came by Friday afternoon."

"When was that?"

"About three."

"How should I know? Probably roofers. Does it matter?"

"I guess not."

"You see anybody in the hall other than that couple or Richard or Randy?"

"No. I didn't even see you . . ."

". . . because you were on the phone with some roofers." We recited the words at the same time.

I thought a minute. "You weren't here during the murder, or you'd have heard something. Right?"

"I guess. Right."

"So where were you?"

"Jeez, Gin. The police asked me that, and I just plain wasn't sure. I'm all over this place all day, you know? How would I know when I went where or why?"

"Okay, so you were somewhere else at the critical time. Do you remember seeing a Dustbuster in the hall next to the Community Room door?"

He wrinkled his forehead and nose. "One of our new ones? In the hall? No. I'd have noticed that. I would have put it away."

"Okay. What are you doing with *Green Eggs and Ham* in your desk?"

"Green eggs? Oh, the books. They're for—come to think of it, that's none of your business."

"Au contraire, mon cher. 'Fess up."

Kevin laughed. "If it'll get you off my back—hey! That's probably where I was: putting the books in Patrice's locker. I always wait until after school, when nobody's around, and I probably did it early because it was Friday. I'll bet that's it."

"That's what?"

"Where I was during the murder."

"Explain."

Kevin leaned against the wall, looking quite at ease. "You promise you won't tell?"

"No deal. Let's hear it."

"Okay, but don't tell Patrice. She's embarrassed enough about learning to read at her age."

"You're borrowing easy-readers for Patrice? To practice? Wow, why didn't she say something?"

"Like I said—she's embarrassed. Lots of adults who can't read are embarrassed about it. Otherwise, they'd probably ask for help. I found out about Patrice when she couldn't figure out how to operate the new washing machine. I told her to read the instructions, and she started to cry. Jeez, I felt like shit. So I made her a deal. She'd try to learn, and I'd keep it between her and me."

"Of course." I knew how he felt. Once I'd seen Patrice leaning on a dust mop outside a classroom listening to the teacher. I immediately assumed she was goofing off, when she probably had been trying to learn something. Dumb, dumb, dumb—of me. I simply had to stop jumping to conclusions.

"Kevin, you're wonderful. And I promise not to tell. In fact if I can help . . . ?"

"Nah. It's covered. She's coming along real fast. It used to take her a week to read three books. Now she returns them overnight."

"But what do you say to the librarian? You're not even married."

"They're for my niece."

"Nice. You're really nice." I felt excessively proud of him, also inordinately pleased that I had suggested him for the business manager's job. He belonged here. I wasn't sure I could say that much for myself.

"So does that mean you no longer think I'm capable of murder?" he asked.

"I never wanted to think that in the first place."

"But you were desperate."

"Yeah." I touched his cheek with my hand. "I really am sorry, Kev." Then I eased my way past him through the door.

"That's what all my women say when they leave."

I smiled all the way down the hall and all the way through the lobby until I was outside.

Then the wind and snow slapped every warm sentiment right out of my head.

Chapter 27

The snow swirled erratically, curling in eddies around my feet. The cement sidewalk across the front of the school remained swept by the wind gusts, but now the grass of our lawn and around the parking lots was crusted gray. It was a dirty snow, the type that reminded me of a particularly soul-wrenching edition of Dickens' *A Christmas Carol* I'd seen on TV as a child. I recalled that Scrooge wanted to make sense of his personal nightmare by blaming it on a bit of undercooked potato.

Currently, in my very own living room, far less logical conclusions were being aired by men and women who should have known better.

"I think we need a consultant, a professional to handle this," somebody remarked as I opened the door.

"Excuse me," I said, hurrying through my ill-chosen, multi-textured decor to the stairs. "Sorry to interrupt." I did not bother to hang up my coat, just raced up the stairs, glanced in on Garry and Chelsea, and plopped down on my own bed, coat and all.

"I thought that was what we hired Mr. Barnes here for. Why go to the expense?"

"Oh? Has he dealt with a murder before?"

"No. No, of course not . . ."

"Has anyone else around here? Any educator, I mean?"

"Well, yes, actually. There was that one scandal . . ."

"And is the school still in business?" That voice I recognized as my husband's. He sounded inordinately calm, I thought, a message in and of itself.

"Yes." This voice came across aggrieved, as if its owner felt no school deserved to survive tragedy or scandal.

"Listen," Rip said, making use of the opening the nay-sayer left for him, "we have no indication at this point that Randy did anything wrong. And no information whatsoever that the murder had anything to do with Bryn Derwyn, except the unfortunate fact that it happened here.

"I understand why some parents are keeping their children home; they're worried about their safety. I might do the same until more information emerged. But this talk about shutting down strikes me as patently premature. Even irresponsible. If we appear to be panicking, the school really will have to close. But if we behave sensibly, I sincerely believe we'll be fine."

"What do you suggest?"

"Institute extra security precautions, mainly to reassure some of the more emotional parents. Do whatever we can to reassure ourselves that the school was not involved in Richard's death. Assist the police in their efforts . . ."

"You sound as if you don't think Randy Webb is guilty."

"There is some doubt. He hasn't been indicted yet. Or tried."

"Well, by then . . ."

"Innocent until proven guilty."

"You can't be that naive."

I had been holding my breath. Now I wanted to yell, "Hey! How about the Constitution?" or something similar. Rip remained appropriately silent, allowing the others to hear the prejudice in the negative Board member's words.

Garry padded into the room, turning on a light and showing me how grim a nine-year-old can look. Adults were not supposed to argue like that, not within earshot of children. It was unnerving enough for another adult to hear. My son snuggled into my right side and I surrounded him with my arm, resting my head against his. Chelsea saw my light go on and wandered in, too.

"What's happening?" she mouthed silently.

I shrugged. "Daddy's winning," I mouthed back, although there was no way to know. She nodded and went back to her room, to her homework or doodles or headphones.

The night table alarm clock said nearly nine, so I suggested that Garry get ready for bed. "Dad will tell us about it later," I assured him, and he nodded and headed for the bathroom.

I stopped listening about that point, giving my own thoughts their rein. Curiously, I began thinking about our house, about the upcoming holiday and how, since the murder, I was especially counting on our favorite family rituals to finish bonding me to the place.

Maybe I needed to adjust my attitude. Maybe if I resuscitated my nesting instinct, finally made the bedspread and drapes to match the green bedroom carpet, tore down my already faded, dust-producing burlap living room drapes and tried again, fixed that closet doorknob, molly-bolted that curtain rod, lifted that bail, toted that barge—maybe I would get over the notion that we were scarcely tolerated visitors in a house that belonged to the school. Maybe then it would become our home, with or without the help of holiday rituals.

Assuming, of course, that circumstances permitted us to stay.

"Mom!" Garry called from the bathroom. "Why isn't there any hot water?"

Half an hour later, Rip woke me with a kiss. I was curled on top of the covers wrapped in my wool coat. "We need another hot water heater," I announced.

"Isn't this one still under warranty?"

"So it is. Tell me, how did the meeting go?"

"They were scared. Some of them actually wanted to talk about what we should do if too many students withdrew."

"One guy seemed positive the school was going under."

"Kravitz. He's a dunce. Nobody took him seriously."

"Except maybe me."

"He's a dunce. Don't take him seriously." I recognized husband talk when I heard it. Rip wanted me to forget that many of the more rational Board members were also preparing for the worst. Was I supposed to believe they, too, were alarmists?

"So you think everything's going to be okay?"

"Yes. If Kravitz puts a muzzle on it. A bunch of them made that point very clear toward the end. Everybody is to wear a pretty face. If we sound confident that Bryn Derwyn will survive—it will. I think Kravitz got the message."

Gymnasts do acrobatics on a balance beam four inches wide. Limber, young girls do flips and back bends and all sorts of tricks set to music. But if they lean too far right or left, the routine is over—beyond remedy.

"So you think the meeting was worthwhile?"

"Yes."

Was my husband still performing? Staying in character for my benefit? "You don't have to bullshit me," I said. "I can take the truth."

Rip's green eyes snapped to attention. "It's not BS," he said. "We're going to be fine." He appeared peeved, and not just because he hates to hear me swear.

"Okay?" he asked. He wanted me to put on a pretty face, too, to stick with the program, to do cartwheels on the beam.

"Okay," I said, because now I knew the front wasn't for me; it was for him.

My White Knight. My genuine good guy. Dreamer. Believer in one person making a difference. All of those things. BS-ing himself that it was all going to work out because that's what he needed to do to bring it off.

I told him I loved him and pulled him close.

He enjoyed what I was suggesting for a moment then wiggled himself loose.

"Kids still awake?" I asked, taking the rejection hard.

"Nah. Sleeping like babies. I just checked."

"So what then?" I'm the sort who demands satisfaction; a magazine quiz told me so.

"I've got to get up at five, babe."

"Why!"

"To decide about school, whether to open or not."

"But I thought . . ." What about the pretty face, the solidarity?

Rip latched onto my thought and smiled. Then he walked over to the window and pushed the curtain aside. "It's snowing, remember? I have to decide whether to close school or not."

The proverbial Snow Day. "I thought the maintenance people decided that, or maybe God."

"Nope. You're looking at him."

"Oh my God," I teased.

"Maybe some other night."

"Damn," I said.

This time Rip seemed to approve my choice of words.

※ *Chapter 28* ※

Our alarm woke us at five Thursday morning. Rip pulled on sweatpants and boots below his bathrobe then went downstairs to listen for any school closings on Philadelphia's news radio while he watched the Weather Channel on cable TV.

When I heard the front door open, I hurried over to the window. By our front light I could see crisp snow-flakes stuck sideways to tree trunks, and the yard glittered with scarcely half an inch accumulation.

Bryn Derwyn's head meteorologist emerged into the light. While his dog drowsily peed on the nearest bush, Rip tested the sidewalk with the toe of his boot. The rubber sole caught, abruptly halting his scuffing motion. Placing hands on his hips, Rip tested for slipperiness once again with the same result. Dog and Headmaster reentered the house. Morale would be low in classrooms all over the Delaware valley.

A minute later I heard Barney's hearty "oof" as he flopped down onto Garry's warm bed. Rip reset his alarm and snuggled back with me.

He slept. I replayed and reworded what I'd heard of last night's meeting.

By breakfast, the sky promised a warm powder blue

that would melt and dry any evidence of winter by noon. Chelsea seemed privately pleased, perhaps because her between-class social life would continue without interruption. Garry groused so sourly I considered introducing him to coffee.

Rip dressed and ate with his usual morning cheer, although he might have been practicing his PR. He caught me loading my favorite plastic Phillies cup into the dishwasher.

"Hey," he said with concern. "I thought you never put that in there. What's up?" He nuzzled my neck.

True, I had snapped at every family member more than once for putting my World Series souvenir at risk. "Hand wash only," I barked, yanking it out of the automatic dishwasher, "or you'll have me to deal with." Thanks to my vigilance, the colorful printing had held up beautifully.

I turned to cuddle my husband and explain. "I'm practicing what I preach: Possessions don't matter. People do."

"Very noble, I'm sure. But do you really want to start with that cup?"

"Have to," I answered. Garry's prized hat was gone, and the only comparable thing I owned was that cup. "If I don't do this, my entire credibility as a mother comes under suspicion."

Rip kissed my forehead and pulled away. "God forbid," he said, heading for the door.

"Tease," I replied. "See you over there—I'm finishing that mailing today for sure."

"And about time, too."

But first I fed Barney, put in a load of wash, made the beds, tidied the living room, and took out chicken to thaw for dinner. Eventually, I showered and dressed in school-employee clothes—today a fringed, long, gray wool skirt, black boots, a teal turtleneck, and an Indian-print blazer in mostly gray and aqua. Warm and stylish, too. Mother would be proud.

About ten I tucked into my long overcoat and trotted through the sunshine into Bryn Derwyn's lobby.

My timing could not have been better, because just as I arrived, Emily Wrigley asked Ruth, the receptionist, if she needed any help. Although the forty-year-old fifth grader was supposed to be in study hall, apparently she already knew everything so she was free.

"Ruth," I called, hurrying to join them. "If you don't have anything for Emily, she can help me with a mailing." Please, begged my eyes, if not my whole body.

"Sure," said Ruth with surprise. Get this kid out of my face and thank you very much.

"C'mon, Emily," I corralled the girl, "we've got envelopes to stuff."

"Uh, okay," said the fifth grader with appropriate suspicion. Usually she couldn't beg an office job. I heard she rearranged desk drawers when people weren't looking.

As I approached the fire door leading to Randy's office, Emily lagged behind.

"What's the matter?" I asked foolishly.

"I, uh, oh. Nothing." She seemed tall, standing by herself in the empty hallway, and I thought of how quickly Garry seemed to grow. In a year or two Emily would hit puberty. She would become preoccupied with new hairstyles and tormenting boys; in the meantime, desk drawers and stuffing envelopes—anything for adult attention.

"Well, c'mon then. We've got work to do."

"Where?"

"Where the envelopes are. Let's go."

Emily sulked along behind me fingering the right-hand wall. When I reached Kevin's office, she was ten feet behind. When I reached Randy's, twenty. The

Community Room door stood several feet further along to the left.

While I waited in the development doorway, Emily sighed dramatically before hurrying inside. If the work had been located in the Community Room, she probably would have run home screaming. Impressionable girl.

With a minimum of dialogue she and I soon became a fold and stuff duo. Emily had done this before, and she was good. Plus she was devoting herself to the chore as if it would stave off world hunger.

"You're scared," I observed.

Behind her glasses, her eyes shone like blue Christmas balls, pretty ones, but fragile.

I couldn't help myself, I pulled her in for a hug. She sniffled on my sleeve.

She had been standing to work while I sat to fold letters. Now I pulled Randy's spare chair over and parked the girl on it.

"I'm sorry you're scared, Emily," I said, my sincerity also chin-deep in guilt. This was a ten-year-old, after all. A precocious, self-important, screaming-for-attention one, but still one hundred percent child. I needed to remember that.

"Are you uncomfortable being in Mr. Webb's office?"

A nod.

"He's not here, Emily. He can't get to you or anyone else right now."

Her silence eloquently reminded us both of why Randy was presently in jail—and who was responsible for it.

"You think he killed Mr. Wharton, don't you? Did you see him do it?"

A negative head shake.

"But you did see something frightening."

A vigorous nod that freed her shirttail from the waistband of her uniform kilt, The Compleat Emily Wrigley. I almost hugged her again; that is, until she told me, "Mr. Webb's hands were bloody. I saw him wiping them on his handkerchief."

"Are you sure that's true, Emily? Are you sure you didn't see something else, or maybe imagine it?"

The fragile blue eyes widened as far as they would go. "No. I swear." Perhaps she protested a little too much, but there was enough you've-got-to-believe-me in her voice that despite my bias, I did.

I stared over her shoulder at the off-white wall for a long moment before I asked, "Where was Mr. Webb when you saw him?"

"In the back parking lot, walking toward his car."

"And where were you?"

"Messing around the swings waiting for my bus."

"When does your bus come?"

"Three-fifty." One of the later ones.

"That's where you wait every day?"

"Yeah. Unless it's raining." Of course.

"Where was the teacher who had bus duty?"

"Cameron Ingles fell and cut his knee, so she took him to get a band-aid. I was the only one left."

Risky decision, I thought, leaving a student un-supervised. Not often done these days.

Emily perceived my concern about the teacher's judg-ment, because she said, "Cameron was crying like crazy, and anyway I was supposed to go get them if the bus came early, but it didn't."

So Randy Webb left the school wiping blood, or to be fair, something red, off his hands at about 3:45 PM on Friday—early for an administrator to leave, perfect tim-ing if he happened to have just committed murder.

Depression completely displaced any guilt I felt over questioning Emily. At last I understood why Newkirk had arrested Randy so promptly. His "witness's" habit-

ual theatrics were absent from her report. Even her normally cocksure chin trembled. In this instance at least,
Emily's desire to be grown up had slipped into hiberna-
tion. She came across as mature enough to know what
she saw but youthful enough not to lie about it. I would
have arrested Randy, too.

Yet something about Emily's information just didn't
sit right.

To get to the back parking lot from the Community
Room, you had to cross the lobby, proceed down another short hall, and go out through double doors. So
why hadn't Randy cleaned himself up at the scene of the
crime? He also could have washed up properly along
the way in either the boys' room or the faculty lavatory
with little risk of being noticed at that hour.

Furthermore, what about the Dustbuster? The absence of ordinary debris around the victim seemed to
indicate a killer with presence of mind, not one who
would vacuum the table and floor and forget to clean his
own hands.

The bell signaling the end of Emily's study hall ended
our time together and temporarily my speculations. I
thanked the girl and told her I thought she was right to
speak up about what she saw. She did not look especially convinced, which convinced me even more that
she was accurately describing Randy's actions.

After she had gone, my face sagged. Kravitz, the
doom-saying Board member, was more right than anyone else realized.

And yet. I wheeled Randy's chair back to his desk and
used his phone to speed-dial his wife. Annie answered
so tentatively that I felt sorry for her all over again.

"At least you're picking up the phone," I remarked
after identifying myself. "Things must be settling down."

"Not really. I keep hoping it's Randy calling for me to
pick him up."

I sighed right back at her. "Next time maybe. In the meantime, I have a question for you."

"There aren't any more envelopes around, if that's what you want. Everything else must be at the office."

"No. Nothing like that. I'm trying to figure out what got Randy arrested, and . . ." how could I point-blank ask why he would have been wiping blood off his hands? And suddenly the words came. "Does Randy ever get nosebleeds?"

"Sure. Especially in the winter when he has a cold. Why?" She sounded quite happy to tell me this.

"Because a kid saw him using his handkerchief to wipe something red off his hands, and I think that's why he was arrested."

"Gin. You're a genius. I found one of his hankies soaking in the sink last weekend, but I didn't think anything about it."

This I doubted. More likely she was terrified that Randy was guilty and desperate to protect him.

"Do you really think that's all they have on him?" she asked eagerly.

"I don't know." Rip was still looking into that Bryn Derwyn, Inc. bank account. "When you spoke with Randy, did he say anything about evidence?"

"No. Nothing."

Probably his lawyer knew what the police had, and both men chose to shield Annie.

"What did you do with the hankie?"

"Finished washing it. Put it away. Why?"

"Because I'm thinking if tests only showed Randy's blood on the handkerchief, maybe the police will buy the nosebleed story." Which, to my knowledge, Randy had not yet aired. He must be among those citizens who fervently distrusted our legal system. And at the moment, who could blame him?

"But I washed it."

"Tests still might pick up traces of his blood. What do you think about offering all Randy's handkerchiefs to Lt. Newkirk?" Of course, if Emily's impression was correct and there had been no nosebleed, such an offer might certify Randy's guilt. I tried not to dwell on that.

"If you think I should," Annie enthused. "Sure. I'll call Newkirk right away. Oh, Gin. You're an absolute angel to help us like this. We owe you big."

"Randy's not out of trouble yet," I reminded her.

"Yes, but he will be. I just know it."

While Annie eagerly built her straw castle with my idea, I considered that maybe Newkirk was right, that killers are rarely rational and are more than capable of vacuuming up hair and clothing lint with bloody hands. Except for one reassuring detail.

I had noticed surprisingly little blood at the crime scene and none on the handle of the weapon. The only way Randy could have gotten the amount of blood on his hands that Emily described would have been to deliberately touch the back of Richard's head—a thoroughly repulsive thought, especially since such an action would have served no purpose.

Several more minutes of stuffing envelopes both calmed me and completed the chore. If I ran the mailing through the postage meter myself, I could drop everything at the post office before I tried to find Tina Longmeier.

Maybe she could give me her slant on the thing with her father. Maybe she'd even tell me why Randy Webb had all but accused her husband of murder.

Worth a try.

Chapter 29

*L*earning Tina Longmeier's whereabouts cost me a case of indigestion. Nobody answered her home phone, which would have been too lucky by half considering her out-and-about reputation. Although I could have asked her father, I preferred not to. Instead I waited half an hour for seventh grade to dismiss for lunch in order to approach Nicky D'Avanzo without causing a fuss.

"Any idea where I might find your aunt?" I asked. All around us middle school kids jiggled and squirmed and yakked.

The young teenager finished collecting flatware on his gray plastic tray then fixed me with a sarcastic, half-smile. In front of him students wound through a doorway past steam tables and beverage coolers. Behind us lay the long lunchroom full of rectangular tables with brown plastic chairs. The few teachers there for supervision, and coincidentally their own lunches, had the relaxed demeanor of prison guards manning the wall.

"You eating?" Nicky asked me.

Not on a bet.

"Yeah, sure," I relented.

"Hey, pal. Let the lady in. It's Mrs. Barnes." The kid

who was next in line was either clueless or deliberately unimpressed; however, he permitted me to butt in. I batted my eyelashes when I thanked him, and he rolled his eyes.

"So where do you think I should look?" I pressed Nicky. I had my tray and my utensils before I got a glimpse of what I would be eating: burgers and fries.

Nicky turned back to face me, his confident stance emphasizing the graceful athleticism I had noticed before.

"Whaddaya want her for?" he asked, his dark eyes challenging mine.

"Coupla questions."

"Like what?" He collected his plate, pushed his tray to the end of the counter where pay-as-you-go cafeterias would have had a cashier, then moved toward the condiment table. When I didn't follow, he turned and questioned me with his eyebrows.

"Like what?" he repeated loud enough to penetrate the din while he pumped ketchup onto his hamburger from a gallon jug. Kids flowed around us like water diverted by rocks.

"Why so protective all of a sudden?" I asked back. "I thought you didn't like her."

He shrugged while a girl nudged him away from the ketchup. "She's family. My grandfather wouldn't want her hassled." *My grandfather,* not Gramps or Pop or any of the other more familiar—and less respectful—names kids were inclined to use. I thought again of the Sicilian hierarchy you saw so often in movies.

"What makes you think I'm going to hassle her?"

Another shrug. "Aren't you?"

"No."

"What then?"

Most of the kids had found seats and were already devouring food. The relative silence allowed me to speak in normal tones. "Now that I think of it, my questions are private. But I can say they don't have anything to do with you."

"Aw, what do I care?" He finally knuckled under. "She's at All Things Bright and Beautiful."

"That accessory shop in the mall? How do you know that?"

"Because she co-owns it. She's there almost every morning."

"When does she leave?"

Nicky glanced over my head at a clock. "About one."

So that was how I got my indigestion, washing down cafeteria food with chocolate milk driving to the mall like a trucker on amphetamines. Time was running out for me, and not just because I might not catch Tina Longmeier at her shop. Randy's Grand Jury hearing was tomorrow afternoon.

All Things Bright and Beautiful stood between a shoe store and Pants Plus on the second floor of the original section of the King of Prussia mall—the everyday "Plaza," not the up-scale, and in my opinion, overpriced "Court."

After parking, I sprinted inside and upstairs then down the lengthy hallway to the right section. Then I caught my breath before venturing between tall, rotating racks of earrings to look for Tina.

The shop had been decked out for Christmas with gaudy sequins and rhinestones and faux pearls available to punctuate any outfit imaginable, assuming you were intent upon glowing in the dark. Behind the counter a slender woman dressed in seasonal red and white wore ten, count them, ten, items of jewelry including earrings, necklaces, bangles, and rings.

"Gee, if we wrapped up what you're wearing I'd be done shopping," I said.

She took that as a compliment, as any good entrepreneur would despite whatever I might have meant. "Are you Tina's partner?" I asked.

"Why, yes."

"Is she here?"

"Just missed her."

"Damn," I said fervently. "Where does she usually park, do you know?"

The woman was no longer flattered by my conversation. She said, "It's the King of Prussia mall. In December. Where did you park?"

Good point. Tina could be slipping behind the wheel of whatever she drove and heading for any of about eight exit areas with access to four major roads (three expressways and a turnpike) or several smaller roads that offered egress from this Mecca of free enterprize. No wonder car thieves from the city used to arrive by the busload—until the cops got smart and started meeting the buses.

"Listen," I said, putting on my most contrite, near-to-groveling-as-I-get demeanor. "I'm sorry I teased you about the jewelry. I get that way when I'm stressed out, and right now I've really got to talk to Tina about, about somebody who's in jail, maybe because of her. So tell me, do you have any idea where she went?"

"Buy something."

"Excuse me?"

"Buy something while I think about it."

The word extortion came to mind, but so did a vivid picture of Annie Webb baking rolls every day until forever, because in Pennsylvania a life sentence means exactly what it sounds like it means. I grabbed a comb with a puffy green velvet bow edged in gold lame.

"Five bucks, plus tax." Tina's partner wore false eyelashes that made her blue eyes look fake, and her blonde hair was the exactly the type you never hoped to find clinging to one of your husband's sweaters.

I paid the woman and waited. With no discernible haste she packaged the bow with tissue and slipped it tenderly into a miniature shopping bag with All Things Bright and Beautiful written on it in gold. She carefully counted change into my waiting palm, then leaned her elbows on the counter and said, "She went grocery shopping."

My face fell, then brightened. "So afterwards she has to go home. Where's home?"

"You really think Tina put somebody in jail?"

"I can't say—yet." We shared a naughty smile.

"That's funny. That's really funny." Wisely, I pretended to share the joke, because Tina's partner immediately warmed up. She even drew me a map leading to the Longmeiers' house.

Unfortunately, the route was so circuitous that by the tenth turn I was wishing for a Ferrari or perhaps a helicopter. The Main Line roads probably weren't designed to keep outsiders out and insiders in, but sometimes they sure drive that way.

The Longmeier home was very California tan stucco with a red tile roof, the sort of house you expected to see among palm trees and eucalyptus, not winter-brown grass and empty maples. I parked at the end of the drive opposite the mailbox. While unsuccessfully trying to digest my lunch, I perked myself up for my chat with Tina by listening to Jimmy Buffett's "Songs You Know by Heart." When the tape rolled around to "Cheeseburger in Paradise," I turned it off. I would fake "perky" long enough to get in the door. After that, I planned to be just as irritable as I felt.

Michael D'Avanzo's daughter drove a Mercedes, that nice scrambled egg color I admire. She steered around my maroon Nissan into the drive and thirty yards further to park beside the house. Then she popped the trunk and started lifting brown grocery bags out of it.

"Tina! Hey, hi!" I called as I emerged from my car and started toward her. "Can I talk to you a minute?"

She stood there with bags in her arms, flummoxed by my approach.

"Gin Barnes. Remember me?"

She narrowed her dark eyes, tilted her head and inspected my long overcoat, black boots, fringed skirt, even the Indian print on what was showing of my blazer. "We've met?"

"Sort of. The copy room at Bryn Derwyn? I'm Rip Barnes's wife, Gin."

"Oh, yeah." Despite what she said, there was no recognition in her eyes. However, considering the circumstances of our previous encounter, that wasn't surprising.

She started to walk toward her kitchen door. I grabbed a couple grocery bags and followed.

"I need help deciding what to tell the police."

She stopped walking for a beat, then proceeded.

"About you and Randy Webb."

"I've got nothing to say." She unlocked her door and slipped inside. For a second I thought she was going to kick the door shut on me, but her arms were full and the motion would have been too awkward.

I hipped my way in beside her and set the bags I was carrying on the center island, which happened to be done in a nice white ceramic tile to match the airy white kitchen. A wide, floor to ceiling window beside a white table and chairs set offered a view of the wooded back yard, but the greenest thing in sight was a potted, five-foot tall avocado tree in the corner.

Tina Longmeier crossed her arms and sighed. She wore a belted black coat that matched her long hair and high-heeled black boots. Her earrings were hammered gold hoops that I'd have bet the Mercedes she hadn't bought in her shop.

"Were you having an affair with him, too?" I asked.

"Too?" Tina said with a scowl.

The "too" had been a gamble and referred to no one in particular; but since Tina had picked up on it, I decided to take a greater chance.

"The police already know about you and Richard."

Tina whitened and went very still. She even reached out her professionally manicured hand to steady herself on the nearest white chair.

Maybe it was the indigestion or a perverse reaction to what Tina had just revealed, but I felt no compunction about invading her privacy. I even began to unload a grocery bag: package of homemade pasta made in a factory, Tree-Free Tissues made entirely of recycled paper. Revealing. Almost as informative as searching a drawer.

"You're sure they know?" Tina finally managed to ask.

"Positive." As soon as I told them. "So what about Randy? Were you having an affair with him, too? Is that why he killed Richard?"

Bright red blotches appeared on Tina's cheeks looking either like an overdose of rouge or a rash. She sat on the chair, put her fist up to her mouth and stared into the back yard where two crows squabbled nastily over an old apple from someone's garbage.

On the bottom of the grocery bag were a box of recycled plastic kitchen trash bags and a bottle of Tums containing calcium. "May I?" I asked. My stomach was so acidy I couldn't help thinking God himself had offered me relief.

I rattled the Tums to get Tina's attention. "Mind if I open this? I had cafeteria food for lunch."

Tina waved her hand in permission and I ingested two tablets in record time. They really do work fast.

"So," I continued. "My question is, do I tell the police about you and Randy, or not?"

Appearing to be in shock, Tina turned to watch me begin on the second bag: celery, a red pepper, cilantro, a thing that looked like an anemic carrot, and a bag of red potatoes. On the white counter they made a beautiful pile of produce, something a *Better Homes and Gardens* photographer might assemble to lend this stark room a focal point. Outside the crows departed noisily, one close behind the other.

"Randy and I . . . were . . . never an item," Eddie Longmeier's wife told me at last. "Whatever you heard simply isn't true."

"Saw, not heard."

She blinked. "I beg your pardon."

"I saw you and Randy in the copier room at school. You looked like you'd just been in a clinch."

"Oh."

"What was that all about?"

Tina untied the sash of her coat and shrugged it off onto the back of the chair. Underneath she was wearing a black turtleneck and a long, narrow skirt, also black. Black was in fashion this year, but the absence of further jewelry suggested that she was discreetly in mourning.

For Richard Wharton, her murdered lover. Now that Tina had confirmed my suspicion, all sorts of possibilities stepped forward.

"Randy. Copy room. When did you say this happened?"

"Early fall. September."

Tina stood and rubbed her arms. Some of her confidence had returned and with it the sensual body language that went so well with her provocative clothes. Although to be fair, over her figure most men would consider overalls inviting.

Her face suddenly brightened. "Now I remember. Randy, well, he somehow found out about Richard, and

I was, you know, trying to keep him from, from telling Eddie."

"I see." She had been bribing Randy with implied sex to keep her husband from finding out about Richard.

"You ever have to deliver?" I asked.

Her mouth dropped open. "No. No, of course not."

"Randy just dropped the whole thing?" I said skeptically. "You sure?"

The red blotches returned with a vengeance. "Eddie never said anything." Yet I could tell she was no longer certain her husband didn't know about Richard. She sank back onto the chair, this time staring at the wall next to the door. I imagined that she was seeing visions of her husband bashing her lover with a shovel—she looked that ill.

"So Randy really had no motive to kill Richard, as far as you were concerned."

"No." Her voice was distant, weak.

"Great. That's great. So you'll tell that to the police?"

"No!" That answer was loud enough to back me up a step. "Eddie . . ."

"Would find out for sure?"

"Yes." Weak again.

"Come on, Tina. Eddie told me himself you and he don't care about each other anymore. What's the big deal? The police have Randy in jail, and he doesn't belong there."

"Maybe he does."

"Maybe he doesn't."

The blotches threatened to turn into hives. Tina's long fingers opened and clenched, opened and clenched. It was time for me to show myself out.

Before putting my car in gear, I took a minute to contemplate Tina Longmeier's kitchen.

I'd done it again, the same thing I've caught myself

doing before. When I was watching the crows, they were all I saw; they might as well have been on big-screen TV. When I was focused on something inside the kitchen, my field of vision included the avocado tree but ended abruptly at the window glass. Ever since I noticed this habit, I've been trying to break it, trying to appreciate the outside view in the context of the inside decor and vice versa.

In Tina Longmeier's emotionally charged kitchen, once again I had failed to take in the picture as a whole. It was an error I could not afford to repeat.

Chapter 30

My nervous bravado expired before I got back to Bryn Derwyn, leaving me with a feeling of desperate urgency bordering on depression.

By the time I burst through the front door of the school into the lobby, I was angry—angry that I felt so helpless, angry that even though Randy and Tina had not been lovers it didn't mean he hadn't killed Richard, angry that the more I learned the more I needed to know.

So what if classes were still in session. I needed information—right now.

"Where's Jacob?" I barked at Ruth.

"I'll beep him," she replied, scarcely raising a brown, professional eyebrow at my abrupt demand.

"Be right back," I replied.

I burst into Joanne's office. She stood behind her desk speaking on the phone, so I used some extra volume. "Could Longmeier's Mercedes have been parked here last Friday afternoon?"

At my interruption she had taken the phone away from her ear. Now she told the caller, "I'll get right back to you. Something's come up."

To me she said, "What's . . . ?"

"Just answer me, please. Did you see the Longmeier's Mercedes in the parking lot last Friday afternoon?"

The older woman shifted on her feet, rested her fingers on the desk top and pressed her lips together.

"I really can't say . . . I was working, you know, but if I had to guess I'd say no."

"What makes you think that?"

Her eyes flicked on and off me like a bird perched too close to the cat. "I had the feeling they were ordinary cars," she said. "Ones we always see. Not strangers. Lt. Newkirk asked me this—"

"I know, and I'm sorry to ask you again, but I'm very worried, and this is important." To my surprise, my eyes filled with tears, and my words hit some obstruction in my throat. Phase Three: utter frustration.

Joanne's lips pressed together like a stern grandmother's. Her eyes softened toward me then tightened in concentration.

Because I was blowing my nose on a tissue from the box on her desk, I almost didn't hear the next thing she said. "Mr. Longmeier's station wagon might have been there."

"What did you say?"

"I said Mr. Longmeier's station wagon could have been here and I wouldn't have given it a second glance. He's always around talking to Kevin. If it was here Friday . . ."

"Yes!"

Joanne jumped from the force of my exclamation. "Yes, it was here. I saw it myself. Oh, Hank, you're wonderful." I grabbed her shoulders and kissed her soundly on the cheek.

"You're sure Eddie was here?" her words challenged me, but her face glowed with reflected joy. "You're sure I didn't put the idea in your head?"

"Of course you put it in my head. I mean you reminded me. I saw it myself and there was something odd about it, too." But that particular memory refused to surface without assistance. If I thought it would help, I would beg the first hypnotist in the phone book to put me under.

"Thanks, Hank. I've got to go."

I waited expectantly at Ruth the Receptionist's lobby altar, too het up to speak.

"Jacob is in the gym," the young woman announced without wasting one second or one word.

"Thanks, Ruth, I'll remember you at Christmas." I'd do better than that; I'd recommend her for a raise.

Eddie Longmeier's station wagon had been here. I could almost picture which parking slot it had been in, two or three from the far end facing the school, near my yard, almost directly in front of the hall which housed the business office, development office, and Community Room. The question now was why hadn't anyone actually seen Eddie Longmeier?

Jacob was up a twelve-foot stepladder doing something to a basketball net. He seemed annoyed that his fingers were not functioning up to his expectations.

When I called him, he initially transferred his annoyance to me. "What! Oh, Gin. I thought you were one of the kids, you know, to tell me something else broke. What can I do for you?" He climbed down as he spoke and now stood before me smiling and fully cooperative.

"Important question." I paused to let that sink in. "What time did you chain-bolt the exit near our house last Friday?"

The maintenance supervisor's head jerked slightly as he realized to what time period I referred. He rubbed his chin whiskers thoughtfully and rocked on his heels.

"The police should have asked that, eh?"

I nodded, agreeing completely. Although the police

probably had not known the school routine well enough to ask.

"Lemme see. I drove the wrestling team to Friends Central and back." He shook his head, no doubt calculating how much the early weekend traffic had held him up on the Schulykill Expressway. "Late. Maybe twenty after four."

Probably after the murder and just before I discovered the body. "You see anyone in the hall? Anyone at all?"

The man shook his bald, dark-fringed head. "Nobody. Not even Randy or Kevin, which surprised me a little. But hey, it was Friday . . ." He watched to see if I reacted to that, but I didn't. To my mind, at least until proven otherwise, Randy had gotten a nosebleed and decided to go home early. Kevin, according to his account, had slipped out of his office to deliver some new easy-readers to Patrice's locker, and maybe stopped to take care of some business in other parts of the school while he was out.

"Did you see Eddie Longmeier around that afternoon?"

"Umm, no."

"His car?"

"No. Sorry."

I thanked the busy man and trudged back toward the lobby.

Why might Eddie Longmeier have been here? To see Kevin regarding plans for the new gym?

Kevin glanced up from the piles of papers on his desk like a bear peering into sunlight from the depths of his cave.

"Did Eddie Longmeier come to see you last Friday afternoon?"

"No. Why?"

I didn't feel like giving him a premature explanation

of my thoughts, so I fibbed and said Joanne thought she saw Longmeier's station wagon instead of me. "I just wondered who he could have been here to see."

Kevin shrugged. "Not me."

Wearing yet another interesting sweater, this time a heather blue, he reminded me of a college student who had crammed all night for an exam. "Get some rest," seemed to be the right line to deliver with my exit.

"I wish." So he was sleeping poorly. I wondered if we had the same reason.

Back in the lobby I slumped into a stuffed chair, rested my head on the cushion, closed my eyes. Ruth was kind enough to ignore me.

In that slouched down, exhausted position I began to recreate Friday afternoon in my memory, detail by detail, inch by inch. I arrived and spoke with Joanne, greeted Emily, proceeded to the Community Room, unloaded some shelves. I decided I needed a Dustbuster and went to get one from Patrice, who suggested using the one from the Faculty Room. Again, I had the feeling there was something I wanted to remember about the Dustbuster, but again, as when Newkirk and I had collected them last night, the detail eluded me.

I replayed myself in the Faculty Room, slow motion this time. Patrice sent me there, told me the slob-teachers would never miss their Dustbuster, or something to that effect. I understood her sentiment, more or less agreed. Then I took the little gray vacuum out of its rack on the wall and did what I do to my own, which was wipe off the dog hairs static electricity always adhered to the nozzle. Except in this case, I remember the nozzle had been covered with blue carpet fuzz and dust, and after I wiped it off a row of scratches along the top of the case remained. I remember thinking that one of Patrice's careless teachers must have jammed it under a cabinet or low sofa or chair.

My eyes popped open. The lobby had filled with several students waiting for rides or passing through on their way to Thursday afternoon's extracurricular activities.

Didi breezed in the front door, swooped toward me ready with a hug, and stopped five feet short of where I now stood.

"What's wrong?" she asked.

I didn't turn my head an inch. "Wait," I said. I pushed out my hand to keep her at bay, but Didi had already frozen. I swear she even held her breath, she read me that well.

Friday afternoon fast forward. I returned to the Community Room. Kevin was gone. Randy asked me to come back. I meant to give him the Dustbuster, but he shut the door before I could pass it inside. So I put it on the floor, went to hear the kids sing. Rip and Nora had their disagreement. Nora quit. Rip asked me to ask Didi to help.

Now I could glance at my best friend, acknowledge her presence. She stared back at me with her whole being. I shrugged out of my overcoat and handed it to her. Then I did the same with my blazer. It was going to be cold as hell outside, but that was what I wanted. I wanted everything the same—needed everything the same.

Didi accepted the coats in silence. I could feel her eyes on my back as I went out the door.

Just as I hoped, the outdoor chill propelled me into the past, to last week when I jogged through the cold Valley Forge winter to go home for Didi's phone number.

Without any curbing to protect the grass strip in front of the school's right front parking lot, cars often parked so far forward there was precious little sidewalk left between them and some low spreading dogwood trees.

That was why, when school was in session, I usually walked home down the middle of the drive, crossing a few feet of grass to pick up the brick path to our house.

Today as I passed the rear bumpers of cars, I compared what I saw with my memory of Friday afternoon. Yes, a teacher's red van was in the same spot to my right. No, there was nothing in this slot to my left. In fact two spots had been empty, but two full before I came to Eddie Longmeier's muddy blue Subaru station wagon.

I crept up to the car in the station wagon's former spot on my toes, hugging myself from the cold, probably shivering, but scarcely aware. I was seeing the Suburu from behind, straining to see it as clearly as I now envisioned the scratches on the Dustbuster, the scratches that had been absent from the ones Newkirk packed so carefully into his evidence box.

In my mind I saw a cover, a sort of gray window shade that matched the Suburu's interior, employed to keep prying eyes off the owner's cargo. That was the oddity, the cover. Eddie Longmeier used his station wagon for business. He carried paint and nails and trowels and rope and, yes, shovels and rakes and garden hoses back there. I had seen his car parked in roughly the same area dozens of times in the six months since we moved to the school, and on no other occasion had I seen his cargo covered.

While I stood staring into my memory, cars pulled into the front circle, children climbed inside, and the cars drove away. The teacher who owned the red van came out, shouted, "Hi, Gin," started the van, and also departed.

My shivering developed into huge shuddering spasms, and still I stared at the trunk of the navy blue BMW that was parked where I was now certain the station wagon had been.

Soon, a woman and her teenaged son, who was whining about going to the orthodontist, approached the BMW. The boy ignored me, walked around, and got into the passenger's seat. The woman watched me askance until she stood by her door, finally concluding that she would have to speak.

"Excuse me, miss," she said. "But we have to go."

I lifted my head to look at her.

"We have to leave?" she both explained and asked.

I registered what she meant, even intended to get out of her way, but then it came and I was so surprised that I shouted, "Yes!" and slapped my hands on her trunk.

"Hey!" the woman yelled. "Stop that. And will you please get out of the way?"

"Yes, yes. That's it," I said, punching the air and scurrying back toward Didi and my coat.

Cavorting giddily, waving my arms in the air, I probably looked totally out of my mind; but who cared?

If I was right about why—I also knew who.

Chapter 31

Didi had run off to rehearsal; but since she stalks a story like a lioness hunts meat, I knew she'd show up later.

Avoiding an inquisition would be difficult, but it had to be done. If I successfully discovered which Longmeier was a murderer, I might never want to admit my role in the arrest. That made discussing my intentions now, even with Didi, unwise if not downright dangerous.

I bundled up in my blazer and overcoat and went home, grateful that Chelsea and Garry would be occupied helping Didi with her music program for at least another hour. Lying over the phone in front of them was out of the question; I didn't even relish doing it in front of the dog. That problem, at least, was easily solved: I opened the door, and Barney cheerfully went out for a romp.

Because of location, the first two Mercedes dealers I phoned should have been negatives, and they were. That left the one most accessible from the Longmeiers' home. Before getting somebody from their service department on the line, I thought through my spiel carefully and steadied my breathing.

"Hi, I'm Tina Longmeier," I said with a rough approximation of her voice, "and, and I feel so silly, but could you possibly help me with a problem?"

Tired and bored, the serviceman on the other end asked me to describe the problem.

"I need to know the amount of a check I wrote you a few days ago. I know it's silly of me not to have written it down, my husband hates it when I forget, but would you mind . . . ?"

He transferred me to their cashier, a woman.

"I'm really very busy," she complained. "Can't you just phone your bank?"

"Not really. The check probably hasn't cleared yet, and anyway, I need to know my balance right now."

I apologized some more, and with a heavy sigh the woman asked, "What day did you write the check?"

"We dropped the car off last Friday." Actually that was the question I wanted answered, the information the spiel was designed to elicit.

"Was the car ready that night?"

"I don't think so." Would a person who committed murder remember to pick up a car? "How about Saturday?" I suggested.

"Not here."

"Monday?" I offered hopefully.

"No, nothing."

"Tuesday?"

"Listen, I've got to go. Why don't you just wait and call your bank?"

I hung up with a scowl. Then I curled up in an armchair and wrapped my coat around my knees. My stint in the school parking lot had chilled me, but not nearly as much as my conclusions about Richard's death.

Barney batted the door, and I let him back in. Outside twilight had begun, so I turned on the Christmas tree knowing that down by the road its twinkling white lights would show more and more clearly through the floor to ceiling window. A visual smile for the Thursday afternoon traffic, a calming touch of family memories for me. I sat on the floor and leaned back against the living room sofa facing the tree.

"Hug?" I asked the dog, inviting him to curl up next to my legs by patting the carpet.

He complied. His golden brown eyes gazed at me fondly then slowly closed as I stroked his silky red coat. Following his example, I scooched a little closer to the floor.

Could I prove my murder theory? No.

Did I have to?

Good question. I squinted my eyes and gave it some thought.

Maybe not. Not if I didn't go through Newkirk.

The cool fur on Barney's right ear slid through my fingers. He twitched the ear back into place, swallowed, and sighed.

Okay, so if I didn't tell Newkirk, how could I do this? How could I remain completely anonymous and still precipitate an arrest before tomorrow—before the Grand Jury could indict Randy Webb and, by association, Bryn Derwyn Academy?

I read somewhere about a half awake/half asleep state of mind called "alpha." In this very specific mind set, this particular place in our head, we did our clearest, most creative thinking. A famous inventor—Edison, if I remembered correctly—had a comfortable chair he used just to relax his mind. He balanced tin pans or something on his arms; so if he fell asleep, they would crash to the floor and wake him.

My decision set off no bells or clattering pans or even light bulbs. Rather I felt sad to the bottom of my soul. If maturity means doing what you believe you must, I was about to put on a couple of decades.

Yet if I brought it off, my plan would cause the right thing to happen. Only one man would know. He might hate me, but he would not expose me.

And if I was mistaken? The same man would consider me a fool, but privately; and my ego could accept that.

I extricated the edge of my skirt from under Barney's head, wrote a note about my whereabouts and what I had planned for dinner, then fished my car keys out of my purse.

Thomas Edison probably didn't own an Irish setter, and I'm certainly no genius.

We work with what we have.

❈ *Chapter 32* ❈

This time I phoned Michael D'Avanzo's home, because now I needed to find him. He was at La Firenze, no doubt surprising his chef with a rare weeknight visit.

Discreet lights well back on the sloping lawn set up the white-columned restaurant like some suburban Philadelphian Parthenon. Although it was just past five on a Thursday night, the parking lot was respectably filled with various luxury cars. Inside, a glance into the bar revealed a mixture of business types, both male and female, there to network to the full extent of their expense accounts or their abilities, whichever came first. My summer luncheon in the private room with Richard Wharton's hand on my leg seemed to have occurred at a different place—in a different lifetime.

Tonight a dark, clean-shaven maitre d' in a tuxedo snapped to attention behind his podium. Beneath my feet the same mosaic warrior poised for battle. Probably because I was feeling vulnerable, I had the uncomfortable sensation he was looking up my skirt.

"Madam?" the maitre d' pronounced with an excellent smile.

I smiled back. "I'm not here for dinner. I just need to

speak to Michael D'Avanzo for a minute." If a soft approach didn't get the desired result, I could always become more insistent.

The man signaled a waiter to watch his post, then on superbly polished shoes disappeared down the hall behind him to my right.

A second man emerged from around the corner, his eyebrows raised in anticipation of my approach.

"I understand you wish to speak to Mr. D'Avanzo?"

"Yes," I agreed.

"Regarding?" the man inquired.

"It's a personal matter. My name is Ginger Struve Barnes."

The man's face began to arrange itself into the proverbial stone wall, so I hastily suggested, "Why don't you just tell Mr. D'Avanzo Gin Barnes is here to speak with him and let him decide whether he can spare me a minute?"

Barrier #2 did not appreciate my suggestion. He conveyed this by stiffening his shoulders, looking down his nose and sniffing; yet he did turn on his heel and step back around the corner.

A moment later Michael D'Avanzo burst into view, his palms spread in welcome, his voice booming hello. He was wearing that delicious lime fragrance again.

"You must forgive Mario his concern for my time, Mrs. Barnes . . ."

"Gin," I corrected him.

"Gin," he agreed. "My employees sometimes like to forget they are not my real family," then he lowered his voice a bit to add, "not that I blame them for their loyalty—I pay them well enough for it, eh? Come, come. A glass of wine perhaps?"

"No. No thank you . . . Michael." I glanced around at the employees deliberately looking away while their ears strained to catch my every word. "Is there somewhere . . . ?"

"Of course. But you're sure a little Bordeaux would not be welcome at the end of a hard day?" Like a suitor mentioning an intimacy, D'Avanzo referred to my sampling of his wine last night after driving Nicky home, an astonishingly scant twenty-four hours ago.

"Do you have an office?" I asked, ignoring the proffered hospitality.

"Yes, but to escort a beautiful young woman, alone, into my very personal space . . . I'm sure Mario would not approve, nor I suspect would your Rip? We shall go this way." He guided me in a firm but polite fashion through a large archway and to the far right of the largest dining area, a long room that spanned the back of the building. Off-white, oval-backed chairs padded with deep rose surrounded both large and small round tables. Brocade swags softened the edges of three walls of picture windows.

The overabundance of glass made the room feel a bit drafty, so I did not remove my coat. Although my chilliness could just as easily have been stage fright.

Michael D'Avanzo leaned his elbows on the table and stroked his hands arthritically. Although no one dined within fifteen yards of us, if we spoke above a murmur we would be heard nevertheless.

"A beverage, my dear Gin?" he asked. "For appearances?" So he had correctly discerned that my topic would be unpleasant and had deliberately maneuvered me into this controlled arena.

I nodded reluctantly. Only a wave was necessary to place the order, which came in the form of a dusty bottle of merlot. We waited while the wine steward went through his routine. D'Avanzo then grunted his approval, the steward poured generously, and D'Avanzo settled back in his seat. He wore a café au lait suit with

cream accessories that complemented his coloring, although I thought the graying black hair and moustache
too startling a contrast for the brown.

He opened his lips, no doubt to say something gra-
cious and intimidating, so I spoke first.

I said, "I think your son-in-law killed Richard Wharton."

D'Avanzo's coloring no longer complemented his
suit. Rather, his face bloomed like a tulip and his tie
seemed to be choking him. Abruptly, he stood, lifted my
elbow with an even firmer grip than before and marched
me through a smaller arch, down a short hall, around a
corner, and into a roomful of walnut and red leather,
clearly the much-protected private office. He slammed
the door with his foot.

After releasing my arm, the restaurant owner strode
past his desk until he faced a painting of Venice, possibly depicting the Bridge of Sighs.

"What do you mean by this, this accusation?" he
asked.

"Just what I said."

Eyes closed, head back, his right hand jumped off the
credenza beneath it like a pianist's playing chords in
staccato. To address me he spoke over his right shoulder.

"You have proof of this?"

"Yes and no."

He whirled to confront me. I had remained just inside
the door, my coat drooping on my shoulders, my purse
dangling from my fist to the floor. D'Avanzo had responded as to a threat but now seemed to realize I was
almost as sorry to be there as he was sorry I came.

He ran a thick, laborer's hand through his perfectly
groomed hair, and instantly became an older father,
more vulnerable to failed hope and excessive pride than

to the bottom line of a spreadsheet or dishwashers who refused to come to work.

"My poor, poor Tina," he said. This was the part I feared most, the powerful need to protect his daughter. My maternal instincts have yet to be driven to their limits, yet I knew those limits far exceeded anything I would do for anyone else, save Rip, my mother, and previously my father.

"Sit, sit, and talk to me," D'Avanzo instructed, obviously resigning himself to hear my worst.

I threw my purse on an overstuffed red leather chair and rested against its cushiony arm. Behind the desk D'Avanzo slumped noisily into a swivel chair on rollers. Light from one brass floor lamp and one red table lamp carved deep shadows into his forehead and cheeks causing him to age by several years. I probably looked just as bad. It's one thing knowing that you have to deliver devastating news, and another matter entirely when you are in the recipient's office, smelling his cologne, listening to him breathe.

Michael D'Avanzo was what my mother always called "a presence," meaning he was one of those individuals who filled a room of any size. He was so vital, so confident, so commanding that everyone else seemed insignificant in comparison. Politicians ascended to the presidency with "presence" and a good speechwriter. Actors and athletes pulled in fortunes with presence and a good set of teeth. And probably Mafia dons intimidated their peers with a combination of presence and a reliable semiautomatic weapon.

My mother was too oblivious to be prejudiced, my father too liberal. Appreciating individuality was my Sunday school lesson, the ABC's of being a Struve. Yet I knew the difference between walking down a center city alleyway during rush hour with hundreds of commuters and walking alone down that alley any other time. The

displaced person in the back doorway of the burger joint
might be harmless to a crowd, not necessarily so to a
lone woman in high heels.

Yet fear is not always so rational. I'm also afraid of
the snakes in the zoo. Not as frightened as I would be of
one slithering toward my feet; but the fear is nevertheless real, and I am not entirely able to control it.

So there in Michael D'Avanzo's office, having already
upset him with intentions of possilby infuriating him, it
did not especially help for reason to remind me that few
Italians are criminals. Just as with other groups of any
description, I also realized that some were.

Let's face it, in the Philadelphia of my youth news of
Mob slayings occasionally eclipsed the sports coverage,
so a man named D'Avanzo possessing both presence
and a painting of Venice naturally might fuel my child-
ish imagination. Although I personally knew the man
only as a flirt who wore tasteful clothes, enjoyed vintage
wine, and adored his grandson, my mind insisted on
waving a file card in front of my eyes—a card that read
"Very *connected* . . . pending clarification." Common
sense told me to choose my words carefully.

"First I have to tell you something about Tina," I
began. With luck, if he took this part well, the second
part would go better.

"Go on."

I squirmed with reluctance. I wished myself home
with my family. If it meant never coming across Richard
Wharton's body, I wished us all back in Ludwig before
Rip even applied for the Bryn Derwyn job.

"Your daughter doesn't really care for her husband
anymore."

D'Avanzo fell silent. He did not move. I could
scarcely see him breathe.

"Go on."

"I guess she felt neglected," a fabricated excuse, but

so common that Tina herself probably even believed it. "She's been afraid to tell you."

"Afraid . . ." His face sagged.

"I don't think they think they can afford to divorce."

D'Avanzo wagged his head in disgust and said something sharp in Italian. "She told this to you and not to me? Why?"

I shrugged.

D'Avanzo shot forward. "I'll tell you why. Because they are greedy, both of them. They know they would have to stop spending money they don't have. They know I would no longer send business toward that pathetic company of his. Pah, on the both of them. Now tell me the rest." D'Avanzo was standing now, pacing.

"For several months your daughter had been interested in someone else." I watched D'Avanzo's eyes. He stood with his thumbs in his pants pockets and his chin lowered glaring at me with those eyes, the patriarch deceived and therefore scorned. I watched those eyes very carefully.

"She'd been interested in Richard Wharton."

"How do you know this?"

Rather than admit I tricked Tina into implicating herself, I told her father I saw her in the copy room with Richard instead of Randy.

D'Avanzo grunted. Whatever emotions he was experiencing were invisible to me. "So you think Edwin found out and killed this man? Is that what you're saying? Eh?"

"Yes. His car was parked in the school lot at the time of the murder, but he didn't have an appointment with anyone and no one actually saw him. I think he used a back door to get in and out. He must have phoned Wharton's office to find out where he was."

"And you say you do or do not have proof of this?"

Although it was extremely important from my standpoint for D'Avanzo to shift any lingering loyalty toward Eddie wholly onto his daughter, he was accomplishing the adjustment so easily I had to wonder whether he ever liked his son-in-law. Instinct again, and my cue to capitalize on it. Follow his stoic example. Conceal my quivering knees.

"I know where to get proof. That's why I'm here. I need your help."

"My help!"

"Yes."

D'Avanzo actually laughed. "Okay, Shirley Jones, tell me about this so-called proof." Did he mean Sherlock Holmes? Was he patronizing me, trivializing the situation? Annoyance began to buoy my waning bravado.

I folded my arms across my chest and explained how the murderer had used a hand-held vacuum to clear the area of evidence. "The Dustbuster I left outside the Community Room door had scratches on the top; but when I helped the police collect all of the ones at school, the one with the scratches was missing. I think your son-in-law used the school's, took it home and replaced it—either with one he and Tina already owned or a new one. I'm hoping the one with the incriminating debris is still at their house."

"This vacuum, the one from the school—you think he went back later to replace it? You believe him that brave, or that foolish?"

"Not necessarily either. He's frequently at the school. That's why nobody remembered his car right away. And if none of our Dustbusters was missing, nobody would necessarily figure out what he did."

"Why haven't you taken this theory of yours to the police?"

"Because I want my name kept out of it," I told him adamantly.

Then I went a little coy, started playing with the edge

of my coat. "Because even if the police believed me, the Dustbuster might not be there; and even if it's there, it may not provide proof enough to convict Eddie Longmeier . . ."

I stuffed my fists into my overcoat pockets, ". . . and because I need Eddie to confess by tomorrow."

D'Avanzo strolled back and forth with occasional glances in my direction.

"I assume you would like to see justice done," I said.

"Ah, yes. Yes. It doesn't do to have murderers running around free. No, no. I'm thinking you could be right about Eddie. Oh yes. You could be right. But you could also be wrong."

"Another reason why I'm here instead of at the police."

"Explain."

"I'd like you to tell Eddie that you know he knew about Tina and Richard, that you know his car was at the school and you know where proof of his guilt can be obtained. Tell him it would be best for Tina and Nicky if he confessed immediately."

From my listener's expression I could see he understood how a confession would minimize talk about Tina's infidelity by focusing on Eddie's far more despicable act. Probably the part about Nicky needed more explanation.

"Why immediately?" he asked.

"You say you're grateful for what Bryn Derwyn has done for Nicky. So grateful that you plan to donate half a gym so both Nicky and Bryn Derwyn will benefit.

"If Randy Webb is indicted at the Grand Jury hearing tomorrow, there may not be any more Bryn Derwyn for Nicky to attend. He may have to go somewhere much less perfect for him." In other words, much less tolerant of his learning style, his behavior, his ego. That at least needed no elaboration.

"A bit extreme, wouldn't you say?" Despite D'Avanzo's outward calm, I could sense a shift in the atmosphere, an ominous movement beneath the surface. My hand reached back to the chair arm to steady me before I answered.

"Overly cautious maybe," I agreed reasonably, "but not unrealistic. Doesn't your restaurant go to great lengths to keep the public's trust?"

"Yes, but I don't see . . ."

"If one person died of food poisoning because of something one of your employees did, what would happen to your business? Could you wait for it to recover? Would it *ever* recover? Even if you fired the employee and scoured the entire building with Clorox, would the public ever forget?"

D'Avanzo appeared to consider that.

I proceeded with my closing argument: "Randy Webb isn't squeaky clean. Rip is checking him out; but if whatever he's been up to gets exposed to the public, even if he didn't murder Richard, Bryn Derwyn loses face. Randy Webb just plain has to step out of the spotlight before it's too late."

While his thoughts temporarily escaped the confines of the room, any semblance of the man who greeted me so warmly disappeared. D'Avanzo's face became a rigid mask, his eyes unforgiving, his whole body a tangible physical force.

The revelation lasted only two or three seconds, so short a time that in the upcoming days I would once or twice convince myself that it had not occurred at all. But, of course, it did.

During that one unguarded moment the restaurateur revealed himself to be the most menacing human being I had yet encountered. The revelation both terrified me and forced me to reassess the magnitude of what I had started.

When I set out, my goal had been to initiate actions that would save Randy Webb and, coincidentally, Bryn Derwyn Academy. My plan depended on Michael D'Avanzo responding predictably.

My trust had been recklessly naive, a realization that made me almost physically ill. Armed with my information, D'Avanzo was fully capable of executing an agenda of his own, one that might in no way resemble my own.

Something would happen tonight.

I just hoped to high heaven it would be what I intended.

Chapter 33

*F*ear is powerful. Fear puts you in your place.

I drove home with my eyes narrowed against the glare of oncoming cars, my fist buried into my painful stomach. While I kept watch for places to pull over in a hurry, just in case, my mind busied itself with Michael D'Avanzo.

Why had he frightened me so? His self-control had been exemplary. If I hadn't caught that one glimpse of chilling calm, I would never have guessed the magnitude of his anger. Indeed, at one point I remembered thinking he had distanced himself from his son-in-law with unusual ease.

My stomach lurched. I pulled over.

When I got back into the car, driving the rest of the way home safely pushed all other thoughts aside. I would have all night to dissect my impressions of Michael D'Avanzo, to second guess myself—to be sick with worry.

"Flu bug," I told Didi and the children as I staggered into the house. "No dinner. Bed." Thus I hoped to avoid answering any probing questions.

Didi cocked her head and perused my condition with a wrinkled forehead, then grabbed my sleeve and ushered me up to my room. There she wiped my face with a cool washcloth and turned out the light. Downstairs I heard dishes clink and water run as she cooked for my family and later cleaned up.

My nervous stomach tormented me for a few hours more, until I was too exhausted to remain awake.

Then Rip came to bed and my eyes snapped open. Where I was and why, where I had been and why crowded my consciousness like air to a vacuum. I would be awake for the duration.

Rip noticed my opened eyes and came over to brush my hair away from my forehead, kiss me and tell me he hoped I'd feel better in the morning. As always, he slept like a rock.

His breathing usually comforted me during wakeful periods, but not tonight. I kept thinking of what I'd told Michael D'Avanzo—and what I had deliberately left out.

In the morning I rested until everyone else had gone. Then I showered and dressed in presentable slacks and a sweater, lingered over tea and toast with the newspaper, which, for once, carried nothing about Bryn Derwyn's troubles. Finally, unable to stand my own company any longer, I climbed into my coat and walked over to school.

Joanne's eyebrows rose. "Thought you were sick."

"All better," I announced with as much energy as I could muster. "Came over to help. Rip around?"

Joanne was too polite to voice her skepticism.

"In there," she said, referring to the mail room.

Rip gaped with surprise. "What are you doing here? I thought you were sick."

"Guess it was something I ate." Crow, perhaps. "I'm fine." Except for the dark circles under my eyes and the impending fidgets.

I explained that the business about Randy's Grand

Jury had me jumpy, and I needed to be around people. "Give me something useful to do—anything," I begged.

"You mean it? You sure you're all right?"

"Yes and yes."

"There are a few thank-you notes to donors that shouldn't wait. Normally, Randy would do them . . ."

"Anything to keep busy."

"Know what you mean, babe." He pulled a fistful of papers out of Randy's mailbox. "Receipt forms and thank-you cards will be somewhere in Randy's office. Just add a personal note at the bottom."

"I know, I know," I told Rip with a smile. I'd noticed the forms during my search. Despite the possibility of shocking a stray student, I kissed my husband right smack in the mail room.

Rip swept into Randy's office an hour later almost stopping my heart with anticipation. Whatever my visit to Michael D'Avanzo instigated had happened. My husband's elation could mean nothing else.

Rip grabbed my hands. "Newkirk just called," he told me. "Tina Longmeier confessed."

The release of tension left me limp. All night long I had obsessed about the hundred ways my strategy could go wrong, but it had actually worked!

"She's pleading temporary insanity—can you believe it?"

A man and his wife have one fight too many. The woman decides to take her lover's pillow talk literally and leaves her husband. The lover rejects her, perhaps even laughs in her face. She flips out, grabs the nearest weapon . . . Sure, I could believe it. I had believed it as soon as I realized what must have been under the Suburu's cargo cover.

"Wow, that's astonishing!" I exclaimed.

All along, the softball photo had lingered in my mind.

No matter that Tina's scowl had projected her distaste for the game; she had been on a team, and everyone on a team is taught how to bat. Just like riding a bike, Tina's muscles would remember the stance, the grip, how the hips held still while the torso turned smoothly for a nice solid connection.

Remembering the covered cargo in the back of Eddie's station wagon made sense out of everything else. To my knowledge Eddie never concealed any of his construction gear, most likely because it would have been of little interest to a thief. So something worth hiding had been stowed back there Friday afternoon.

I reasoned that if Tina was the driver, the cargo could have been suitcases, packed with the intention of leaving her husband. Yet as logical as that scenario seemed, it wasn't anything I could prove.

Although I wasn't thrilled about undertaking the risk, sending Michael D'Avanzo to accuse his son-in-law of murder was the only way I could imagine securing a confession. If Eddie Longmeier happened to be guilty, Michael D'Avanzo was perfectly capable of forcing the man to turn himself in.

However, I considered it much more likely for Eddie to throw Tina to the police. Despite my inconclusive call to the Mercedes dealer, the probability of her guilt seemed far, far greater. The nature of the murder implicated her.

For Eddie Longmeier to have killed Richard Wharton, the crime should have contained at least some element of premeditation. To my mind, the coincidence of catching Richard at school and grabbing the nearest weapon simply did not fit. Furthermore, it presumed that Eddie cared enough about his wife to want to eliminate his rival, and nothing he said or did suggested that. Eddie and Tina remaining married for financial reasons made much more sense to me, just as Richard's rejection of Tina made sense.

After the authorities became aware of her guilt, I trusted that they would be able to substantiate it—Eddie would confirm that she had driven the station wagon that day; if indeed there was a Dustbuster somewhere in their house, the police could confiscate it after Tina was safely in custody. I grabbed Rip's sleeves and practically danced. If those possibilities didn't pan out, surely there would be something else.

That morning the shock and titillation of Tina Longmeier's guilt spread through the school like viral spring fever, but after lunch everyone dealt with the surprise by acting as normally as possible. For Rip and me that meant questions and answers about my assigned thank-you notes, which were not as easy as they sounded.

Randy arrived about one-thirty to find us huddled over the work on his desk. He virtually beamed with self-congratulation.

"Hello, boys and girls," he bubbled. "Great to be back."

Rip offered his hand. "Rough deal," he told his Development Director with sincerity. "Glad you're finally free of it."

"Shouldn't you be home with Annie?" I asked. I couldn't bear the thought of him leaving her to come to work so soon after his release. If Rip had been jailed for even a second, our reunion honeymoon would probably last for months.

"Yeah, I guess. I just had to stop in. You know, because I can." Then he grinned even wider. "Work must have piled up. Miss the old boy, did you?"

Rip and I exchanged uncomfortable glances. The school had yet to suffer noticeably from Randy's absence.

"Excuse me, Gin," Rip said to my surprise. "I do have to get some work to show him." With that he departed, leaving Randy and me to stare at each other.

"Oooh. Mysterious," Randy joked.

I laughed to dispel the discomfort of Rip's abrupt exit. "So what got you off the hook?" I asked conversationally. Not that I expected him to know.

He happened to know plenty. "It's the damnedest thing. Husband gave the cops a blood-spattered skirt he found in the street. Said he found it when crows picked apart one of their trash bags, scattered food and junk all over the place. Dumb luck Tina didn't go out there first. Anyway, the guy had stashed the skirt away for a rainy day, if you know what I mean." Randy's leer seemed to suggest coercion of some male/female nature, which in Longmeier's case probably meant divorce negotiations. "Anyhow, the wife confessed before her lawyer showed up."

"Really?"

"Yup. Cursed Richard Wharton up and down. My attorney's source said she actually made Newkirk blush."

"No kidding." I would have enjoyed seeing that.

Then another thought occurred to me. "Will the confession hold up?" I wondered aloud.

"Who cares? She did it, and I'm out." The man couldn't resist a touchdown jig across the end of his desk. It was a bit callous, but quite forgivable.

Also, he was right, in a way. Now it was entirely up to the professionals—forensics technicians and attorneys —them and a jury of Tina's peers.

While waiting for Rip to return, I stood up and offered Randy his chair. He had imprinted himself on his work space, and he seemed to feel as proprietary about it as I soon hoped to feel toward our present house. So what if the Christmas tree had not yet worked its magic.

Something would. Eggnog and carols, presents, possibly Spring. Now that this shared nightmare was over, maybe the place would warm for me.

Rip re-entered the room and solemnly spread a sheet of letterhead in front of Randy. At the bottom of a typewritten message was a sentence in feathery blue ink.

"What's this?" he asked. A sudden sheen of sweat suddenly glossed his face. Resting on the desk, his hands involuntarily grabbed at nothing. He stuffed them hard into his pockets.

"It's your pink slip, Randy," Rip told him. "I think you know that."

"But . . . ?" said Randy. He appeared totally flummoxed, and after what he'd just been through, I was surprised that Rip was coming on so strong.

"As you can see, it's your letter to Agnes Borkowski," Rip elaborated, perhaps to force a response. I recognized the name of a Philadelphia woman known for her generosity, whom recent rumors mentioned as becoming slightly eccentric or possibly senile, depending on the source.

Randy's mouth opened, but no words came forth.

I leaned closer to read the letter over his shoulder. It was a solicitation pitch very similar to the many I had signed, except this one was typed on one of the sheets of "Bryn Derwyn, Inc." letterhead I found at Randy's house. Across the bottom the addressee had answered, "Sorry. Changed my mind due to recent events. Perhaps another time. AB" Apparently, Agnes was not so doddering as rumor had it. She had been astute enough to eschew the phoney return envelope, instead returning her note to the school's proper address. Score one for Agnes.

"Any more of these I should know about?" Rip inquired.

Randy tried to swallow, but his throat refused to work.

"Which euphemism would you like me to use, Randy? Moved on to greater challenges? Preferred not to return after your unpleasant incarceration? Family illness? Personal problems? All of the above?"

Randy nodded.

Rip and I left quietly, so Randy could clear out his desk in private.

"No second chance?" I asked, thinking of Annie and their boys.

Rip stopped walking and glared at me. "Would you prefer that I send him back to jail? Because if that stupid scheme of his had gone any further, that's where he was headed."

"Sorry. You're right. I was just feeling sorry for his wife. Their marriage is already shaky."

Rip jerked his head toward me. "Where on earth did you hear that?"

Flushing instantly, I muttered something vague about overhearing a conversation.

He peered at me in a curious way, and I memorized that expression, internalized it thoroughly so that in the future I would remember not to make such a mistake again. I even did a mental inventory of what I could and couldn't say about my activities throughout the past week.

At the time, I thought my inventory was complete.

Chapter 34

Tina's confession should have washed me clean with relief, but for some reason I still felt unsettled and vaguely worried. Aftershock maybe. Exhaustion, for sure. Perhaps if I just finished the notes Rip asked me to write I would feel better. So, running on willpower, I did just that.

Then, despite a combination stress/insomnia headache, I forced myself to grocery-shop and then to cook a whole meal—pork chops, spinach, baked potatoes, salad, rolls, and purchased brownies. Putting on a rather self-satisfied smirk, I congratulated myself for coping so gracefully with the day's events. However, when my family gathered around the dinner, I scarcely remembered having prepared it.

Just in time for dessert, Newkirk appeared at the door, a battle-weary hound wishing to be patted on his head. Working such peculiar hours (and I was sure he considered himself to be working) I wondered when he ever saw his wife and kids.

He accepted a brownie and coffee. Without removing his coat, he settled with them in a living room chair. By silent agreement, Rip and I left Garry and Chelsea at the table and followed his example.

Newkirk worked at some walnuts with his tongue and said, "Lucky turn of events, wouldn't you say?"

Rip and I merely listened.

"Thought it was your guy Webb for sure, but it just goes to show you . . ."

I rearranged myself into what I thought would look like a more relaxed position while internally bracing for exposure.

Then I decided this was one anxiety I might as well deal with head on. "Any idea why Longmeier finally came forward?" I asked.

"Well now, that's the interesting thing," Newkirk replied. "The way Longmeier figured it, a husband can't be forced to testify against his wife, so why bother turning her in? Except last night his father-in-law paid him this visit, the point of which was to accuse Longmeier of doing the murder." The investigator took another bite of brownie and washed it down.

"So . . . ?" I prompted.

"So the husband figures keeping quiet about the skirt is no longer in his best interest. Did you know he had her blood-spattered skirt? Well, not so much blood as . . ." He eyed the brownie in his right hand and the coffee in his left. "Never mind."

Newkirk shook his head and proceeded with his answer. "Anyway, Eddie wasn't about to take the rap for his wife, not for a second, especially since he found out she'd been fooling around with the victim. He figured it was time to turn her in."

"Why last night? Any idea?" My insides flip-flopped. I kept glancing from my husband to Newkirk, from Newkirk to my husband.

"Something about the Grand Jury thing today. Supposedly, D'Avanzo didn't want to see an innocent man railroaded."

"You buy that?" Rip asked.

"Sure. Some folks are decent, contrary to popular opinion. You got another brownie in there?" He jerked an elbow toward the dining room. I gave him the package to take home.

Before he left, he paused to deliver his intended message. "Sorry about all the, you know, trouble this caused. You've got a nice little school here. Hope it'll be okay."

"It is a nice little school," Rip agreed. "And it would help a lot if you'd tell all your friends."

"Be my pleasure."

Rip shut the door and smiled. "He seemed happy," he said, sounding surprised. "I almost liked him."

"Yeah, he's not such a bad guy, for a cop," I agreed, ironically, of course. "His social skills still need a little work."

"Yours, too." Rip frowned. "I wanted another one of those brownies."

That night I blamed the caffeine in the chocolate for keeping me awake until four AM. I used the time to debate the wisdom of keeping silent about my part in Tina Longmeier's confession. By morning I still hadn't decided what to do.

On Saturday, I concentrated on finishing neglected chores, such as re-stapling the ruffle of an overstuffed chair Barney had mistaken for a pull toy in his youth. I scrubbed the edges of the dishwasher door with an old toothbrush. I touched up the stain on Garry's headboard where the movers had chipped it. I even unpacked the last two boxes of Rip's mother's china—stuff we never used, and never expected to use. Then I refilled the boxes with stuff I removed from our hutch.

I went to bed exhausted—only to stare at the ceiling until dawn.

All day Sunday I felt like cow cud, ached, didn't have enough concentration to read a cereal box, and snapped at Garry when he asked for more milk. Other than that, I functioned fairly normally.

Since Thursday night's holiday concert was only five days away, I did take time in the afternoon to brave the Community Room closet, again with an eye toward making those old school store items saleable. If I bought votive candles and set them inside those shot glasses with the Bryn Derwyn logo, touted the oversized T-shirts as nightshirts, stuck a couple napkins from home through the scarf rings to give people the idea— maybe some of this junk would sell after all. The baseball hats still looked good, and the eyeglass cases. I even wrote Jacob a note about where to find that big spool of telephone wire I found in there before.

Throughout my entire time in the empty school working at the "scene of the crime," I succeeded fairly well at blocking any thoughts about Richard Wharton's murder. That ordeal at least, was over. And yet, my fear from Thursday night refused to leave entirely.

Michael D'Avanzo was a wealthy and powerful man, capable of expansive warmth and sudden, marrow-curdling menace, and I had manipulated him into causing the arrest of his own daughter. Instinctively, every cell in my body anticipated retribution.

True, I could confess my role in Tina's arrest and get protection for my family, but there were costs to consider on either side of that fence. What if, God forbid, Rip misinterpreted my motives? What if he somehow saw my frustrated need to set things right as a lack of confidence in his ability to preserve the school? If he ever decided to think that, would I ever be able to convince him otherwise?

At no time in my private investigation had I considered myself to be undermining my marriage. That was a risk I would never choose to take. I had no tangible evidence to support my fears regarding Michael D'Avanzo—not a word, not a gesture, nothing but pure instinct. My head and heart weighed the odds and chose to keep my role in Tina Longmeier's confession a secret.

Assuming Michael D'Avanzo permitted me to.

The possibility existed that he still thought that I believed my own story. Maybe he appreciated that it wasn't my fault his daughter responded violently to Richard's rejection. Perhaps he blamed himself for spoiling her. Maybe he blamed Richard Wharton.

But maybe he blamed me for how it all turned out.

As the days blended into the nights, I developed dark, haunted circles beneath my aching eyes. Despite plodding through the simplest of household tasks, I refused to see a doctor. A doctor would prescribe pills. Pills would cause me to sleep. If I was unconscious, no one would be looking out for my family.

On Monday morning, I kept my eye on Chelsea and Garry through the kitchen window until their bus picked them up. I even stepped into the front yard, ostensibly to supervise Barney's AM outing, but really to see Rip safely into the school.

On an intellectual level I knew what I was doing was exactly as worthwhile as looking under the bed for the bogeyman. Occasionally, your nervous system just plain insists on seeing for itself.

That evening Didi, Rip and our kids arrived home about five-thirty in a jolly bunch. Rehearsal must have been hilarious. It sounded as if Garry and Chelsea had won "assistant" status and had made friends with some of the Bryn Derwyn students.

As usual, Didi looked at me and went straight to the point. "You look like shit."

"Guess I've got a flu bug after all."

"Nauseous?"

"Now and then," I admitted. "Not too bad."

"You hungry?" She pressed her wrist against my fore-head. I knew it to be cool and dry. We both knew wrists were unreliable thermometers.

"Oddly, I am a little hungry."

Didi shrugged and steered the kids toward setting the table, a task I had not yet managed to do.

I turned to Rip. "So what's got you pumped up?" I asked.

"Am I? Maybe I am. Some key students came back, and it looks as if others will follow."

"That's great."

"Yes, it really is. Now I just have to dazzle them with my footwork, get them excited about coming back next year."

My husband, the educational visionary. "Should I start calling you Merlin?"

"You better not!" he teased.

Then he circled my shoulders from behind and kissed my hair. "I'm worried about you."

"I'll be fine. What else happened?" I turned to drink in the sight of his face.

He shrugged and said, "Nicky D'Avanzo was absent," then he added, "but I doubt if that means anything."

On Tuesday Rip found out exactly what Nicky D'Avanzo's absence meant. His grandfather had transferred him to public school. Evidently, the "perfect match" was a relative description, literally. The letter of withdrawal cited social difficulties stemming from his aunt's arrest as the reason for the mid-year switch.

"Would other kids really be unkind about that?" I asked.

"Sure, given the chance. Except they didn't have much chance. Tina turned herself in Friday, and Nicky hasn't been to school since."

I was awake anyway, so I brooded about that one all Tuesday night.

On Wednesday D'Avanzo phoned Rip to personally deliver the bad news about the gym.

"I'm sorry, but the project no longer interests me. I'm sure you understand. My regards to your lovely wife."

I spent Wednesday night and the early hours of Thursday morning on a mental treadmill, imagining that I was chasing after my own sanity.

Thursday afternoon, apparently Eddie Longmeier stopped by Rip's office to inquire about the school's intentions regarding the contract with his company.

"I've got to make plans, you know." Life goes on.

Rip said he reminded him that Bryn Derwyn's development director "departed suddenly," and further explained that without D'Avanzo's pledge the board had chosen to shelve any work on the gym project until summer.

"Obviously, we can't let you break ground until we have the money to pay you," Rip told the contractor. "I'm sorry."

"Yeah, sorry. There's a lot of that going around."

Thursday, December 16, was the day of the holiday concert. Vacation wouldn't start until noon the following Wednesday, but Rip expected any classroom learning to be in limbo between now and then. "I just hope all these high spirits don't cause any damage," he remarked at breakfast, adding that since that bus incident, "the destructive pranks seem to have stopped." He knocked on our wooden dining table.

"Maybe because police were around so much," I observed. "I hope you're not letting down your guard."

"Not at all. Those extra security measures are here to stay."

I breathed a little easier. Extra precautions still made sense. The nervous parents whose children, for the most part, had returned to class just this week, would insist on continued vigilance.

To get a jump on the store display, I went over to school almost as early as Rip. Didi was already there, wearing a lavender mohair dress and shiny brown boots. She looked so much like a froufrou wedding confection that I felt like coffee grounds in comparison.

To tempt non-participating teachers and students to attend that night's performance, Bryn Derwyn's temporary music director planned to have the fourth grade sing "Joy to the World" at morning assembly. No one's political sensibilities were even slightly offended though, because the lyrics to Didi's version started, "Jeremiah was a bullfrog," and went on from there. Everybody clapped along. Some of the audience sang, and across the room from me Rip jitterbugged with the French teacher. Personally, I couldn't imagine where he got the energy.

It was all I could do to move the loaded underwear tree aside and set up the school store on a table in the center of the lobby, even with Didi's help.

But by ten we were done. I sank onto the nearest chair to admire our eye-catching conglomeration of red, white, and Bryn Derwyn green. Sweatshirts, notebooks, and other school-store staples filled out my collection of novelties.

Ruth and Joanne would watch over the merchandise for the rest of the day. "Go home to bed," Didi ordered. "I'm worried about you, girl,"

"Yeah, thanks," I said.

Then, just thinking out loud, I added, "this probably won't last much longer."

✸ *Chapter 35* ✸

My accomplishments for Thursday afternoon were
few. When insomnia erodes your nights, anxiety
devours your days. So using soap opera background
noise to keep me focused, I managed only to wrap an
assortment of small Christmas presents Rip and I had
chosen for the people at school. Fudge in a pretty tin
box for the cook, a wool scarf for Patrice, a bottle of
Jack Daniels for Jacob, that sort of thing. Rip would
hand them out just before vacation next week, friendly
gestures in return for theirs.

The packages looked pretty under the tree, which I
lighted at twilight in an attempt to warm my soul and
get me into the spirit of the season. Then I fixed a hamburger, noodle, and tomato sauce casserole the kids call
Cowboy Stew. Didi, this week's permanent dinner guest,
and all of us Barneses needed something quick so we
could rush back to school for the evening program.

"C'mon, tell me," I coaxed my best friend as we all
ate. "Just a little hint. What will we be seeing tonight?"

Nobody said a word, not even Rip, who had pronounced yesterday's dress rehearsal, "Unique."

We postponed dessert for later, and everybody
whisked their empty dishes into the kitchen where I

stood and fed them to the dishwasher, including my plastic Phillies cup, which was showing signs of wear from rubbing against the racks. I experienced mixed emotions about that.

Everybody was already out the door, so I hurried to catch up, wriggling into my long, red wool coat, grabbing my purse, unplugging the Christmas tree, slamming the door, and checking the lock.

Half a dozen cars had already been parked in the lots. Inside the lobby a very polite man I didn't recognize helped me out of my coat and hung it on the portable rack opposite the auditorium door. I thanked him, regretting that I didn't know his name. Maybe if I saw him later with his child I could figure out who he was.

Mostly at the urging of the children, many families arrived early enough to tour the school and admire their son's or daughter's classrooms. By six-thirty the lobby contained quite a crowd.

I had already assumed my post behind the school store table. An efficient mother named Jean had volunteered to help with the cash box while I filled orders and wrote receipts. Business was brisk from the moment we opened until the last minute before seven, when the show was scheduled to begin.

I locked the cash— already hundreds of dollars—in Rip's office and slipped into the back of the sloped auditorium to watch. Rip used the microphone at the podium to briefly explain how Didi had been asked to take over production of the show at the last minute. "She had very little time to work with, but I'm sure you'll all enjoy the results. Let's all give Ms. Didi Martin a big thank-you in advance."

The near-capacity audience applauded heartily.

Completely at random, the stage filled with children wearing bright colors, but nothing remotely alike. Like friends gathered for a party, there were about fifteen elementary-aged kids, a dozen middle schoolers of both sexes, and five additional girls from the upper grades—probably the only dedicated singers.

The cover of the photocopied program consisted of a star penciled at the upper left corner with a roughly drawn box and a broom down at the bottom. "Bryn Derwyn Holiday Concert" was printed across the box.

Suddenly the lights dimmed almost totally. Standing on a chair in the back corner behind all the parents, Garry switched on a flashlight and held it high.

"Twinkle, twinkle little star," sang the mishmash of voices on the stage, "how I wonder what you are . . . I wish I may, I wish I might, get the wish I wish tonight."

The stage lights brightened, and a girl wearing a fedora with "Press" stuck in the band held out a toy microphone to the tallest boy. "What did you wish for?" she asked.

"Snow day," he replied.

"How about you?" she asked another boy.

"I wished for a box and a broom," he told the audience.

"And you?" the reporter inquired of the tiniest first grade girl.

"World peace," she replied.

From somewhere offstage I thought I recognized my daughter's voice saying "Whrrrrr" into a microphone. The chorus began to shiver and watch the ceiling. Everybody briefly sang, "Here comes Suzy Snowflake."

Then the older boy brought a chicken-wire frame on stage with a few clumps of black tissue stuck in strategic spots and a carrot near the top. All during "Frosty the Snowman," everybody took turns stuffing white tissues into the chicken wire until the thing actually looked like a snowman.

Off went "Frosty," and on came a large box and a broom. The first grader, a darling urchin dressed in purple, climbed into the box and began swinging the broom back and forth. "Row, row, row your boat," commenced, and the audience was invited to join in.

Next the box was placed with the open top facing forward from the back of the stage. The largest boy positioned himself in front of it with the broom. A tape of the "Skater's Waltz" began, and a rainbow of girls tip-toed to the music. Chelsea sat Indian-style at the front edge of center stage so that people in the first row could see over her. She directed the dance, which no one had had time to memorize properly, using two lolly-pop-shaped signals, one red, one green. Hop left, skip right, turn in circles. Half the girls went the wrong directions. The other half started late. Finally, they skipped off stage left, with the exception of two stranded skaters who exited to the right.

As the tune continued, the boys ran out wielding hockey sticks. One of them tossed a red balloon into the fray, which they all tried to bat into the box with their sticks. However, the first time the goalie tried to save it with his broom, the balloon popped.

Next Garry took up the lollipops and attempted to direct the boys in a choreographed sort of pandemonium. Clunk, clunk went the hockey sticks as they hit the floor almost in time with the music. Hop, hop, hop the teams went in a ragged crisscross to the opposite side of the stage. Two kids tripped, setting off a burst of laughter, which spread like chicken pox. Any appearance of a rehearsed routine dissolved. The song played itself out while kids blushed and laughed along with the audience.

Finally, the goalie recovered enough to hand several performers a piece of straw from the broom, which each person proceeded to add to his or her outfit. A girl with a long French braid stuck hers sideways across the braid. A boy managed to wear his like a moustache.

Others put theirs in a pocket, sticking out of their hair, across the front of their collar.

Wearing dangling earrings, a flowered smock, hot pink tights, and aqua socks, Elaine Wrigley climbed up on a chair. Using her piece of straw for a baton, she conducted the chorus in a taped version of, "I'd Like to Teach the World to Sing," which sounded like semi-orderly hollering. The audience added its voice to the din.

Just as Didi no doubt intended, a few adults gasped at the beginning of the "Jeremiah was a Bullfrog," edition of "Joy to the World." Since I'd heard that song during morning assembly, I slipped out to prepare the school store table for the exiting rush.

Behind me the auditorium door closed on a stage full of kids dancing to the rock 'n' roll beat with three hundred parents clapping along. I felt buoyant, the best I'd felt in days.

Wilson Flagg, the maintenance supervisor who quit last summer, stood alone in the middle of the lobby. His face was waxen and tears poured from his eyes.

For a split second only the incongruity of his being there struck me. Then his crazed appearance registered, and I rushed to grasp his thin arms, to secure his attention.

"Wilson, what is it? What's wrong?"

He lifted his streaming eyes to take in my face.

The applause in the auditorium peaked, Wilson muttered something about "911."

"You called 911?" I asked to be certain I heard him right. "Why, Wilson? What happened?" I held his arms tight in my hands. I realized I was shaking him. "What happened?"

The applause ended, followed by a quieter babble. I could hear sirens screaming in the distance.

"I got your dog out, Missus," Wilson told my face. "But there was an awful explosion. I had to run. I had to run, but I came in here and called. Honest. I called it in. It wasn't me this time." The man fell from between my hands down to his knees. Nearby sirens wailed.

The auditorium door was heavy and slow on its compressor, but for once it seemed like nothing to open. Rip was at the microphone, thanking the stage crew.

"Rip!" I shouted, and he stopped mid-sentence.

"It's our house." Three hundred heads swiveled to gape. Dozens of people leaped from their seats.

"Tell Garry and Chelsea to wait by the school sign. Tell them," I screamed, willing my children to be safe with the force of my volume over the other now shrieking voices.

People poured around me. Some women cried. I heard Rip's amplified voice beg everyone to remain calm, remain calm. "Exit in an orderly fashion. It's only the house next door. The school is completely safe."

Wilson had become a sobbing heap in the middle of the lobby. Before I reached him others had already passed by, sprinting for the doors.

Someone tossed something to me, something pliant and red. A coat. My coat. I put it on and ran out along with the others.

The first fire engine had arrived.

Chapter 36

I ran down the middle of the parking lot toward our house, stopping only when I felt the heat. Great rumbling, crackling flames billowed from the living room window. More spilled out of our bedroom and still more flicked out of the roof vent on the school side of the house. Rolling smoke clouds darkened a slate-gray sky.

Activity swirled around me, but I stood shivering, unable to cry out or even to move.

Nearby, an authoritative man wearing heavy gear and a white hard hat urgently waylaid everyone passing by, asking something they seemed unable to answer. When he stopped Sophia Mawby, she impatiently wrenched her arm free and pointed at me.

Hurrying closer, he cupped his hand and yelled, "Is anyone in the house?" His face was so deeply-lined by the flickering light, he appeared to be in agony.

"No," I shouted back.

"You're positive?"

I nodded emphatically. "Not even our dog."

The man turned and ran ponderously in his thick boots while shouting into a radio. He disappeared be-

yond an enormous chrome and red fire truck glowing
with reflected flames.

The huge vehicle filled the space between the two
rows of parked cars at far edge of the lot. A five-inch
hose ran from its side between the cars and down the
length of the driveway to the hydrant a hundred yards
below the front of our house.

Behind me, people continued to rush from the school
building. Some parents carried their children, others
dragged theirs forcibly by the hand.

More sirens screamed and died in the din of the fire
as additional trucks stopped all the way down at the
curb. The police allowed no through traffic, and no Bryn
Derwyn cars were permitted to leave. When the parents
discovered their cars were trapped by the fire hose,
many frantically argued with the police. Even at a distance their jutting jaws and clenched fists were unmis-
takable.

I was immune to their anger, indifferent to their fear.
I was the only stationary object in the center of a spin-
ning world. If I could just cling my family tight enough
to me, maybe I could prevent th planet from unrav-
eling.

At last Rip, Chelsea, and Garry came into sight. Didi
followed close behind. I went to them, but they were
orbits unto themselves.

"Barney," Garry shouted at the night. "Where's Barney?" Rip tried to constrain our son, but with the added
strength of fear our nine-year-old tore himself from his
father's grip.

"Barney's out," I yelled. When I caught up with my
son, I implored him to go down to the school's sign and
wait for Rip and me. "Please," I begged, but the boy
whirled away, staggered and whirled again.

Yet he did head down the driveway. He would be
safe. That was all I cared about, all I needed to know.

Rip and Chelsea, too.

I caught and hugged our daughter, but she, too, squirmed herself free. Her face showed the same stunned immobility that was my own first reaction to the fire.

Pouting, sniffling, she lowered her head and walked, hands stuffed into the pockets of a gray wool coat much too large for her. Yellow flames glistened in the tear streaks down her face and glowed in her fluffy hair.

Didi spoke to her like a comrade—wise woman to wise child. Chelsea nodded and waved to dismiss my friend's concern. Didi watched after her a moment, then broke off to trot through the stragglers in Garry's wake.

An amplified voice shouted orders in a surprisingly businesslike tone. "Crew number one, run a one-and-three-quarter line to protect the southern exposure." My pulse added its own urgency to the command; "southern exposure," referred to the school building.

Rip approached me, a wildness in his eyes beneath the control. "C'mon honey. Go down to the field. Stay out of the way."

He meant me to join the crowd that had been herded onto the practice field down in front of our house. A yellow tape had been strung across its width just below the parking lot.

"C'mon, honey. There's nothing we can do." My husband folded me inside the arms of his down jacket.

I nodded and wiped my tears. Smoke and the beginnings of smoldering stench stung my eyes, my nose.

Rip held me at arm's length and searched my face for a long moment. Then he squeezed my arms and loped off to corral a student who had sneaked under the tape for a closer view of the action. Rip spoke earnestly to the boy, holding his shoulders much as he had just held mine.

Beyond them three hundred fifty people shivered and

stared. The firelight revealed the round, astonished faces of those nearest me, set in the colors of their clothes—purple and green ski jackets, camel-colored overcoats, a few women in long, dark furs. Behind them the others became milling, shifting silhouettes—moths and butterflies and their shadows.

"Crew number two, take the deck gun around back and darken down that fire."

I started to walk away. Just as I turned down the length of the driveway, the interior of the house crumbled inward, thundering onto the slab that was the foundation. Next, two exterior walls fell with a windy, gusty roar. Another followed.

Breathing hard, almost sobbing, I hiked myself up on the rear bumper of a station wagon to see. Only the lone brick and plaster chimney reached skyward with the smoke.

Down on the ground a small army of volunteer firemen hosed the roots of the flames. Helmets covered the tops of their heads and air packs covered the rest, reminding me of World War I gas masks or those androgenous warriors from the Saturday cartoons—futuristic space heroes fighting to save the Barnes family's dwelling and everything around it. Ironic. Astonishing. Hopeless.

I hopped down and shrugged to loosen my neck. Jogging now for warmth, I circled the playing field to join the back of the crowd.

This close to the street I could see the neighbors on the opposite sidewalk gawking around the edges of the five fire engines that consumed all of the school's curb space. For the same reasons that no cars could leave, the fire trucks were unable to park any closer.

At the back of a white ambulance, paramedics treated a couple of bruised children shaken up during the exo-

dus. The vehicle was nosed into the end of the drive at a
zany angle, which struck me as off-balance and untidy.

I continued past the paramedics, stepping over the
thick fire hose as I crossed the drive and proceeded up
onto a little knoll. The main parking lot utilized the
whole left front yard of the school, and in the streetlight
I noticed a few families huddled together inside their
cars, peering out at the spectacle. From that distance it
looked like overeager ants waiting on a flaming marsh-
mallow.

Feeling six sleepless days and nights weary now, exhausted deep into my soul, I leaned against the post of
the lighted green-and-white Bryn Derwyn sign.

The night was winter cool this far from the flames,
with chilly breezes gusting around the onlookers like
agitated, invisible spirits. My face would be chapped for
days, raw and sore from my frozen tears.

Although my kids had not come to this spot as I had
hoped, they were somewhere safe. That was all that
mattered. Even Barney was out, for all I knew frolicking
his way from yard to yard across town. He had tags.
Someone would return him.

Stuffing my right hand into my coat pocket, my cold
fingers came across a piece of paper. Shopping list? Dry
cleaning ticket? I drew it out intending to tear it up.

The penciled block letters doused me in sweat:

"OLD CHRISTMAS TREE LIGHTS ARE DANGEROUS. YOU
SHOULD HAVE TURNED YOURS OFF."

An anguished noise emanated from my throat. While
I thought a gentleman was helping me with my coat, an
arsonist had been planting an oblique warning.

What I dismissed as yet another act of kindness had
been the same man making certain that his message got
delivered. Simple, and thoroughly effective.

I swallowed great frigid gulps of air—two, three, four
gasps before my knees crumbled and I was on the

ground clutching my stomach and writhing with horrible hysterical convulsions.

A neighbor woman ran over shouting, "Help her. Help her. She's having a fit."

Others encircled me as I rolled and gasped for breath.

A man in a white uniform pinned me still. Another wrenched open my coat, tore down the sleeve of my blouse and injected me with something.

Oblivion beckoned, and I succumbed.

✵ *Chapter 37* ✵

When I woke, the edges of my eyes were painfully dry, and the base of my head felt like it had been clubbed. Also, my back was stiff.

I lay on a rough-woven sofa under a blue blanket. Rip sat beside me on the floor, his head in his hands, a yellow blanket across his lap.

I was exceedingly glad to see him, yet wary. Holding myself together, if only to function as a semblance of my self, seemed tantamount just then. If my husband gave me so much as one odd glance, lifted one worried eyebrow in reference to my "fit" of last night, I thought I might truly unravel.

"Where are we?" I asked.

The rest of the sofa cushions seemed to be under Rip. He wore men's pajamas that were a size too small. Mine were too big. My muddy clothes and red coat had been folded onto a maroon brocade armchair. Judging by the outdated decor and musty-fruity smell, we were in an elderly person's living room. Seeing the couple's history so lovingly preserved in their possessions hurt more than I could ever have imagined.

"Wilson Flagg's."

I glanced around again in awe—long living room

stretched into a dining area, lace curtains, dust motes in the slanted sun, alcove into a sideways kitchen, white porcelain sink just visible under a back window with a hanging plant. Rip could have told me we were in Oz and I'd have believed him. Bryn Derwyn's irascible former maintenance man's house I could not believe.

"Yeah. I never realized he lived right next to the school, did you?"

"No." Although Wilson and Rip had worked together only a month.

I glanced through the side window across the room to my left. The playing field where the fire police shepherded the crowd was right out there past some bushes and a maple tree. Also in the visible distance was the Bryn Derwyn sign, the location of my collapse.

"Rip, I have something to tell you," I blurted before my husband's proximity could sabotage my resolve. I looked hard into his eyes and told him I thought I was responsible for the fire.

"Oh no, honey. That's impossible." His face was at my level, his unshaven cheek within reach of my fingertips, close enough to weaken my backbone. Better hurry and see how he took a half truth before I told him everything.

"I might have left the Christmas tree on."

I hadn't, but I might have.

"No," Rip protested. "I will not let you think that." To my distress, his eyes filled up. "Let's not talk about that anymore. Not ever. Okay?"

His naked vulnerability unnerved me. His pain made me physically ache. Certainly every person's emotional strength and physical endurance had limits; but so far, my husband's had been out of my view. Illness scares with the kids, near misses on the road—my husband never flinched. Furthermore, he had just coped with a murder and the possible failure of his school without wavering.

For him, the loss of our home apparently went too far.

Considering how I responded last night, the fire had clearly gone beyond my limit, too. But that was last night, and this was today. In so many words Rip had just told me he couldn't bear to discuss the fire. So I would never, ever bring it up in front of him. I would deal with the children's concerns in private and keep their father out of it. Later Rip and I would talk it through, but in the meantime I would permit him to cope in his own way.

And I would cope in mine.

The kids bounded down the stairs, Garry's jack-in-the-box disposition just as springy as ever. Chelsea looked bewildered, pale, and unnaturally tired. Both wore the same clothes they had worn to help with the concert, but they carried a pile of pants and sweaters for Rip and me to try. Apparently Wilson Flagg had been helping them root through his closet.

He followed behind with a slower, heavier tread. "Good afternoon," the former maintenance supervisor greeted me. He no longer was the balding, stoop-shouldered nemesis who refused to fix our bedroom ceiling. Now he was simply contrite. Embarrassed about something, too.

"Afternoon?"

"One-thirty," he confirmed.

I glanced at Rip in amazement. "You missed quite a lot," he remarked. "Go get washed up and I'll tell you. But hurry, because the fire marshal needs us to go through the house with him at two-thirty."

I winced at the official sound of that.

"Just routine," Rip assured me. I fervently hoped he was right.

I showered and towel-dried my hair and even helped myself to a couple of aspirins from Wilson's medicine cabinet. His clothes, brown corduroy pants, and a soft oxford shirt, looked ludicrous on me, but they felt comfortable over my own underwear. The fire marshal would probably understand that what I'd been wearing had been rolled around in mud.

Over scrambled eggs and coffee, Rip and the kids filled me in.

The blaze had been under control within twenty minutes, but the fire fighters had done another two hours of "overhaul," checking for embers.

"They used long poles to stir everything up," Garry announced, clearly proud of his knowledge. "But boy did it stink."

"How do you know, young man?" Rip demanded. "I thought you came over here with Didi."

"She let me watch for a couple minutes. Chelsea waited by the road. It was really steamy and yucky, Mom."

"Dear Didi," I remarked.

"Yes," Rip agreed. "She was going to take the kids home with her, but I thought you'd want to see them as soon as you woke up. Wilson has bunks up in his attic for his grandchildren."

"Thanks, Wilson," I managed over a suddenly tight throat, "for everything." The old man nodded.

"You, too, Rip." He knew I meant the part about seeing the kids right away.

"What about Barney?" I asked.

"After she settled you and the kids down with Wilson's help, Didi took it upon herself to track down our dog. Since we no longer had a phone, the family who found Barney had to call the dogcatcher. I'll go pick him up in a couple minutes.

"By the way, your Mom expects us to stay with her until we figure out what to do with ourselves."

"You called her?"

"Yeah. Woke her up. I didn't want her to hear about us on the news."

I smiled my admiration and gratitude, and Rip smiled back. Then I realized it was Friday. "What about school?" I asked.

"Canceled. We used the snow chain to tell everybody. We'll open again Monday."

"Phew. You've been busy."

"And now I have a dog to pick up. Mind if the kids come along? We'll be back in half an hour."

I waved them away. Chelsea hugged me before she went. She seemed much too silent, something I would address as soon as possible.

Wilson served me another cup of coffee in a yellow-and-white mug. Then he sat opposite me at his dining room table, a lovely oak one sporting a doily and a pot of plastic ivy.

"How long has your wife been gone?" I asked gently.

"Ten," he answered.

I sipped my coffee. It was strong and fresh, exactly what I needed. "What did you mean last night when you said, 'not this time'?" I asked.

He shrugged his left shoulder apologetically and sighed, I thought with relief. Then he opened his right hand above the table.

"Sometimes I would drop things," he said. "Once in a while, I'd be somewhere in the school, tools all around me, and I couldn't remember how I got there—or why. I could figure it out easy enough, but it rattled me, you know?"

I nodded but didn't speak, not wishing to interrupt what seemed to be a difficult confession.

"Bill Bodourian treated me real good. Like a friend,

you know? When he left and your husband took his place, well, I got it in my head to blame him for my own troubles."

"That's a natural enough thing to do," I suggested.

"You think so?" he asked as if the thought surprised him. But then he hadn't had a woman to talk to for ten years.

"You did a little more than blame Rip for your troubles, didn't you?" I suggested.

Wilson Flagg raised an eyebrow, but he did not flinch.

"You also poured coffee on Joanne's computer keyboard," I said, referring the incident that made Joanne question her own mental faculties. "And poured water in the bus's gas tank?"

Wilson lowered his head. The muscles in his jaw rolled as he gritted his false teeth. "You going to report me?"

I thought of all he'd done, including saving our dog and trying to save our home, and the idea of him carrying out another prank became unimaginable. Wilson Flagg almost felt like family.

"No. Of course not," I answered. Perhaps Rip could think of a chore or two that wouldn't rely on an arthritic hand or a perfect memory—parking cars for special events, or dust-mopping the gym in the mornings—a more tangible way to respect an old employee's pride while supplementing his pension. We owed this guy.

Out on the porch Barney, Rip, and the kids clattered up to the door. Wilson moved somewhat stiffly to let them in, but then he had had an awful night. We all had.

"Fire marshal's here, Gin," Rip told me. "How about we go meet him and keep this beast out of Wilson's nice neat living room?"

"Sure," I agreed. Then I took the old man's arthritic hand, and kissed him on the cheek. His stubble was three days old, and he smelled like my grandfather. The pang of nostalgia braced me just enough to put on my muddy red coat and go out to face the fire inspector.

He met us on the playing field, a stolid man of about fifty who looked vaguely familiar—the lines defining his face, the shape of his mouth.

"Good afternoon, Mrs. Barnes," he greeted me, for some reason favoring me over my husband. Unusual I thought, and disquieting.

He handed me a card. "DAVID SMITH, FIRE MARSHAL," it said. "CODE ENFORCEMENT."

Rip caught my eye. "I told him you knew a lot more about the house than me." Perhaps that explained why Smith chose to concentrate on me. I certainly hoped so.

"Sorry to bother you at a time like this," he said, "but we often find the homeowner's input quite helpful." All of us began to walk up the playing field toward the house.

"In what way?" I asked, suddenly remembering. He was the first official person I'd seen, the one who had asked whether anyone was inside. Now I realized that he probably had been in charge.

"To determine the cause," he replied matter-of-factly.

When we got to the yellow crowd-control tape, I faced forward to lift it over my head and for the first time in full daylight took in the destruction of our house.

The sight hollowed out my insides, lungs and all. What had been a pleasant looking, putty-colored structure with green trim, a brick walk, and tall, wide living room windows was now a heap of rubble. Some first floor studding remained, but little above that height, just the brick and stucco chimney and a third of a back wall. The evergreen bushes out front were charred stumps littered with glass and blackened trash. Even the near branches of the oak tree above the picnic table had been singed.

I couldn't imagine that one single item would be salvageable. Everything we used, everything carried forward from our past, everything that was familiar to our everyday life seemed to have been consumed.

The closer we approached the more items defined themselves. Bedsprings, the refrigerator, and other metal kitchen appliances, all blackened carcasses standing in a mire of sodden debris. The smell of wet ashes reached us even twenty yards away.

For the concert I had worn navy blue flats and stockings. The closer I walked to the house the more the winter-damp grass soaked my shoes and chilled my feet until they ached. David Smith's thick rubber boots made me remember the gardening boots I kept in the shed, which luckily remained intact. I excused myself to go get them. Without socks the boots would be freezing cold, but at least they were dry and would save my only shoes from the filthy muck I'd be sorting through.

My only pair of shoes. Thoughts like that would stab at me for months to come. At least the few Christmas presents I'd stored in the shed remained untouched, a collection of colorful plastic bags. Amazing to think that Christmas was exactly a week away. Even more amazing to think how little I cared.

"I'll keep Barney and the kids out front," Rip told me. His mood was bleak, although the sharp sunlight and the awful smell may have contributed to the ravaged appearance of his face.

Chelsea walked over to sit on the picnic table like an orphan, shoulders drooped, hands stuffed into that oversized gray coat she somehow acquired. From between the trees, Beth, the arrogant girl who ostracized Chelsea on the school bus, approached and began to speak to her.

"That's the silly girl who offered us a garden hose," Smith remarked. "Can you imagine?"

When I glanced again, Beth was gone and Chelsea looked less forlorn. Shoulders squared. Chin up.

"She dusted her off," I told Rip. "I'll bet you anything."

Somehow Garry had found a tennis ball and was throwing it to Barney, who was on a long leash made from an old clothesline. Our son must have had the presence of mind to grab his own ski jacket from wherever he stashed it during the performance, for he was wearing it now.

I thought of the arsonist tossing me my coat as I ran from the school, and my hand closed guiltily around the note I must have jammed back into my pocket. David Smith gave me a probing glance, but without x-ray vision or clairvoyance, my worry probably appeared natural. Whatever he was thinking, the investigator immediately began to step through the remains of the house toward the former laundry room area. I released my breath, which condensed in the chilly air.

"C'mere a sec, Mrs. Barnes," Smith said. "See this?" With a gloved hand he threw some charred boards aside to reveal what used to be our clothes dryer. He opened its door.

"A little smokey, but this ain't it."

I saw what he meant. The outer shell of the dryer was charred while the inside paint remained light colored, merely stained near the openings by brown streaks that had seeped from the outside in.

David Smith unzipped his official-looking black jacket to free the small 35mm camera dangling around his neck. He proceeded to take a picture of the dryer. Beside it the hot water heater stood its ground beneath hunks of collapsed outer wall. I asked whether it had been responsible for the water on the floor.

"Nah," Smith demurred. "That was probably us."

Figures, I thought bitterly. Just when we got a good one.

I made my way around boards and bedsprings, fragments of furniture, bits of glass, forcing down sentiments, kicking aside emotions, until I reached the corpse of our dishwasher. I opened the door with one finger. Inside, among some broken dishes, some whole, a few lumps of smelly plastic adhered to the metal racks.

"My Phillies cup melted," I said aloud. Emotions roiled. The floor seemed to shift.

Smith stood nearby, watching me.

Watching *me*. Did he think I set the fire myself?

Then with sudden clarity I realized that was exactly what I needed him to think.

The pressure to behave perfectly further unnerved me. Tears began.

I tossed up my hands. "Sorry," I said with ragged breath. "My Phillies cup melted."

"Understandable," Smith said reasonably, releasing me from his riveting stare. "Probably reached twenty-two hundred degrees in here . . . in about ten minutes."

I wiped my face on my now sooty sleeve. "What exploded?" I asked.

Smith waved a hand. "Your house."

"Beg pardon?"

"Your house," he repeated. "Flammable gases collect at the ceiling, neighbor breaks in the back to get your dog, air rushes in, fuels the fire and bam, she explodes, blasts out the windows. Called a 'flashover.' When fire gets in between the trusses like you had, that's pretty much it. We can't even come into this kind of house—walls collapse."

In other words, anyone trapped inside would have stayed trapped inside. No wonder he had been exceptionally relieved to learn we were all out; there was nothing anyone could have done if we had not been. The realization made me feel nauseous.

Smith snapped three more pictures then picked his way around the bedsprings toward the former front door, now an empty frame.

"See these low burns," he said, stooping down to indicate a particularly dark area beneath where the Christmas tree had been. In front of us stood tall, rectangular metal window frames twisted by the falling walls but still displaying some jagged shards of glass.

"Here's where your fire started." Smith fished around in the ash muck with his gloves and lifted a black, double strand of wire. "Christmas tree?"

"Yes."

"Figured as much. In front of the living room window and all that."

"I put the lights on at dinnertime, but I thought I unplugged them when I left."

Smith stood to snap some pictures of the tree area, then stooped again to shoot a small sooty box with two pieces of metal protruding from it—the outlet and parts of the plug.

"Yep. Sorry to say, it looks like the lights were on."

Pick a lock, plug in some Christmas lights, touch a lighter to a package under a tree. Instant conflagration. No trace.

I began to huff, but fought for outward control. Inside my head I screamed "bastard" and worse, internally cursing the arsonist Michael D'Avanzo had sent to avenge his daughter. Never mind that she was a murderer, she was still Daddy's girl, and don't anyone forget it.

My anguish emerged in a sobbing moan, the sort you hear at funerals caused by war. Rip hurried to usher me away but I pulled loose and staggered into the yard.

Smith followed, watching me, deciding about me. I could feel his thoughts.

I began to pace.

"Gin," Rip called, his voice fraught with concern.

I turned. Chelsea was up from her observation post on the picnic table, fists at her side. I was scaring her. Garry stood still, the tennis ball forgotten in his hand.

I turned. The school spread before me, unharmed. I turned back. My children and husband and dog were there, also unharmed.

In a sudden moment of insight I realized what their safety meant. More than living proof of a grandfather's gratitude, the sparing of my family meant that Michael D'Avanzo accepted some of the responsibility for his oldest daughter's downfall. Pride required that I be apprised of his generosity. Conceivably, the price for manipulating Michael D'Avanzo could have been much, much higher.

Now that I understood, I could also forgive.

Rip moved closer; David Smith hung back.

I eased into my husband's arms. The children, too, came near and Rip and I hugged them.

"It's all right," I said. "It's over."

❊ *Chapter 38* ❊

I added a basket of potato chips to the assortment of junk food on the aluminum folding table. Then I moved it. Then I moved it again. Kevin Seitz's "'Afternoon, Gin," startled me into spilling the whole basket.

Looking especially boyish in his casual clothes, the young business manager pinched a couple of chips off the table with a wry smile, ate them, then wiped his fingers on his jeans. Together we surveyed the Bryn Derwyn teachers gradually gathering in the school's outdated gym.

"Quiet," he observed. Today was December 22, the last school day before Christmas vacation, and by noon not a student remained in the building. Only three hours later the place felt as if it had been abandoned for years.

"They'll be back in two weeks," I said. Most of them would. Only three students had been permanently withdrawn because of the murder, Nicky D'Avanzo included. Next year was a different matter; next year depended on Rip.

"What? Oh, no. I meant the teachers are quiet."

"Ummm." While I stared at the desultory gathering, Kevin stared at me. Although I was trying to get used to that, I had not yet succeeded. At least he wasn't dripping with sympathy like most of the others.

"You look like a gypsy peering into a crystal ball," he remarked.

The astuteness of his observation unsettled me. Despite knowing better, I still expected this party to provide some clues about the future of the school. Had the murder and the subsequent loss of our house bonded Rip's constituents into a team? Or had they become even more pessimistic and divided?

Would Bryn Derwyn become the warm sanctuary portrayed in the brochure? Or was the place so terminal that nobody dared to whisper about it?

"It's just an office party," Kevin reminded me. "Lighten up."

I snickered at my old family friend. "Obviously you have no recollection of my last attempt." I referred, of course, to the September debacle in which Jeremy Philbin got horribly blitzed.

"Au contraire, mon cher," he mimicked me. "I'm just glad it's too cold out for badminton." He winked and sauntered away, swigging Coke from a can.

"Smart ass," I muttered. My having briefly suspected Kevin of murder had eliminated any trace of pretense between us.

"I heard that," he said without turning around.

Joanne Henry appeared at my side. She picked up a pretzel and wiggled it between her thumb and forefinger. I noticed some of the salt fell off.

"You didn't need to do this," she remarked sententiously.

"Oh yes I did," I told her. Should I explain about needing order in my life? Should I remind her the invitations had been sent before the murder and its aftermath and I was damn well going to deliver, even if it was only pretzels, potato chips, and canned soda?

Joanne's face told me that no explanation was necessary.

"You got anything stronger under that table?" she teased.

"No such luck," I said. "Jeremy Philbin cured me."

Her eyes lingered on me a minute, formulating her thoughts. "He checked into rehab this afternoon. I drove him over."

"Oh, Joanne, how tactless of me. I'm sorry."

"Forget it. After what you've been through, you're entitled to say anything you please."

"Just not in front of a reporter."

We smiled at each other fondly. "Thanks for everything, Hank," I said, quickly turning away before I got teary.

Although I'd slept away great chunks of the days since the fire, my emotions were like Hawaiian weather, quick showers that blew up quickly then just as quickly disappeared.

"Cute outfit," she remarked. I wore black slacks and a multi-colored sweater, hand-me-overs from the Bryn Derwyn Community's "Barnes Family Relief Drive." As early as Monday, Joanne had collected great heaps of donations, which had filled and refilled a bin in the school lobby all week.

An only child, I had never been comfortable wearing other people's clothes; but now I regarded each item as an embrace. Unfortunately Chelsea, the self-conscious pre-teen, refused so much as a used shoelace. An emergency run to the mall had taken care of essentials for her and business clothes for Rip. To Garry, wearing borrowed, broken-in stuff was like throwing a pig into slop.

Music squawked over the loudspeaker then hummed down to a more listenable volume. Didi had brought her brother's collection of oldies tapes. Her initial selection was "Sea of Love."

"How's your mom?" Joanne asked over the maudlin melody.

"Very glad we found a house."

"Already?"

"We were motivated." With one guest bedroom at my mother's and four guests, we had all begun to feel like sardines.

"Where?"

"At the end of Beech Tree Lane. It's a real handyman's special." Garry's pronouncement that it was "Right up my alley," had produced yet another Hawaiian shower; he had said the very same thing about the campus house.

"You're happy about that?"

"Very. If I'm going to get up close and personal with a toilet tank, I need it to be *my* toilet tank, if you know what I mean."

"No, thank goodness, I don't." She was dainty, with perfectly styled gray hair, professional nails, and yet another immaculate knit dress. What made me think she would understand the joy of wielding a wrench? I wouldn't even try to explain how much I was itching to refurbish the eclectic odds and ends of furniture we'd been offered.

"We only put a bid in this morning, but already it feels like home."

Joanne nodded. That she understood.

Much to my relief, the fire marshal, David Smith, had pronounced the fire accidental, clearing the way for an insurance payment to the school. Part of that would go toward helping us with a down payment on our own home, but most would be put toward constructing the gym—on the site of the burned down house. Boards of Directors were nothing if not logical. Most of the time anyhow.

I poked an elbow toward the clusters of teachers, who

for all I knew were grimly discussing their most irksome students. "This looks about as promising as grass on a ski slope," I told Joanne. "Better see what I can do."

I waited for Rip to break away from the librarian.

"What?" he said, his brow creased by the depressing statistics on overdue books.

"This party needs resuscitation."

Rip glanced around. "They're probably taking their cue from us," he decided.

It figured. Our party, our mood.

"Be right back," I said. "Don't go away."

I ducked behind the curtain to the corner where Didi had set up the tape player. She was chewing a nail, frowning at a row of tapes. She wore red overalls over a green striped turtleneck. Her blonde hair was clipped to the top of her head.

"What do you think, Gin. 'Santa Baby?' or some Elton John?"

"Rock 'n' roll and keep it moving."

Didi's eyes sparkled. " 'Wake Up Little Suzie' ?"

"That's the idea."

I was back at Rip's side in time to see the eyebrows jump when Didi hit the switch on the Rolling Stones, who still couldn't get any satisfaction.

My husband, the beleaguered headmaster, barked with laughter and pulled me onto the fold-out dance floor. Beaming with mischief, Didi took Kevin Seitz's hand and began to demonstrate exactly how sensuous a pair of red overalls can be.

While the four of us giggled and cavorted like deranged teenagers, I could sense the straightjackets dropping off the faculty's backs one by one. A few began to dance. Most just smiled with pleasure over our silliness, tolerant parents enjoying their kids.

Or vice versa. Whatever.